PRA...
THE HOUSE IM...
House ...

"I love Devon Monk's books. There is something about each story that sucks the reader in completely and doesn't let go . . . an excellent story. Devon Monk is incredible at weaving a tale that makes the reader excited, crazy, and astonished all at the same time." —Fiction Vixen

"Original and intriguing . . . [a] kick-ass heroine, powerful, near-immortal beings, fun sidekicks, and [an] original world."
—All Things Urban Fantasy

"I didn't want to stop reading. *House Immortal* kept my interest every second." —Yummy Men Kick Ass Chicks

"A fresh and unique world. . . . Devon Monk once again proves she's a powerhouse in the genre." —A Book Obsession

"*House Immortal* brings *Frankenstein* into a new world, and Devon Monk puts it together excellently!" —Drey's Library

"[Tilly] is exactly the type of heroine I enjoy reading about: She's intelligent, independent, compassionate, and totally kick-ass. . . . Definitely one of my favorite reads this year."
—Short & Sweet Reviews

"Monk has a way with putting a unique twist on a story . . . absolutely wonderful." —Bookworm Blues

"Monk has a way to create worlds that feel like our reality mixed with a kick of fantasy." —Seeing Night Book Reviews

"A unique, new series with intriguing characters, a power-hungry villain, and an original, well-built world."
—Urban Fantasy Investigations

"Interesting, well-developed characters, a kick-ass plot with more twists and turns than you can even guess, and incredible world building. . . . *House Immortal* is the start of what looks to be a fantastic series." —Book Briefs

continued . . .

INFINITY BELL

A HOUSE IMMORTAL NOVEL

DEVON MONK

A ROC BOOK

ROC
Published by the Penguin Group
Penguin Group (USA) LLC, 375 Hudson Street,
New York, New York 10014

USA | Canada | UK | Ireland | Australia | New Zealand | India | South Africa | China
penguin.com
A Penguin Random House Company

First published by Roc, an imprint of New American Library,
a division of Penguin Group (USA) LLC

First Printing, March 2015

 REGISTERED TRADEMARK — MARCA REGISTRADA

ISBN 978-0-451-46737-9

Printed in the United States of America
10 9 8 7 6 5 4 3 2 1

For my family

ACKNOWLEDGMENTS

I would like to thank my awesome editor, Anne Sowards, for once again helping to make my stories shiny and strong. I'd also like to thank the many wonderful, talented, hardworking people inside Penguin who have gone above and beyond to support and create this book. To my agent, Miriam Kriss, thank you for all that you do. And to the excellent artist, Eric Williams, thank you for bringing Matilda and her world to life.

As for my two amazing first readers, Dean Woods and Dejsha Knight—I hope you know how much I truly appreciate all the talks, feedback, and support you both offer so generously and on such ridiculous deadlines. I promise to work on the deadline part. A big thank-you to my wonderful family, one and all. You people are crazy, and I love you. To my husband, Russ, and sons, Kameron and Konner, I've said this before, but I will always mean it: I love you. Thanks for being such amazing people and the very best part of my life.

But mostly, dear readers, I'd like to thank you for letting me share this story, these people, and this adventure with you.

1

I thought you were an angel burning in that dark night. I thought you had come to save me. Maybe you did. But I never wanted you to die for me.

— *from the diary of E. N. D.*

The sound of the seaplane's engine growling low and loud as it came in for a landing jarred me awake.

I sat, still half asleep, reaching for my duffel, my gun, or anything I could use as a weapon. The seat belt dug into my hips painfully, and a warm, soft cloth slid down away from my chin.

"We're coming into San Diego, Matilda," my brother, Quinten Case, said from behind me.

Right. Seaplane, running for our lives from the Houses who thought we were behind the murder of Oscar Gray and Slater Orange. Houses who ruled all the resources in the world, and were, at this moment, using those resources to sift through the world to find me, my brother, and Abraham Seventh.

To be honest, the chances of us slipping their notice

weren't great. The chances of us slipping their notice before the Wings of Mercury experiment—an old time machine my ever-so-great-grandfather had built—triggered and killed me, Abraham, and all the other galvanized in the world was right near zero.

Still, I was a Case. And we Cases never gave up when saving the world.

It was dark outside. Night. I must have slept for hours. The rest of the blanket covering me fell away as I lifted my hands to rub at my face.

"How much longer?" I asked.

"Just about to land."

I straightened and dug at the knots in my neck, rubbing the ache out of it. Then I glanced back at my brother. He sat with a blanket around his shoulders, cradling a thermos cup between his hands. His dark curly hair was mussed, as if he'd been pulling his fingers through it. Even in the low light, he was too thin, too pale.

Captivity had not sat well with him, somehow sharpening his features and movements and cornering that restless-genius mind of his.

"Coffee?" he offered.

"I didn't know we had any on board."

Corb, who sat in the rear of the plane, raised his voice over the lowering rumble of the engines. "We were saving it for when we made land. A victory celebration."

The big man and his pilot wife, Sadie, had come to our rescue and smuggled Quinten and me out of Hong Kong in their little seaplane. They'd also rescued my farmhand, Neds Harris, who was sleeping in the seat next to me, and Abraham Seventh, the man I might be stupidly falling in love with and who was passed out in the cargo area.

Travel had been less than kind to Abraham. He had a sort of rugged handsomeness about him, dark wavy hair above a broad face with piercing hazel eyes, and a strong jaw covered in scruff. But now his skin was yellow between the bruises that covered it. The stitches that held him together, crossing his face, neck, torso, arms, and legs, had nearly disintegrated in just a few hours. Loose threads poked up out of his skin like sun-seeking maggots in rotted fruit.

At first we'd thought he'd been soaked in Shelley dust, a substance possessed by the heads of Houses and used as a means to control galvanized—people like Abraham, people like me, who were made of bits stitched together. Shelley dust on the skin would burn through the stitching.

Then Quinten had found the bullet holes in Abraham's chest. Abraham had been shot with Shelley dust, which meant it was doing as much irreparable damage to his internal organs as his stitches.

Quinten thought we could negate the dust's effects if we got him to a doctor soon enough. I didn't know how soon would be soon enough. But I knew he didn't have much time left.

Along the tattered lines of Abraham's broken stitches were new, thin silver threads holding him together. That thread was my father's own invention, made of nanos and minerals right out of the soil and water of our farm.

Quinten had sewn Abraham together last night with the spool of thread I'd packed with me. So far Abraham had remained in one piece. The thin silver stitches were precise, clean, and beautiful in their way. My brother had an artist's hand with stitching.

I should know. He was the one who had stitched me together when I was just a little girl.

But along with the unstitching, Abraham had lost a lot of blood. Too much. The heavy blanket we'd wrapped him in was soaked with it, and it was seeping out of holes we could not patch.

At least he couldn't feel pain. None of the galvanized had full sensation.

Well, except for me.

"Matilda?" Quinten held out the cup.

I pulled my thoughts away from Abraham and took the steaming, fragrant drink from my brother. Coffee wasn't my favorite hot beverage, but right now anything liquid and warm would do me fine.

I took a couple sips, the bitter liquid spreading through my empty stomach like a heat wave, then noticed Neds were watching me.

Neds Harris was a man put together in the nonstandard configuration of two heads side by side on one body. He'd been with me for two years now, and had left my off-grid farm when the Houses had discovered not only that I was off grid but also that I was something they wanted to own.

I offered him the coffee.

Right Ned took a sip of it, offered it to Left Ned, who shook his head. "I'm good," Left Ned said.

The plane dipped suddenly and I almost missed them handing me back the coffee cup.

"Need some help up there, Sadie?" Left Ned called out to our pilot.

"From you?" she called back. "I can handle this with two eyes twice as good as you could with four."

"Except I wouldn't hit every pothole in the sky," Left Ned muttered.

"I heard that," she said. "Not another peep out of you, or I'll tell my husband to escort you overboard."

Neds held up their hands in surrender, although Left Ned was grinning. They both settled back a bit and closed their eyes.

I took another sip of coffee and passed it back to Quinten. "How are you feeling?"

In the dim light my brother's sharp features were a little blurry, but I could make out that irritated frown of his. "I've been thinking about what we need to do."

When Quinten used that tone of voice, nothing but trouble came of it.

"Get Abraham blood?" I suggested. "And cleanse his system before his organs fail?"

"No. Well, yes, but not that. The break in time. How to fix it. We talked about this," he admonished, as if I'd been sleeping through a class lecture.

"No," I corrected, "*we* haven't had time to talk about anything. We've been running. I guess just you and your genius were comparing notes in your brain again."

He slid me a quick smile. "All right. Well, we need to talk about it."

"Now?"

The plane bucked again, and Sadie corrected with a tip of the wings that had me grabbing the armrest of my chair to keep from sliding into Neds.

Neds, eyes still closed, chuckled and Sadie cussed.

Outside the windows I could barely see the city lights through the fog. I sure hoped Sadie had a better view than I did.

"Maybe after we land," he said.

Better idea.

We held on tight as Sadie brought the plane down into the water, slowing against the drag until we had turned and were trolling over to the dock.

San Diego glowed distant and fuzzy in the fog that was so thick, it seemed to swallow the world whole.

"This is it," Sadie said, her hand busy over switches and toggles as the little plane came to a rest alongside an unlit dock. She unlatched her seat belt and shifted in her chair so she could look back at all of us. "As far as we can get you. I wish we could do more...."

"You've been great," I said. "Above and beyond, and then some. Thank you so much for all of your help. I don't know what we would have done without you."

She smiled. "A friend of Neds is a friend of ours. Always."

"You are good people, Sadie," Right Ned said around a yawn. He rolled the stiffness out of his shoulders. "And a decent pilot. I owe you one."

"You owe me nothing," she said. "Just see that you stay alive."

"I'll put in an effort," Right Ned said.

Corb opened the rear door and the plane shifted and rocked as he exited and lashed the vessel to the dock. The sharp salt and oil scent of the bay wafted, cold and wet, into the plane.

Left Ned nodded at me. "Give me a minute to find us transport. I'll be right back." He unlatched the side door and hopped out onto the pontoon then over to the dock.

It was a little strange having Neds do all the legwork to get us home. I was usually the one coordinating escape routes for the people of House Brown. I knew all the ins and outs for the off-grid families to avoid the direct gaze of the other powerful Houses who didn't think House Brown or the people in it should have freedom or a voice.

But my knowledge and contacts had not been enough. Neds knew Sadie and Corb, and, with them he had gotten us out of Hong Kong. He said he knew people who could get us across the country quickly and without notice.

I didn't know if those people were a part of House Brown, or were perhaps people like Sadie and Corb, who flew so far under the radar, they didn't even claim House Brown.

What I knew for sure was we had to be moving, and quickly for everyone's safety. Anyone helping us right now was putting himself directly in the line of fire.

"What about Abraham?" I asked.

Quinten glanced down at the unconscious man. "We'll carry him. Hopefully Neds can find an accommodating vehicle."

In just a couple minutes, Neds did find an accommodating vehicle. A dark late-model box van with two seats in the front and plenty of cargo space in the back.

Between Neds, Quinten, Corb, and I, we strapped Abraham securely to the stretcher, then transferred him from the plane to the van.

I was glad it was dark and foggy and that the dock was secluded. But security cameras could be anywhere. We needed to be gone fast.

Quinten took the driver's seat, a stocking cap on his head, covering his curls. He was already rolling away from the dock before I got the side door closed.

Neds rode in the back, sitting on the floor next to Abraham. I decided that might be a good place for me to stay out of sight too.

"Gloria's?" Quinten asked.

"End of the world, she'd be top of my list of safe harbors," I said. I didn't know why he had to ask me. He'd spent time with her. I'd never even met her in person.

"I think," he said, "well, it may be *an* end of the world, but there could be a fix. We can fix it. Us Cases. You and I. That's what I need to tell you. I think I know how. Brilliant, actually, but we don't have all the pieces yet, so there are some challenges involved."

"Pieces to fix Abraham?" I asked. "Or save the world?"

"No." He glanced up in the rearview mirror, and I wasn't sure quite how much sanity shone behind his eyes. "Time. We need to fix time." The way he said it made me feel like I was a second-grader who hadn't learned to count yet.

"We can do that? Fix time?"

"I think . . . yes."

Impossible? Probably. But, then, it wouldn't be the first impossible thing my brother had done. I was living proof of that.

"All right," I said, "We'll fix time. But first we need to get to Gloria's for Abraham, right?"

"Yes," he said. "Of course, yes." He turned his attention back to the foggy road, taking us away from the harbor and toward Newport Avenue.

I stared at his reflection in the rearview mirror. He carried a tightness around his eyes, and in every line of his body, really. As if he expected something to jump out at him from each dark corner we passed. I just hoped captivity hadn't rattled his brain too hard. It had been three years since I'd seen him, and his imprisonment could not have been easy.

Gloria's place was about thirty minutes away, a squat, square building crammed between an antiques shop and a restaurant space that constantly rotated through owners, unable to stay in business long enough for the new layer of paint to dry.

The faded sign above her shop windows said she sold books and odds and ends. While I knew she did do that, she also had one of the most advanced secret medical facilities known only to House Brown beneath her shop. We made sure it remained secret and advanced by sending her monetary support, equipment, and tech whenever we could get our hands on it.

Because of that and Gloria's skills, a lot of people in House Brown had received care the other Houses would never have provided.

I'd never been here, but several years ago, Quinten had spent a year working with Gloria, learning basic and maybe even some advanced doctoring from her.

He'd never told me why he'd decided to leave her tutelage. That was not long after our parents had died, when he had been intent on absorbing the best on-the-road education House Brown could scrape together for him.

He parked the van back behind the shop. "I think this is bad . . . well, not the worst idea," Quinten said, "but it might not be a good idea."

"Fixing time?" I asked.

"No." He frowned at me and shook his head slightly as if he couldn't understand why I wasn't following his mental leaps. "Coming to Gloria," he said. "She's . . ."

His voice faded and his eyes went distant.

This was no time for him to check out.

"She's what, Quinten?" I asked.

He shook his head again, and this time his eyes cleared. "I suppose it doesn't matter. We do have wounded, and some of us are House Brown. All right. Stay here a second. I'll make sure she wants to see us."

He got out of the van, and Neds and I sat in silence a bit, the engine ticking off heat in the cooler air of the night.

"This might be a strange question," Left Ned said. "But how much do you trust your brother?"

"Completely," I answered truthfully. "Why?"

"Besides I don't know the man?" Right Ned answered. "He just seems like he's got an awful lot of things buzzing around in his head and not a lot of it making sense."

"He's been gone for three years. A prisoner." I had to pause so I could swallow down my anger. "Might take him more than one night on the run to pull himself into civilized manners."

"It's not the manners so much that bother me," Left Ned said. "Does he seems . . . right to you?"

"Not to say your brother's a problem," Right Ned amended. "We just want to know *you* think he's in his right mind. That he's the same man you could trust when you last saw him three years ago."

"He is," I said. "I trust him."

"Good," Left Ned said. "Because if I were thinking of turning us in, it'd be here, now that we've reached the mainland. And it'd be at a House Brown safe house like Gloria's."

"Really, Neds Harris? You were a spy for House Silver."

Left Ned winced at the tartness of my tone, and I regretted letting the words carry anger. I was tired. I was worried.

Abraham was as near to dying as a galvanized could be. My brother wasn't wholly himself.

"Ex-spy for House Silver," Right Ned said quietly.

"I know," I said, drawing my fingers through my hair. "I'm sorry. I trust you. You did just drag our butts out of the fire. I don't think any of us should be doubting our motives. We're pretty much all in this together. Unless you want out, which I'd totally understand."

"No," Right Ned said. "My point is that we were spying on you and you trusted us. Just like you trust your brother now."

"He's saying you might not be as good a judge of people as you think you are, Tilly," Left Ned said.

"I got that," I said.

I stared out at the dark edges of buildings against the night sky, thinking. Quinten had always been a little distracted when he had his head in books too long.

I was used to his nonlinear trains of thought. But he was my brother. He'd done everything in his power to save me when I was hurt and dying as a child. He'd spent his life protecting me. I knew he was easy to laugh, had a hell of a singing voice, and hated losing at board games.

And I knew without a doubt that he loved me and would never betray me.

"No," I said quietly, "I don't think I've ever trusted anyone like I've trusted my brother. I like you, Neds, even after I found out you'd been keeping an eye on me for Reeves Silver. But my brother . . ." I pushed my hair back behind my ear with one hand, the stitches that lined my wrist glowing with mercurial light in the darkness.

"I've always trusted him. Looked up to him. He's a force of genius in my life who never got anything wrong."

"He got captured and imprisoned," Left Ned noted. "Not a lot of right about that."

"I know," I said. "He's made mistakes, but morally he's solid. I still trust him. I always will."

Neds nodded. "That's good enough for me," Right Ned said.

Left Ned didn't say anything. I was pretty sure he didn't agree. But it was nice of him not to say so.

And, ultimately, we didn't need trust. We just needed to save the world.

2

HOUSE ORANGE

Slater Orange knew his enemies, these heads of Houses who gathered in this small, private, fortified chamber. He had once been one of them.

They were mortals who wielded the power of their station, their Houses, and the world. Mortals looking for the key to eternal life—a key he had found.

Slater wore the galvanized body that had once belonged to a servant of his named Robert Twelfth. He was almost used to Robert Twelfth's stitched body now that it had been carrying his mind, his thoughts, his life for more than a day. And while the body wasn't born of House Orange bloodline, it had bestowed upon him the one thing all the other heads of Houses would never be strong enough to claim: immortality.

When he had been Slater, head of House Orange, he had changed the laws that ruled his House. Now the power he had once wielded as the head of House Orange was his, even though the other Heads of Houses thought him to be the lowly galvanized Robert Twelfth.

"This meeting will now come to order," John Black, House Defense, said.

All the heads of Houses sat at the curved table that edged the chamber, a wall at their back and a clear view of the other people in the room. The heads of Houses had never trusted one another, though they hand in hand and more often knife in back, ruled the world together.

Slater—or Robert, as he must be called now—stood at the other side of the room, four of John Black's men next to him and unseen laser-locked weapons aimed at his head. He was the enemy here, the other, the galvanized.

But not for long.

His gaze ticked over the gathered: four women and four men. Troi Blue, House Water; Aranda Red, House Power; Kiana White, House Medical; Feye Green, House Agriculture. Troi Blue, who appeared to be twenty but was decades older than that, carried the most power of them all. She looked just as angry and on the edge as the rest of those who were gathered here today.

Of the remaining heads of Houses—Gideon Violet, House Faith; Welton Yellow, House Technology; John Black, House Defense; and Reeves Silver, House Vice—Slater was only remotely concerned about one of them: Reeves Silver.

Reeves Silver was the snake in the apple orchard of this world. He had appeared upset over the killing of Oscar Gray, who had been the head of House Gray, and shocked at the murder of Slater Orange, but Slater knew that was a ruse. Reeves Silver had been making deals, connections, and bribes within the Houses for years on end.

He was, in his own way, positioning himself to rule

them all. And only Slater had the brains to see through Reeves Silver's lies.

He played the stage, patient as a spider, waiting for the strings of his web to tremble with the struggles of his foes. Years of blood stained Reeves Silver's hands, though he had kept his brutality carefully hidden and blamed on others.

Yet now he sat with all the eyes of the Houses upon him, to hear judgment on the murder of Oscar Gray perpetrated by his galvanized, Helen Eleventh.

That shooting, along with Slater's own false murder at the hands of Abraham Seventh, had terminated the treaty between the galvanized and the Houses.

To say that the Houses teetered on declaring open war upon each other was not overstating the tension in the room.

Slater had his stake set in that conflict too. He was the only person in position to rule House Orange. He had made sure of that before he was transplanted into the galvanized body.

In time, he would have the power of all the Houses. He would rule and see Reeves Silver deposed, killed, and buried.

"It is clear from the treaty between Houses and galvanized," John Black continued in his low voice, "that the murders of Oscar Gray and Slater Orange have made said treaty null and void. This leaves us with the decision of punishment. House Black will hear from each House. House Black will also note that House Gold, Money, has exempted itself from these proceedings, citing their non-involvement in galvanized ownership. House Blue, please begin."

Troi Blue wore a pale blue dress that made her coal-black skin glow with a youthful sheen. Her hair was braided away from her temples to reveal flawless, innocent features.

Slater knew she presented herself in such a manner to flaunt her manufactured youth, the formulas of which she had bought at heavy cost from House White, Medical.

"It is House Blue's stance that all galvanized shall remain imprisoned, bodies separated from brains, for fifty years," she said. "At such time, we shall reassess their use to the Houses."

"House Red agrees." Aranda Red, Power, was quick to echo House Blue's decree, which wasn't like her. It was no secret that she lusted to replace Troi Blue as the most powerful House leader. Why side with her now?

Slater frowned. He had been perhaps too concerned with getting rid of his disease-riddled body to pay attention to the shifts in allegiances among the Houses this past decade.

"House Silver also agrees," Reeves Silver said. "With an option to free the galvanized before the end of their sentence if their skills are needed."

"I agree," Feye Green said. "House Green agrees," she amended. "With a further modification. We will allow reassignment of galvanized to the Houses when and if they regain their freedom."

"Yellow is opposed," Welton Yellow said. "Just because Reeves Silver's galvanized shoots someone in the face doesn't mean all the galvanized have gone crazy. One mistake should not be a debt all the galvanized pay."

Of course that boy would be opposed to locking up

the stitched. He treated his own galvanized, Foster First, as if he were a robot toy built for his amusement. Welton Yellow had never taken ruling his House seriously. Unfortunately, there were very few other members of House Yellow stable enough to be put in charge of all the technology in the world.

"It is how the treaty is written," John Black said. "If one falls, they all fall."

"House Faith also opposes galvanized imprisonment," Gideon Violet said. "And further suggests that we each, as individual Houses, decide and carry out the punishment of the galvanized under our keep."

That wasn't a surprise from the head of the House that ruled all faith and faithful activities in the world. Gideon was showing his age, and perhaps his favoritism for Clara Third, the galvanized who had served his House since even before the beginning of the treaty.

"Medical opposes body-removal imprisonment," Kiana White, head of House Medical, said. "Removing their brains from their bodies will lead to mental instability. If we want the galvanized to remain viable for our use, we will offer them the same imprisonment conditions as humans."

"House Defense also opposes," John Black said. "There is language in the treaty that can be argued against a combined sentencing. Which means this decision rests four to four. I move we incarcerate the galvanized in humane prisons while we sort through the matter. We will reconvene on the issue when Houses Gray and Orange are in possession of ruling members to put forth a voice.

"Is there a claimant to House Gray?" John Black asked.

"I claim head of House Gray." A man stepped forward into the room. Hollis Gray, Oscar Gray's younger brother.

Slater had seen the smooth-faced, snake-thin man many times and knew, as all the Houses knew, that he had stabbed and slandered his way up the ladder in House Gray, positioning himself to take over when his brother stepped down.

But what Slater had never noticed before was the satisfied smirk Aranda Red hid away at the sight of him. She wanted him in place as head of the House. She might have even been behind Oscar Gray's killing.

Wasn't that interesting? He had thought Reeves Silver had killed the soft old man, but perhaps Reeves had been hired to do so.

Reeves did so like a game.

"Hollis Gray," John Black said. "You are the next in line to succeed House Gray. Are there any objections?"

It was only a perfunctory question. The Houses had long ago decided it was best to let each house choose their own successors. After a moment of silence, John Black continued. "Welcome to the head of House Gray, Hollis Gray."

Hollis simply nodded once, putting forth a cool smile that did not reach his dark eyes. "It is my honor to fulfill the duties of House Gray," he said. "All contracts currently in place between Gray and other houses shall remain so for ninety days. After which term they can be negotiated."

Also standard procedure. Hollis Gray strode to the table and took the empty seat there, next to Gideon Violet.

"Now we must move on to the issue of House Orange rulership," John Black said. "Robert Twelfth, please step forward."

Slater crossed to the center of the room and stood under the gaze of those who had just hours ago been his peers. No: his inferiors. They all thought they were above him now. But they were so very wrong.

"The records of House Orange clearly state Slater Orange intended for you to speak as the head of House Orange. Permanently," John Black said. "In light of the recent deaths—both Oscar Gray and Slater Orange—at the hands of galvanized, we are reluctant to allow you to stand as head of House, no matter what Slater Orange signed into law."

"I assure you, I have only the interests of House Orange in mind," Slater said.

"You have not been asked your opinion," Troi Blue snapped. "Stay silent until you are asked to speak, galvanized."

Slater tipped his head down, hoping it might look like obedience, even though he was fuming inside. How dare she speak to him as if he were nothing? He had done something none of them had dreamed to achieve: transferred his mind into a body that would never die.

He was immortal.

Troi Blue and the others would die, no matter how many chemicals they injected to keep their false youth. He was above them. He had always been above them.

John Black continued. "Unless another House wishes to assume the debt and responsibility for Robert Twelfth as head of House, we shall place House Orange and all dealings with and from House Orange on hold until such time as a new head of House is in place. Will anyone stand with Robert Twelfth of House Orange?"

Slater knew the answer to that question. None of the Houses would stand by a galvanized acting in a human role. And yet the law within each House was not within another House's control. Lawfully, by House Orange laws, he was already head of that House and it was a mockery to think they could take that away from him.

"I will stand with Robert Twelfth."

Slater turned, surprised, and gazed at Reeves Silver.

The man was lean, tanned, and wore his white hair as a sort of prize, even though he didn't appear to be much older than thirty. His gaze was unreadable, self-satisfied, and brief, before he turned his full attention to the other heads of Houses.

"House Silver will stand responsible for Robert Twelfth's decisions with House Orange for a full year," Reeves said. "If he fails, we will settle his debt and appoint a suitable head of House from within House Orange."

The silence in the room said more than words could. Reeves Silver never did anything out of charity. Of course, neither did any of the other heads of Houses. There was something in this for him. But for once, Slater didn't know what it was.

"So witnessed," John Black said. "So shall the decision stand for review in one year from this date.

"As for the matter of the galvanized, they will be surrendered to House Black for imprisonment until a final vote is taken."

"I didn't agree to that," Welton Yellow said.

"Nor did I," Gideon Violet said.

"Gentlemen." John Black dropped the formalities. "I

don't give a damn what you want. Two heads of Houses are dead—killed by galvanized. Turn yours in to me so they can be locked up and observed, or be prepared to step down as head of your House. You know it's within my abilities to force this issue."

"Come to my House to force the issue, then," Gideon Violet said, "and you will be refused. The galvanized who stands with me is not a killer." He stood and stormed out of the room.

"Well"—Welton Yellow clapped his hands together once—"this has been fun. Just a delight. Good day, all."

"I expect you to bring me Foster First, Welton," John Black said. "Or I will come for him."

"Will you? I wonder how many men you will be willing to lose when you try to take him from me."

"Do you really want to find out?"

Welton and John glared at each other; then Welton smiled, smug as a cat. "I think I do, actually. Sorry, John, but Foster is mine to care for. He will never be thrown in prison. Not while I'm alive. I'd prefer if you didn't fight me on that. It will only end up messy for us both."

John studied the boy. Slater knew the head of Defense had a soft spot when it came to Welton Yellow. John had been a friend to Oscar Gray, who seemed to see the good in every worthless and weak person in the world. Too many years had softened the head of House Defense. A weakness Slater intended to exploit.

"You know it's my job, Welton," John Black said evenly.

"I know."

"Then I will be seeing you soon."

"Looking forward to it."

"Is there anyone else who wants to make this difficult on themselves and their House?" John Black asked.

No one answered.

"Good. This meeting is convened." He stood, glanced at Slater, glanced at Reeves Silver, and shook his head. Then he also walked out of the room.

"Robert," Reeves Silver said as the other Houses left the room. "Attend me."

Slater narrowed his eyes at the man who thought he was his owner.

This might not be how Slater intended the takeover of his own House to play out, but these circumstances would still work in his favor. Reeves Silver was a liar, a thief, and a clever man.

But, then, so was Slater. Reeves Silver wouldn't be a problem once he was dead. Slater would see that day come very, very soon.

After all, he had already put plans in place to kill Abraham Seventh and Matilda Case. The best assassins in the world were on their trail.

One more death on his hands would be no trouble at all.

3

The world was different when you found me.
Now I'm a part of the fight, a part of making
things better.

—from the diary of E. N. D.

Quinten Case opened the back of the van. "She's in," he said breathlessly, the curls of his hair sticking up around the edge of his stocking hat. "Let's go. Keep your faces down, and don't talk until we're clear."

"Do you think we're being watched?" I asked.

Quinten shrugged. "We're in a city, so one must assume."

I covered Abraham's face; then we scrambled out of the van, keeping our heads tipped down. We carried Abraham quickly across the concrete parking lot, the earthy scent of a wood fire hanging thick on the stillness and fog. We entered the back room of the shop.

At first glance it looked like a receiving and mailing room for a legitimate business. Boxes, tape, and other packing goods filled the shelves. It smelled of paper and glue and just a hint of moth repellent. It wasn't a large space, but the ceiling had enough lights to chase most of the shadows back to the corners.

Corners into which cameras were mounted.

The door automatically locked behind us with the teeth-vibrating hum of black-market tech snapping on. Gloria had enough scrubbers, locks, and blocks to keep the Houses off our trail for days.

If we had days.

"This way," Quinten said. He strode down the aisles of boxes and bookshelves.

Left Ned gave me a raised eyebrow and a look.

I answered both by starting off after my brother.

Neds and I handled the stretcher, me at Abraham's head and him at his feet. This place was a lot bigger than I'd thought. It was also spaced so that it was fairly easy to maneuver a stretcher through the corridor.

Finally, Quinten turned right, down an aisle that was narrower, created by shelves with file boxes stacked tight and high on both sides.

At the end of the aisle was a wide wooden door. I didn't see any cameras, but that didn't mean they weren't here.

Quinten tapped on the door, and the door slid into a pocket in the wall.

Gloria, whom I'd only ever seen on screens, gestured for us all to enter, then closed the heavy door behind us.

Her face was smooth, dusty olive skin framed by long, straight hair that shone glossy black. Gloria's eyes were bright, brown, and wide. She was shorter than I expected, a bit curvier at the bust and hip, and even more beautiful in person.

"Matilda," she said. "Please put him there for now." She pointed at a wide table on one side of the room. "We will need to be quick." She crossed to the computers near that table and flicked through screens.

The room was clean, white, clinical. It didn't look or feel like a back-alley kind of operation. This was a top-notch medical facility. The machines, equipment, lights, and cabinets with glass doors that revealed carefully labeled containers weren't homey, but the place was well stocked and capable of handling all sorts of medical disasters.

"I can scramble your signals out to a five-mile radius," Gloria said.

"That's not far," Quinten said.

"It's the best I can do. You wouldn't have been tracked over water—the signal is too erratic—but here on land, they will try to lock on to you. The faster we debug you, the better."

"Debug?" I asked, easing Abraham, stretcher and all, onto the table. His skin had gone a deeper yellow, with bluish shadows around his eyes and mouth. If we didn't get that Shelley dust out of his system soon, it was going to do irreversible damage.

"Every House bugs their people," Gloria said. "Quinten is carrying four bugs. How many Houses did you get loaned out to?"

"Several," he said with a sigh, pulling off the beanie and dragging fingers through his curls.

"And Mr. . . . ?" she turned away from the screen and gave Neds a questioning look.

"Harris," Right Ned supplied.

"You have one bug."

He nodded.

"But you don't, Matilda," she said. "So that's lucky for you."

"What about him?" I asked, pointing toward Abraham.

"His vitals and systems are under such distress right now that I can't tell."

"Shouldn't we stabilize him?" I asked.

"First we have to pull those bugs. Or I won't have any time to fix anyone, because we'll have half a dozen Houses knocking down the doors."

Quinten stepped forward. "Do me first."

Her gaze searched his face and I thought there was a question there, the way her eyes settled unflinchingly on his. I thought there was an answer in the tip of his head, the softening of his mouth, which her gaze slipped down to study.

I had no idea what they were not talking about.

If I had to guess? My brother had spent time here for more than just the medical training she offered. He had spent time here for her.

What else would have brought such sudden calm and focus to him? What else would have shadowed his eyes with old pain?

"It will hurt," she said quietly, still not looking away from his mouth.

"I know." His lips slipped up into a rueful smile.

She seemed to remember that they weren't alone in the room and straightened a bit. "This way, then." She took him to what appeared to be a lit shower stall at the far side of the room.

That was my cue to look away. Seriously, if my brother was about to get naked, I didn't want to see it.

"You knew about bugs?" I asked Neds.

He shrugged. "Didn't think about it, really," Left Ned

said. "It's so commonplace. You get owned by a House, you get bugged. Everyone's bugged."

"I'm not. House Brown doesn't bug," I said.

"Yeah, well, House Brown isn't so much a House as a handful of people who don't have the sense to stop fighting a war they lost a long time ago."

"Freedom isn't something you give up on when you're tired," I said, as the implications of bugging clicked through the tumblers of my brain.

"That means House Silver knew you were out on my farm for two years," I said.

"He sent me there to keep an eye on you," Right Ned said, as if admitting a guilt he would rather forget. "Didn't take a bug to track me down."

"And every time Quinten came home, he was sending a signal to whatever House had last claimed him?"

"Maybe. Maybe not," Left Ned said. "Your place has scramblers like I've never seen before. I've told you this before: there's something in the soil out there, Tilly. Something that messes with the laws of the world."

"Why, Neds Harris," I said, putting a little grin behind my words. "I thought you said you didn't believe in magic."

"I don't. But there's strange nanotech in your dirt and mixes of minerals that *do* things to things."

Things like Lizard, who was stitched up out of reptile parts the size of a house, wings included. Things like the pocket-sized sheep that never aged and grew wool that could catch up and save spare minutes of time.

Things like the life thread spun out of the minerals and who knew what else in the creek, and onto spools in my father's laboratory beneath our old pump house.

The same thread that held me together and made it so I could feel.

The same thread that was holding Abraham together.

All of it coming from the land my parents had tried to keep secret and refused to give up, even when it meant their death.

"Sadie and Corb were with us," I said, catching a quick glimpse of Quinten stepping into the booth and lifting his arms out to the side, his stance wide. He still had his clothes on, so that was good.

Gloria closed a door that became a screen and displayed his body as if it were made of a map of roads and twisted electrical wires.

"And?" Left Ned asked, bringing me back to the conversation.

"If anyone was tracking our bugs, they will find Sadie and Corb."

"You heard what she said," Right Ned said. "Can't track over water. And don't worry about Sadie and Corb. They know how to lie low. They knew what they were getting into. It isn't just your head that has a price on it, Tilly. Abraham is the one person the Houses will turn the world inside out to find. They'd like to get their hands on you, but he's an accused murderer."

"He didn't do it," I said.

Right Ned nodded, but Left Ned just looked down at his shoe the way a person does when he's trying to be polite enough not to point out that you're fooling yourself.

"I'm sure you're right," Right Ned said.

Which sounded like he agreed with his brother more than with me.

Abraham was so still on that table, I couldn't even see his chest rise and fall. My heart clenched in fear, in sorrow. I didn't want him to die. Didn't want to watch him suffer.

What I wanted was to touch him, to wake him up and see that sardonic grin on his face and spark of humor in his eyes. I wanted to tell him it was going to be okay. I wanted to ask him if he really did go into House Orange and kill Slater Orange for the heinous treatment Slater had given Robert Twelfth, a galvanized who was Abraham's dear friend.

Abraham was the galvanized who had led the other galvanized through the Uprising that had put them at war with the Houses. He'd also been the one who had led the galvanized into the peace negotiations and the eventual treaty that had bargained away galvanized rights for the chance for human freedom—House Brown freedom.

I'd seen him angry. I'd watched as he casually cut off a man's ear just for talking to him wrong.

So, yes, I could imagine he could be pushed to killing someone without suffering a lot of regret. Especially that sadistic prick Slater Orange.

But if Abraham were found to have murdered Slater, it would dissolve the treaty between the galvanized and the Houses they served. It would send the galvanized into prisons, or, worse, they could be reduced to nothing but their immortal brains, locked away conscious but alone for years.

I couldn't see Abraham risking himself and risking the other galvanized that way.

I rubbed my hands over the cold shiver that ran down my arms. That kind of isolation would drive anyone mad.

"Mr. Harris?" Gloria said as she helped Quinten out of the booth. "You're next."

Quinten had always been an almost manic force of energy in my life. While he was capable of holding very still and being very quiet and thoughtful, when left to his own devices he defaulted to smiling, laughing, and going on long, muttering rants about things I never could understand.

My brother was charismatic, caring, and brilliant, all of which had made him the de facto leader of House Brown.

But the man who walked out of that booth was a shaken pale shell of the man in my memories. His eyes narrowed in pain as he pushed away Gloria's concern, walked to the nearest chair, and eased himself into it.

Left Ned took up a lungful of air and let it out quickly. "Faster, the better, Doc," he said as he strode into the booth.

"I'll do my best," she said.

I walked over to Quinten. "Are you all right?"

He sat with his forearms resting across his knees, white sleeves rolled up, as was his habit, his dark gray vest unbuttoned, his hair wet across his forehead. He laced his fingers together and hung his head, every line telegraphing exhaustion. "Yes," he said, not very convincingly.

"Can I get you anything? Water?" I put my hand on his sweat-dampened shoulder, and he put in the effort to tip his head up and squint at me.

"I'll be fine. It just . . . stings."

"You're shaking."

"It stings a lot."

I rubbed his shoulder gently, wishing I could do more for him.

I glanced over at Neds. The road maps and wires that spread out through his body were more compressed and knotted than Quinten's.

Gloria didn't seem the least bit bothered by that. She tapped at an intersection of lines at the side of Left Ned's neck, and that area grew larger. I didn't know what she saw there, but it must have been what she was looking for. She pulled out a small instrument shaped like a cross between a pair of scissors and an oversized medical syringe and set it carefully against the screen. The lines and roads lit up, and Neds stiffened as if they'd just been shocked.

Left Ned grunted through clenched teeth.

She twisted the device, like she was twirling a fork in noodles, then yanked.

Left Ned grunted again, and Right Ned sweated in sympathetic pain. That one bug did more than sting. And my brother had had four bugs removed.

"Maybe you should lie down," I said.

"Maybe you shouldn't worry so much," he said.

I made a face at him, and he managed a smile.

"Just a moment longer while I look for any other bugs," Gloria said softly as she manipulated the screen though several other settings.

I didn't know how we were going to get Abraham in there. He wasn't conscious. He couldn't stand. At least he wouldn't feel the thing being removed.

"That's it," she announced. "You are clean. You may step out, Mr. Harris."

She opened the screen and Neds walked out of the booth a lot more steady on their feet than Quinten. Left Ned threw me a glare, like this bug thing was my fault, but Right Ned just rolled his eyes, letting me know his brother was in a surly mood.

"Now," Gloria said, strolling over to me, "let's have a look at your companion. I'll need a set of hands."

Quinten pushed against his thighs, trying to stand, but didn't make it.

"I got it," I said, pressing down on his shoulder. "Rest." He didn't argue, which was just another sign of how much the procedure had taken out of him.

I walked over to the table where Abraham was lying. "Don't know how we're going to get him in the booth."

"We aren't," she said. "This won't be as pleasant, but he's galvanized and unconscious. He shouldn't feel anything."

She opened a drawer at the foot of the table and pulled out a roll of shiny translucent material. We each took a corner of impossibly thin material, drew it up off the roll, and spread it across Abraham over the blanket that still wrapped him.

I was careful not to touch his skin, even though none of his skin, except his face, was exposed, for fear my touch would make it so he felt his injuries.

Touching me gave the galvanized the ability to feel their bodies, which were usually numb. I thought it had something to do with the threads that stitched me.

"Just tuck the film under his chin," Gloria said, "and back around his neck as far under as you can reach."

I tried to keep the material between my fingers and Abraham's skin, but when I accidentally brushed the nape of his neck, he moaned softly.

Just like back at the farm when he'd come to me hurt

and bleeding. Just like when I'd first seen the bare skin of him, his shirt cut away so I could tend his wounds.

I'd fallen for him then, a wounded creature I thought I could heal. Then I'd fallen for the man who had stood with me while my world fell apart.

"Shouldn't we get him blood first?" I asked.

To my surprise, Gloria glanced over at Quinten, her expression shifting out of the studied frown to something softer. Worried.

Quinten had leaned back the chair and was scrubbing fingertips over the back of his head as if massaging a headache there. "Blood can wait, I think," he said. "It's more important that we get the bug out first. Then we'll do the fluid push. After that, blood."

I raised my eyebrows at Quinten.

"What?" he said.

"I never thought of you as an expert in the medical field," I said. "Gloria is a doctor."

"Yes," he agreed. "For people. She hasn't worked on many galvanized."

"None, in fact," she said.

Oh. There wasn't anyone more familiar with how a galvanized was put together than Quinten. After all, he was the only man alive I knew who had actually built a galvanized: me.

Gloria got busy scanning Abraham, which took a lot longer with him lying on the table and maybe also because he was galvanized.

Unlike Neds and Quinten, whose road maps were lines of continuous colors that all made a sort of sense, the lines that made up Abraham's different parts were a hodgepodge of color and loops and knots that branched off or ended abruptly.

The uneven joining made it look like order had been at the bottom of the priority list when he'd been put together.

Looking at all his parts, at how different they all were, I thought it might be better that he couldn't feel. Maybe being numb was a kindness so the galvanized weren't in constant pain from their grafted bits.

Gloria found the bug in the webwork that was centered in his chest and pulled out the scissor-syringe device.

"His heart?" I asked.

"No, but very close," she said.

I touched the back of her hand and she paused, searching my gaze. I don't know what she saw there; maybe fear.

"I'll be careful," she said. Then she pushed the tip of the instrument deep enough to puncture the film, twisted, and yanked.

Even though he shouldn't be nearly conscious enough to feel it, Abraham moaned. I hated that he had felt it at all. I hated knowing how much worse it would have been if he were awake.

The bug wriggled. A pulse of raw electricity spun and unspun in a knot that dangled between the blades of the device in Gloria's hands, dripping sparks and blood. She squeezed the handles of the instrument together and sliced the knot in half.

A loud snap and the smell of burned wires filled the room.

"Nicely done," Quinten said. "Quick. Clean. Now let's see to flushing his system, and then blood." He groaned but was on his feet.

Before I could tell him I didn't think he was recovered enough to be tending to someone else, he gently but unceremoniously moved me aside.

"What can I do?" I asked as he and Gloria began pulling out drawers and piling tubes and other items on top of Abraham.

"I'd kill for some food," Quinten said. "Gloria, do you have anything, or should we go out for a supply run?"

"Plenty in the kitchen," she said. "Help yourself."

"That way, Tilly." Quinten pointed, and I realized my brother had a rather intimate knowledge of the layout of the place. The way he and Gloria were working in sync with each other even though they weren't talking, on top of how they were avoiding looking in each other's eyes for too long but couldn't help but sneak glances at each other, got me wondering a few more things.

Like how much of my brother's other annual trips had been spent here with her. I could ask why he'd never told me this about her—that she was his girlfriend—but Quinten wasn't the only one who was hungry.

"Feel like giving me a hand in the kitchen?" I asked Neds.

He leaned one hip on a table near the debugging booth, his arms crossed over his chest. Left Ned was scowling, which is to say he had on his normal expression.

Right Ned watched me with that spark of curiosity in his eyes. That was pretty normal too.

"Isn't it your turn to cook?" Right Ned said, following me.

I grinned. "We get back to the farm in time, and I'll do more than cook. I'll bake pies. Every fruit I can get my hands on. But since we're here . . ." I pushed through the door Quinten had pointed at and stepped into a tidy, compact modern kitchen. "Let's check the cupboards and see what's fast and easy."

Neds found a couple of big cans of soup, and I pulled out a loaf of bread, cheese, and olives, and sliced up some fresh tomatoes. Didn't take long for a meal of soup and grilled-cheese sandwiches, enough for all of us, to be spread on the table,.

"I'll see if they're done," I said.

Right Ned tipped his chin in acknowledgment. He hadn't bothered waiting and was already chewing on a bite of sandwich, while Left Ned slurped down some soup.

The rich cheese, warm bread, and toasted butter smell, along with the fresh fragrance of tomatoes, made me want to dive face-first into my portion of the meal.

Instead I strode out into the other room, apparently quietly enough that my brother and Gloria didn't hear me coming.

Of course, it might also have been that kiss they were both so engaged in that distracted them from the sound of my footsteps.

4

This journal is for you. It is my apology, my chance to make up for what I did to you.
—from the diary of E. N. D.

I supposed the polite thing to do would be to leave them some privacy. Give my brother and Gloria time to finish off that kiss as slowly as they wanted. But I hadn't ever seen my brother kiss a woman.

And it had been years since I'd had something to tease him about. Yes, we were running for our lives. Didn't mean we were dead.

"Soup's on!" I said, loud and cheery.

It was all kinds of fun to watch my brother's shoulders tighten up like I'd just snapped a string on his back.

"Oh, goodness," I said. "I see you're both busy. Sorry to interrupt."

He didn't respond to me, but made a rather loving and slow disengagement from Gloria. His fingertips tightened just slightly on the side of her face, as if he regretted having to let her go like a drowned man regrets being out of air, before he stepped back a bit so none of him was touching any of her.

It was so tender, I almost felt bad about breaking them up. Almost.

"Matilda?" he said, still looking into Gloria's eyes. "What is it?"

"I thought you were hungry," I said. "We made soup. And sandwiches."

Gloria nodded, so slightly I almost didn't catch it.

Quinten finally turned to me. Frustration heated his eyes. I gave him a grin and he sighed.

"We are hungry," Quinten said. "I am," he corrected, his stomach growling. "Thank you *so* much for letting us know the food is ready."

"Sure," I said, ignoring his sarcasm. "How is Abraham?" He seemed to be resting beneath a clean sheet and light blanket, the machines next to him feeding fluid into his chest.

"Doing well enough." Gloria's voice was a little husky. She cleared her throat and walked away, her back toward me and Quinten, as if she had something important to do that would keep her hands off my brother.

Okay, now I did regret interrupting.

Sorry, I mouthed to Quinten, but he just shook his head, his faint smile promising revenge.

"We set up a push of fluids," she continued in a businesslike tone, "and chemicals that should neutralize the Shelley dust. After that, blood. He should wake soon."

"Do you know how soon?" I asked.

"A few hours?" She glanced at Quinten, and they held that gaze a little too long before he nodded.

"Perhaps by morning, I think," he said. "At the earliest. He'll sleep the night."

"So, we'll need a place to stay," I said.

"You can stay here," Gloria said. "I expected it, really."

"Do you have room for us all?" I asked. My brother had gone awfully still again, and I could guess what sort of thoughts were running through his head about a night spent here. With her.

"I suppose we could double bunk if we need to," I pressed innocently. "Maybe the two of you could share a room?"

Quinten blushed red up his neck and threw me a look that said he was going to make me pay for teasing him so hard.

I couldn't stop grinning. It was sort of delightful to see my older brother blush up and get prickly just because I'd noticed he had a girlfriend.

I mean, good for him and all that. I didn't expect him to live a life of solitude. He'd mentioned other women he'd briefly dated. But he had never brought anyone home to the farm. He'd never even told me that there was a woman out in the world whom he still cared for. I liked Gloria, had worked with her off and on over the years by radio and vid feeds.

I was a little disappointed he hadn't wanted to tell me about their relationship.

Maybe he hadn't wanted to bring her home because he would have risked her knowing about the land, the odd creatures that we kept on it, and, of course, his odd little sister: me.

Or maybe this thing, whatever it was between him

and Gloria, was private and precious to him. Something a little sister shouldn't be tormenting him over because his heart was already tormented enough.

I couldn't help it; I glanced at Abraham. Okay. So maybe I understood not wanting to tell someone about feelings that were taking root in you before you knew what sort of thing they were going to bloom into.

"We could find another place to stay," Quinten said, not looking at Gloria, his gaze burning instead into me.

I suddenly realized it might have been a tactical error to annoy the supergenius. He was probably already plotting his revenge. And he was both a creative and clever man.

"We don't want to put you in more danger," he said.

"No need," Gloria said a little too quickly. "There are sleeping quarters upstairs. A half-dozen beds. You aren't the first visitors in the night who have come to me for medical attention. I always have room." She pressed her hands together, but her eyes were for Quinten alone.

He took a careful breath and schooled his face. I was amazed at how quickly and calmly he shut off any indication of his emotions. He turned toward Gloria.

"Please," she said. "I want you to make yourself at home. What I have is yours."

"Glory," Quinten said quietly. "We don't want to cause you any trouble. And we are in so much of it."

"You haven't. You won't," she said. "No matter how much you're in. Please stay. I want you to."

From the silence between them, from the stillness that said they would both be running into each other's arms if a certain person weren't also in the room, I knew this was more than just a stolen kiss. Whatever Quinten had with

Gloria was wrapped up in a past that seemed filled with regret.

For both of them.

It wasn't like he could stay to mend those regrets.

Maybe we shouldn't have run here. Or maybe he'd wanted to come here for this last good-bye.

"Okay, then. Well, so," I said awkwardly, no longer feeling up to teasing him. "There's soup ready when you want it." I turned to leave.

"Soup sounds wonderful," Gloria said, walking past Quinten and over to me.

"There's no rush," I said. "We can keep it hot if you two need a little time to"—I waved my hands in the air— "catch up."

"I haven't eaten since breakfast." She pressed her warm, strong hand against my arm kindly as she walked past me. "I think a little hot food will clear my head."

I watched her walk down the short hall to the kitchen.

My brother was going to kill me.

"Matilda," he said in a warning tone.

I twisted on my feet to look back at him. "Did I interrupt something important?" I asked with an innocence I had no right to claim.

"Yes. But it's not what you think."

"Really? Because I'm pretty sure most medical procedures end with a handshake, not a tongue down someone's throat."

He tipped his head, raising one eyebrow. "Are you done? You know I can make you regret every word."

"Oh, I don't know." I grinned, warming up. "You have been gone for three years, Quinten Case. Seems like I have an awful lot of teasing all stored up in me, bursting to get out."

"Obviously," he drawled. "Do you think you can control yourself long enough that I can eat? I'm starving."

"I'll do my best," I said. "No guarantees."

He shook his head, then walked up to me and draped his arm over my shoulder, squeezing me gently. "You are a pain in the neck, Matilda Case. I missed you."

I slipped my arm around his too-thin waist as we walked toward the kitchen.

It had been a long, long time since we'd been together. I leaned my head briefly on his shoulder that smelled faintly of Gloria's perfume and was just happy that he was alive. "I love you too," I said.

"I know." He planted a kiss on the top of my head. "Thank you for saving me from House Orange," he mumbled softly into my hair. He gave me one last squeeze, then stepped back to hold me at arm's length and give me a disapproving glare. "It took you long enough."

"And you're welcome." I made a face at him. "It's not like you had a bug on you I could track, you know."

"Yes, well, we'll have to come up with some other kind of system if it ever happens again."

"Which it won't," I said.

"But if it does."

"It won't," I repeated.

"We will have another way to find each other," he said. "I'm done with bugs."

We walked into the kitchen.

Neds had finished off his share of the meal and was standing by the coffeepot with a mug in his hand, waiting for it to finish perking.

Gloria sat at the small table in the middle of the kitchen where we'd set out the meal. She looked up as we walked in. "I was just telling Mr. Harris . . ."

"Just Neds," Right Ned said.

"I was just telling Neds," she said, "that the cleansing process on Abraham appears to have gone very well. His vital signs improved immediately, and with the addition of blood, he should be much better soon. Galvanized are very resilient."

"That's good," I said, relief unknotting in my stomach. I knew logically that galvanized couldn't die unless someone went to a lot of effort to destroy the brain. But to rely on that logic without physical proof was a leap of faith I'd been holding my breath on. It was hard to look at Abraham and not see him as a dying man.

"I'd like to know where he got that thread that's holding him together," she said, giving the thread that was visible on my hands a pointed look.

Quinten sat across from her and filled a plate and bowl with food. "Family recipe," he said, lifting the sandwich up to his mouth. "Experimental, secret, and all that."

"Just like everything else about your family," she said. "Experimental, secret. And all that."

He chewed and tipped his hand side to side, shrugging one shoulder. Gloria just gave him a small, intimate smile.

I took my place at the end of the table, my back to the door, and dished out my food.

Quinten wasn't the only one who was starving. Other than a few sips of thermos coffee, I hadn't eaten anything in almost twenty-four hours.

I dug in, and the conversation fell silent while Quinten and I polished off the rest of the food.

Neds put cups down for all of us and filled them with thick black coffee.

"Fresh cream in the icebox," Gloria said, pointing.

Neds retrieved that and gave us each a dollop.

Like I've said, coffee isn't my drink of choice, but the heat and caffeine was a welcome chaser to the meal.

Neds stood near the stove, passing one cup of coffee between his hands as both Right Ned and Left Ned took turns drinking from the cup.

"What's the bunk situation?" Left Ned asked.

"There are beds upstairs." Gloria sat back in her chair with her coffee and tucked one foot up under her leg. "Plenty of room. Not a lot of privacy, I'm afraid, but clean sheets and warm blankets."

"A king's accommodation, if you ask me," Right Ned said. "Thank you. I'm turning in. Are we taking shifts to watch Abraham?"

"I'll do it," I said.

"There's no need." Quinten rubbed at the bridge of his nose, as if the food had reminded him of how tired he was. "He won't wake. He won't move until morning at least. And by then we'll need to travel. No matter his condition. If he can't travel, we need to find him a place to recover."

He paused to give me a look. I didn't know if he meant here with Gloria or somewhere else in the city, but I had only one answer for him.

"No. We aren't leaving him behind. Anywhere. If Gloria is found with him, she'll be thrown in jail. I don't want that; you don't want that; and I'm sure she doesn't want that."

"I understand the risks," she said.

"No," I said. "I won't risk you, nor will I risk losing House

Brown's valuable medical resource you have here. This is too important for too many people."

Quinten narrowed his eyes.

Yeah, well, he wasn't the only person who could use logic to his advantage. And I was not wrong on this matter.

"All right," he said. "We'll find a way to keep Abraham with us if we can." He lifted one finger from around his cup to stop me from saying anything. "And we'll make every effort to see that he heals enough to travel so we can keep him safe."

Left Ned grunted as he pushed off the counter and walked toward the door. "Good luck with that," he muttered. "Ain't any part of this world not looking to take him out. Lost cause, if you ask me."

"We didn't ask," I said after the door swung closed behind him.

"He's your friend?" Gloria asked me.

"Right now he's a man who sees a storm in every drop of rain," I said. "Don't mind him—he gets cranky when he doesn't get his beauty sleep."

I pushed up away from the table and yawned. "I think I'd better get some sleep too. Down the hall to the stairs?"

"Yes, it will be on your left." Gloria said.

"Thank you. For all you've done today. I appreciate your putting yourself out for us. And I'm sorry for back there, when I interrupted that kissing you two were in the middle of."

There was a beat of silence. One more.

Finally Gloria chuckled, a soft, musical sound, and Quinten sighed heavily.

"I should apologize for my sister. She seems to need to be a child about this."

"What?" I said with mock anger. "I wasn't being childish. I was offering a proper apology."

"It's fine," Gloria said. "I appreciate your sincere apology."

"See?" I pointed at Quinten. "She understands the need for manners."

"Unbelievable," Quinten said. "Go. I'll be up in a bit."

"Don't hurry yourself on my account," I said as I walked out of the room. "All I'll be doing is snoring."

The door swung shut. I paused for just a second. It would be easy to listen in and see what happened next between my brother and the good doctor, but I had a pretty clear idea. Besides, the food sat heavy in my stomach, and even the warm coffee couldn't fight off my drowsiness.

I yawned again and walked down the hall to the stairs, then trudged up them.

The entire upper floor was open, the slant of the roof angling down on each side. A fair amount of storage was up here. Over half the loft space was filled with cots that had small tables with lamps next to them. Not a single window was to be found, and I recognized the bulky black-box scramblers up in the rafters. Their presence was particularly comforting considering our current situation.

A door all the way to the left of the room was slightly ajar, just the hint of yellow light escaping to draw me toward it.

Neds were already in bed, boots shucked at the foot of their cot, shirt tossed over the footboard, and blanket pulled up over their shoulders. From the rhythm of their breathing, they were asleep.

I wandered to the lit room, hoping it was a bathroom, and almost groaned in delight. It was a full bathroom with a standing shower and bathtub.

I shut the door, stripped off my duffel, clothes, and boots, and turned on the water. It took a little while for it to get warm. As soon as it was hot, I stepped in and scrubbed the sweat, fear, and anger of the last day and more off me.

The impossible task in front of us just seemed more impossible the more I thought about it. I'd been desperate to get out of the city with Quinten and Abraham. I'd promised Oscar Gray I'd keep Abraham safe. It had been his dying wish. . . .

I swallowed and brushed away the tears mingling with the shower.

I was doing the best I could to fulfill that wish. I was trying to save the world from the Wings of Mercury experiment.

Quinten had told me he was looking for our grandmother's journal while he was at House Orange. He said it held valuable information we needed.

My brother was also convinced that the Wings of Mercury experiment had broken time more than three hundred years ago. And that when time mended—by his calculation, in just a few days—all the galvanized would die.

I'd die.

I knew the Houses might have guessed we were heading to our farm. It was a foolish thing for us to do, but Grandma was there, under the care of Boston Sue, whom I'd found out was a spy and hired gun for Reeves Silver, head of House Silver.

Grandma might be hurt or she might just be bait.

She might have the information that was in her journal somewhere in that forgetful mind of hers.

I couldn't leave her alone and at the whims of House Silver. I had to make sure she would be safe and taken care of if I died.

Any way I looked at it, my chance of surviving this was pretty low. Quinten hadn't broken the law. Neither had Grandma. If I could, I'd make sure they came out of this alive and free.

Neds too.

I didn't know if Gloria's water consumption was being monitored, so I made it quick and washed my hair with soap that smelled like lemons and honey, then got out, dried, and debated getting back into my travel clothes.

If something went wrong tonight, I didn't want to be running in my pajamas, so I got into clean undergarments and put on my jeans and T-shirt, stuffing the long-sleeve shirt and vest into the bag.

I searched the vanity drawers for a brush or comb, found one of each, and took the time to comb my wet hair and then braid it loosely so it wasn't a frizzy menace in the morning.

I slipped out of the room and into darkness. Neds hadn't moved. Quinten was nowhere to be seen. I put my duffel down next to a bed near the stairs and pushed under the covers, the pillow cool and fresh against my cheek. I didn't think I'd sleep.

I was wrong.

5

HOUSE ORANGE

"Close the door and have a seat," Reeves Silver said, as if he were inviting in an old friend. "Can I offer you a drink?" He poured scotch in a glass and held the bottle over a second tumbler.

"No." Slater Orange did as he was told, latching the door, then taking a seat across the desk in Reeves' personal office. He tugged at the cuffs of his shirt, an old, telling habit.

Reeves' eyes lit up when he saw that.

Slater dropped his hands into his lap. "Why have you called me here?"

"Because you and I are partners now," Reeves replied affably, his blue eyes too blue in a face comfortably lined with the lies he told. "Rulers, ruling House Orange side by side. Unless you fail so miserably we must find your replacement."

Slater remained silent.

"Oh, now, have I hurt your feelings? Don't you see how this will work? Our partnership?" Reeves asked. "Fine. Let me try this again. This stunt you've pulled," he waved a finger at Slater, "is impressive. You took a far greater risk than I expected you to take, Slater."

"Robert," he said plainly.

Reeves bit down on a smile. "Let's not play games, Slater. I always thought you were conservative when you made your moves. I certainly never expected you to go to these extremes with your power play. Death? Rebirth or whatever you call that horror you've done to yourself? I believe I've underestimated you all these years, and I am not a man who underestimates his peers. So, a toast. To the surprise of you." He lifted his drink and sipped.

He sat back, fingers pressed together, waiting for Slater's response.

"My name is Robert," Slater said again.

"Are we going to do it this way? Are you expecting me to prove to you that I know you are Slater Orange pressed into that"—here he waved his fingers again—"body?"

"Why would you think I am anything other than Robert?"

Reeves leaned forward again. "I know you, Slater. I might have underestimated your desperation, your sickness, your access to whatever technology it took to implant yourself into that body and brain, but I know you're in there, one hundred percent Slater Orange. I know the stink of you, the hunger of you. I see it behind your eyes. I smell it on your skin.

"And," he said in a conspirator's whisper, "I'd love to know how you did it. But we can save that for later. Right now, here, today, I want you to understand one thing: I own you."

"I can't be owned," Slater said. "I am the head of House Orange. It is the law."

"What is that saying? Good men don't need laws, and bad men always find a way around them? I can claim you. And, really, I already have. Maybe not publically. Not yet. This"—again the finger waved, this time to indicate the two of them—"works for me. Your deals, payments, dues will go through me and my House. Do you understand me, Slater? I own you and your House."

When Slater didn't respond, Reeves set down his tumbler. "I looked into the members of House Orange who might take over ruling. There have been dozens of deaths over the past decade. Subtle, accidental, untraceable misfortunes have befallen every person who could take the throne. The only conceivable candidate left is a ten-year-old boy, who would of course need guidance until he is of age. Guidance I am assuming you would provide until he too was killed. Clever," he said. "Not a long game, but it might be long enough to buy you time to win the trust of the Houses. Or to buy their trust."

"What do you want?" Slater asked.

"You. You are useful to me. I want to give you power—enough to keep you happy and silent. House Orange in your hands. Isn't that what you want? Power for as long as that galvanized body may live?"

Slater's ambitions were much higher than that. He would own Reeves. He would own all of them—and the world. Sooner, much sooner than Reeves suspected. He had the journal Quinten Case was searching for. And in it was the solution he needed: how to control time. But he needed Quinten found and brought to him. Alive.

"Yes," Slater agreed. "I want to rule House Orange."

Reeves narrowed his eyes. Slater held a blank expression, wondering if the head of House Silver could read that partial lie. He did want to rule House Orange, but that was just the beginning of his desires. Desires that began with killing all the galvanized but himself and torturing Quinten Case until he gave him the control over time.

"Good," Reeves said, settling back. "Then we are in agreement. We'll be in touch. I expect you to open your database to me. I want full access to your House and history, partner."

"Of course," Slater said.

Again the pause while Reeves considered him.

Slater waited. Was he giving in too easily? Was he making Reeves suspicious?

"Why Abraham?" Reeves asked.

"What?"

"Why did you set up Abraham Seventh as your murderer?"

So far, Slater had been very careful with this conversation. He had not acknowledged that he was, in fact, Slater and not Robert. He had not agreed to anything that could be used against him if this conversation was being recorded—as he assumed it must be.

He was not going to slip now.

"His fingerprints are on the gun," Slater said. "Perhaps you should ask him why he killed Slater Orange."

The corner of Reeves' mouth curved up. "Maybe I will." he said. "I am looking for him, you know. Abraham and Matilda Case and that brother of hers she seemed so desperate to set free from your House."

"Why?"

"Would you like to guess?" Reeves' eyes burned hard, every muscle in his body tense.

Did he know about the Wings of Mercury experiment? Did he know Quinten was searching through the House histories to find a way to manipulate time?

"John Black is in charge of finding criminals," Slater said smoothly. "Perhaps you should leave their capture to him."

"Of course. But if I happen to find them before him ... well." Reeves tipped his glass to his mouth again. "I will be sure to keep Abraham alive, and maybe that new one—Matilda. But Quinten isn't worth my time. Unless you know of some reason why he should stay breathing?"

Slater remained silent. He was furious but refused to give in to his anger. The answer to that was his secret.

Slater possessed the journal Quinten had been so set on finding. And in it he had discovered an odd and detailed description of the Wings of Mercury experiment.

The experiment appeared to have broken time and also created the galvanized. If Slater's calculations were correct, that break in time would mend in just a few short days. That, he believed, was what Quinten Case had been desperately looking for.

Slater assumed time being mended would affect the world, perhaps even catastrophically. But what he feared most was what the mending of time would do to the galvanized—to him.

Quinten had the answers he needed.

Reeves Silver tipped his glass in a toast again. "I see we have nothing more to say on the matter. Well, then. My men will escort you out."

The door opened and four of Reeves' men, heavily armed, stepped into the room. "See that he is returned to his offices. Comfortably."

Slater stood. Reeves might find Abraham and Matilda, but by then they would most certainly be dead at an assassin's hands.

Already one of the deadliest men in the world was on their trail. But Slater would never allow Reeves to get his hands on Quinten Case. Not yet.

"Oh, and, *Robert*," Reeves said, emphasizing the name. "Until I look over House Orange standing contracts, I want you to excuse yourself from any and all decision making. All House Orange business, money, and resources will be funneled through me. Until you learn the ropes of ruling, of course," he said.

"Of course," Slater replied stiffly. He was going to enjoy destroying this small mortal man. He was going to enjoy breaking him into pieces and sprinkling his bones over the ashes of his House.

He turned and, with armed guards surrounding him, left the room.

6

It took Quinten years before he could look at me without sorrow. I understand. It was my fault he lost you.

—from the diary of E. N. D.

The sound of footsteps climbing the wooden stairs woke me from strange and restless dreams filled with thunderstorms, church bells, and jail cells. I opened my eyes and watched a barefoot Quinten pause at the top of the stairs to get his bearings before heading toward one of the beds closer to the bathroom.

His shirt was unbuttoned and untucked from his pants and his hair was mussed. I guess he and Gloria had taken the time to settle their relationship questions in a most intimate manner.

Good for them.

I tried not to feel envious. The end of the world, or at least the end of my world, was ticking down to days and hours. I'd never stolen more than a single kiss in my life, much less done the sorts of things that would leave me staggering to bed half dressed and messy haired.

I wanted that.

I took a deep breath and let it out. When life settled down, if it settled down and I actually had a life left, I would make a list of things I intended to do and go out and do them. Sex was going to be right up at the top of the list.

Of course, if Quinten was right, we had to do something to stop the break in time mending so I could live.

The Wings of Mercury experiment our great-and-then-some-grandfather had set off was supposed to be an experiment for traveling in time that had instead killed all the people within a fifty-mile radius, except for thirteen unlucky souls.

Those survivors had gone on to become the galvanized, me—the most recently revived—included. Something about fiddling with time had given the galvanized immortality—or that was the theory I'd heard.

My brother was convinced that it wasn't immortality that was given to the galvanized; it was a life extension.

An extension that was going to be up in the next couple days.

I rolled onto my back and stared at the ceiling, too many thoughts scuffing through my mind. I didn't want to die, but if that was the only outcome of this crappy turn of events, then I wanted to make sure that my life had been worth something. That I had done some lasting good for the people I cared about.

House Brown had never been recognized as a voice in the world. I wanted that to change. I wanted my life and death to mean something, and I wanted that something to be House Brown's freedom.

But I had no idea how I could make that happen in such a short time.

I rolled onto my side again, trying to get comfortable. My thoughts churned and scattered, stealing any possibility of sleep down restless paths. I gave up. There would be no more sleeping for me tonight.

I pushed away the blanket, picked up my boots and duffel, and made my way quietly down the stairs. I checked the clock in the kitchen. Only a couple hours until dawn. Too early to make breakfast; too late to go back to sleep.

So that narrowed my activities down to either pacing or planning for our survival.

To plan I'd need info and a network. I didn't want to use any of Gloria's equipment in case it triggered a search.

Great. Pacing it is.

I slung my duffel across my chest but left my boots on the floor. I didn't think they would be able to hear me from upstairs, but just because I couldn't sleep was no reason to keep the others awake.

Only three days left to live. That one truth, that one horror, twisted around inside me, tangling me up in hopelessness. I wanted to shout at the heavens until some great force listened to me. I wanted time. More time.

But all I had was anger. All I had was fear.

I paced over to where Abraham was lying. I didn't touch him. My touch brought him pain. Well, not when he wasn't wounded, but in this state, if I touched him and caused him to have full sensation, he'd be screaming his lungs out.

So I stood there resting my hand on the mattress, holding on to the edge of his blanket.

"You have screwed up my life, Abraham Vail," I said quietly. "You showed up at my kitchen door, bleeding, wounded, and mixed up in a world I was doing my best to stay hidden from. I should have told you to move on and take your complicated world right along with you.

"But I didn't. I couldn't. There was something about you that made me want to help, made me want to know why your eyes were so sad even though you couldn't feel pain.

"And look where it's gotten me. I'm running. Still running. I'm all out of tricks up my sleeve to make this right. For you, for House Brown. For anyone."

Abraham, being unconscious, didn't have a lot to add to the conversation, but maybe all I needed right now was a really good listener. A comatose man three pints low on blood fit that bill pretty handily.

I surveyed the room, spotted a chair, and brought it over, setting it next to the table and then sitting down.

"What am I supposed to do? House Brown relied on me and on Quinten to keep them safe. If I die . . ." I took a breath, let it out. "I suppose the world will just go on without me, won't it? No big loss."

"No," Quinten said quietly from the hallway. "It would be a very great loss. To the world. And to me."

I wiped at my face, at the tears that were threatening to fall. I didn't want him to know how scared I really was.

"What are you doing up?" I asked. "You barely got to bed."

"I slept on the plane." He walked into the room, plucking up a chair as he did so and setting it down across from me. His shirt was still untucked and mostly unbuttoned, his sleeves rucked up to his elbows. He must have smoothed his fingers back through his hair, setting most of it into a semblance of order.

"We need to talk," he said.

"We need to plan," I countered.

That stopped him, and he frowned while taking a moment to consider me, as if he'd forgotten what I looked like.

I wasn't the same little sister he had left behind. I'd been taking care of a farm, stitched animals, an elderly grandmother, and all the crises that cropped up with House Brown for three years without him.

I'd followed a wounded man into a city and politics that were so far over my head, I didn't want to know what could have gone wrong, just for the chance to save my wayward brother.

A girl had to have guts to do that sort of thing.

And I had guts.

"All right," he said, "we need a plan. But first you need to know some things."

"About Gloria?"

He clasped his hands together and looked down at them. "That's . . . private, Tilly."

"You like her."

"Yes," he said, still not looking up.

"Do you love her?"

He finally lifted his eyes. He didn't have to use words to tell me the answer to that question. He was so in love with her, the pain of it shadowed his eyes.

"Okay. I won't ask anymore," I said.

"I want to talk about the Wings of Mercury experiment," he said, switching smoothly into teacher mode. "The easiest way to think of this is that the Wings of Mercury experiment fell like a hammer and shattered a moment in time."

"You've told me that already."

He gave me a look and I shut up.

"What I've spent the past three years at the Houses searching for is the journal that lists the calculations that went into the experiment."

"How will that help?"

"Once I have those calculations, I can—we can—mend time. Fix it." He waited, maybe for me to be amazed or impressed, but I had no idea what he was talking about.

"I have no idea what you're talking about."

He scratched at the stubble of his jaw, then pressed his fingertips against his lips as he stared up at the ceiling. A moment later, he looked back at me.

"Time broke. A piece of it flew off like a ball on a rubber string, and now that piece is winging back to its rightful place in the flow of time. When that happens in three days, all these extra years the galvanized have been living . . ."

"Three hundred years," I said.

"Three hundred years," he agreed, "will come due like a bill that hasn't been paid. The galvanized will die."

"And so will I."

His lips went tight, a white ring spread around them. "Yes. When you were little, when you were eight years old and dying and I implanted your mind and thoughts into the galvanized body you're now wearing, I didn't know about the experiment. I didn't know time was broken. I need you to understand that, Matilda. I never would have done this, done this to you, if I'd known about the time experiment."

I reached over and took his hand in mine. He looked so sad, so worried.

"Of course I know that," I said. "You *saved* me, Quinten. You were only thirteen. You didn't know what would happen. And no matter how this ends, I love you. You gave me years I never would have had."

His eyes glittered and he wiped at them quickly, as if I hadn't noticed. Then he smiled and it was his "I've got a plan" look. "This doesn't have to end. You don't have to end. Your life doesn't have to end, and the galvanized don't have to die. We can fix this. We can fix time."

"Don't you think us Cases have done enough damage trying to control time? Our great-grandfather was the madman who started this whole mess."

"Yes, he was," Quinten said, his growing excitement clear and his eyes shining with something more than tears: hope. "That's my point. His calculations must have been off by just a fraction, but when one is meddling in time, one must be precise."

"All right, Einstein, you've lost me," I said. "What are you talking about?"

"We can, if my theory holds true, change the calculations of his experiment and make it so that time didn't break. It will simply stretch, as he intended. And since we will have allowed it to mend in this time space, the galvanized won't die. You, my dear little sister, will not suffer an early death."

The fire of fanaticism lit his eyes and words. In front of me was a man who had spent years tracking down the solution to a very complicated problem. A man who had sacrificed his own freedom to find that solution, and very possibly a man who had gone a little off his rocker in doing so.

"I knew this would happen someday," I said.

"What?"

"You. Losing your mind."

"I haven't—"

I grinned at him.

He just pointed one finger at me. "The calculations of Alveré Case's experiment were so close to being correct. I was finally able to put the last pieces of the puzzle together when I was working for House Orange."

"Working? I thought you were a prisoner."

"Well, yes. I was that too, but he gave me unlimited access to his histories."

"House Orange histories told you there was a way to fix time? That sounds like trustworthy information."

"This new thing of yours?" he said. "Doubting everything I say? I can't say that I'm a fan of it."

"If you don't like it, then don't take off and leave me alone with no way to contact you—with no way to know if you're alive or dead—for three years."

He sat back at that, surprised at my words.

I was surprised too.

I swallowed and reached out for his hand again, holding him, knowing he was here, real.

"Three damn years, Quinten." My voice faltered down to a whisper. "I thought you were dead."

"Matilda," he said just as softly, "Tilly. I'm sorry I didn't contact you. I couldn't. Not even at the beginning. They were watching me so closely, I knew they'd find you. But this was so important—"

"Nothing's more important than us. Nothing's more important than family. The people you love."

He seemed to fold down into himself, the manic energy gone. It was worrisome how quickly he looked pale, thin, and exhausted. His three years spent at the Houses had not been kind to him. "I was doing this for you."

"I know. I know that. It's just..." I shook my head. "*You're* important to me. More important than ... anything." How did I explain to him that he may have just gambled away three years of our lives? Three years with him I'd never get back.

"And you're important to me," he said. "You understand that, don't you?"

I squeezed his hand and let go again. There was no use wasting more time on regret. "Yes, I understand. So, we're in this together now. How can we fix time?"

"It's ... a little hard to explain," he said. "And without the journal—"

"Grandma's journal."

"Yes. Without that I can't be one hundred percent sure, but my best guess is if we can stand in the eye of the experimental storm at the exact moment time returns to mend itself, we will be able to cross through a ... brief opening. Then all we have to do is find the Wings of Mercury machine and change the calculations."

I waited. Then shook my head. I didn't understand what he was saying.

"You know where the experiment took place, right?" he asked.

"I didn't even know the experiment was anything more than a legend until a couple days ago. So no. I don't know where it happened."

"On our land. Our property. That's why we've kept the place out of House control and in the family. That's why the nanos and minerals act so strangely. That's what Mom and Dad died for." He swallowed around the catch in his voice.

I missed Mom and Dad something terrible, but Quinten had been a lot older when the Houses had come out to our property, killed our parents, and ransacked our home, looking for Dad's research.

Quinten had been gone, studying, when it happened. He'd always blamed himself for not being there to save them. And even though I hadn't thought about it for years, he had often told me that he would give anything to find a way to bring Mom and Dad back to life.

"Tell me this isn't about Mom and Dad," I said. "Quinten, you know you can't bring them back. No one can."

"You can't begin to know what I can and can't do, Matilda," he said, drawing himself up stiffly. "I have stared down death and dulled its blade. You are breathing because I refuse to believe in the limits of genius."

"I know," I said sitting back and studying the anger and righteousness he always resorted to when he was deeply, deeply frightened.

"You're brilliant," I said, "and I love you. I know you love me." I lifted my hands and turned them so the light ran across my stitches. "I have lasting proof of that. You've probably saved Abraham's life too. But Mom and Dad? They're gone, Quinten. And even if we could . . ."

What could we do? Dig up their graves and try to stitch them into functioning bodies? I supposed if anyone in this world would know how to do that, it would be my tenacious brother.

"Even if we could somehow find their bodies and

bring them back, I'm not sure they'd want to live that sort of life, whatever that kind of life would be."

"I'm not talking about bringing them back," he said. "Not right now. What I want is for you to believe that we can change what happened all those years ago. If we can get back to that origin point in space—on our property— and also activate the countermeasures I've put together for the time event, we can go back in time. We can thread the knot before it cinches tight. Once back in time, all we have to do is get to the machine and adjust the experiment."

"Traveling in time?" I shook my head. "Quinten, I don't know. No one's done it. And even if we did, aren't we risking making the world even worse than it already is?"

"I'm doing this for you, Matilda," he said. "Yes, I wish Mom and Dad were still alive, and if there's any chance that can happen, I'll take the chance. But if we don't try to adjust time, to slide through that gap and go back to the origin point of the event, then you *will* die. That isn't a theory. That is an absolute I have spent years trying to change. And I . . ." He swallowed again, shaking his head, his voice down to a whisper. "I can't endure that."

"Okay," I said. "I don't want to die either. So we're in agreement there. You think if can we get home and trigger something . . . What did you build—a bomb?"

"Not a bomb. Do you know the timetable in the basement control room?"

The control room was where we received and sent all transmissions for House Brown, and where we tried to coordinate staying ahead of the other Houses while trying to keep the people who claimed House Brown safe.

"You never told me what it was. I thought it was some kind of clock."

"It is, in some ways. I built it to predict the exact moment when the time event would trigger. Once I knew when the break was going to self-heal, I knew that I'd have to rework the calculations of the original experiment and spot the error our great-grandfather made. It wouldn't have been difficult if I'd had all the information, but since I never found the journal . . ."

"I thought you said you pieced together information."

He shrugged. "I didn't find the journal. Just bits of it. So without the journal, this will be a little more difficult."

"Holy crap, Quinten. So you're just winging this? Making best guesses while you're going to try to alter time? No. Very no. Our grandfather already screwed up time, killed hundreds of people with that experiment, and caused all manner of hell for the thirteen people who survived his meddling. We're not going to repeat that mistake."

"It is not a *guess*." He sounded offended. "I found bits and pieces of reliable information here and there, stored away in different House histories. Enough to know that other people over the years have tried to track down all the information on this experiment."

"Why did Grandma have the information in her journal anyway?" I asked. "How did she get it?"

He shook his head slowly. "I would love to know the answer to that."

I glanced over at Abraham, who still looked more dead than alive.

"All right. We're going to alter time. One more time: how?"

"We get to our basement and trigger the timetable, which should generate enough power to catch the moment time mends. In that moment, a portal through time should open. Then all I need to do is step through."

"You? Alone? And you'll be where exactly?"

"When, is what you really want to know. 1910. Before the Wings of Mercury experiment is carried out."

"And what do you think you can do in 1910?"

"Find our grandfather and convince him to change his calculations."

"Change them to what?"

He leaned back and ran his fingers through his hair. "I'm still working on that."

7

Quinten and the others talk about me in hushed voices. What I am. How worried they are about hiding me from the others.
                    —from the diary of E. N. D.

I'd heard a lot of crazy things in my years. I'd seen my fair share more of impossibilities that turned out to be probabilities, and probabilities that went on to become realities. But time travel?

"You're going to go back in time," I said.

"Don't say it like that."

"Like what?"

"Like you don't believe me."

"Well, I'm just trying to understand the details."

"Someone was going to break the code on time travel," he said. "I don't know why it couldn't be me."

"Sure, you're smart." At his scoff, I added, "The most brilliant person I know."

He gave me a grin. "Go on."

"But you're going to walk in on what I assume was a

secret, or at least private, experiment and jiggle the handle?"

"It's mathematics. You don't jiggle the handle. You make minute corrections to the equation."

"By walking into a stranger's lab and telling him he forgot to carry the one? I know you've worked out the math on this, but have you thought through the practical nature of actually traveling through time?"

"Of course."

I narrowed my eyes, but he held my gaze. I thought he was bluffing.

"You worked out all the details of approaching our great-great-granddad, telling him he was wrong, convincing him you aren't an escapee from the loony bin, and talking him into adjusting the formula—"

"Calculation."

"—whatever—on an experiment he wouldn't even have done yet? You really think he'll believe you're from the future and that you have his best interests in mind?"

"As one scientist to another, he'll believe me. The recalculation will be proof enough."

I sighed and unbraided my hair, running my fingers through it as I did so. "There's no guarantee he will believe you."

The shadow of fear clouded the blue of his eyes, and I regretted my words. I'd seen my brother worried, angry, sad. I'd never seen that shade of fear in him.

"It will work," he said. "It will have to." Desperate words, softly spoken.

"Okay," I said. "If it has to work, then we'll make it

work. We need that journal. Do you have any idea where it is?"

"It's possible Slater Orange has it. He told me he did, but he may have been lying."

Slater Orange. The man who had implanted himself in Robert's body and accused Abraham of murder. "Did he tell you where it is?"

"No."

I shook my head. "Here I thought getting you out from House imprisonment would be the worse of my problems."

"Just the straw that brought the camels tumbling down, I'm afraid," he said.

I stared at Abraham. He was part of that tumble.

"He will recover, Matilda," Quinten said as he stood, and groaned, rolling his shoulders. "The question is when and how well. But he will wake. And if he has enough time, I believe he will heal."

"Thank you for helping him," I said, still watching Abraham. "I know he's a stranger to you, but it means a lot to me that you did what you could for him."

"How did you meet?" he asked.

I glanced up at him. He had on his interested, patient-brother expression, his hands loose and at his sides.

"He knocked on the kitchen door. Neds about blew his head off." I smiled, remembering a day that had happened less than a week ago but that felt like years ago.

"Why didn't you tell him to leave? You must have known he was trouble."

"I suppose I figured as much. He was bleeding. Gutted like a fish. He passed out on the floor, but not before telling me that he had come to save our dad."

"From what?"

"Turned out to be an old message from Mom. She sent it hoping someone in House Gray would come to her rescue. Rescue Dad and us too, before they got killed."

He stepped a bit toward me and pressed his hand on my shoulder. I placed my fingers over his, our shared grief resting between us. "Are you going to try to get some sleep?" he asked. "It's still a while until dawn."

"No. I think I'll sit here for a little longer in case he wakes up. I don't want him to be alone. I owe him that."

"Even though he was the one who got you into all this trouble?"

I shrugged. "All this trouble was bound to happen someday. I'm glad he was the one to go through it with me."

"So, your care for him is more than an obligation?"

I nodded.

"Do you love him?" he asked more quietly.

I still hadn't taken my eyes off Abraham's too-still form. Did I love him? Yes, I did. But things had happened so quickly. Maybe I was assuming things that weren't there. Hope for a love made more needful by the ending of my world.

"There hasn't been time for that," I said. "Not really. I think . . . yes. I do. But I don't think we'll have time to really find out. You know?" I offered a smile, but couldn't hold it for very long.

He squeezed my shoulder once, then let go. "Whatever time you have, take it, Tilly. Love doesn't last. Not for people like us."

He meant House Brown, I supposed. Unclaimed, off radar, and on the run. Or maybe he meant just us

Cases—people who broke rules, defied authority, and messed with time itself.

"People like you and Gloria?" I asked.

He was quiet, his gaze caught on the ragged edge of a painful memory.

"Yes," he finally said in a whisper. "People like Gloria and me."

His eyes ticked down to me and made me regret bringing up the subject.

"Isn't there a way you can apologize to her?" I asked. "Make it up to her? Tell her how you feel?" I didn't even know what had happened between them, but I hated seeing my brother like this.

"I have done what I can. We've said what can be said. Now I'm going to catch what little time there is left. For sleep," he said.

He turned and started across the room toward the hall.

"Don't leave her," I said.

He stopped but didn't look back at me, didn't turn.

"If you love her, then take whatever time you have. Good times, bad times. Live it with her. You've left her behind before. For years, Quinten, but I see how she looks at you. I've seen what she feels for you in her eyes. And if I don't make it"—his shoulders tensed at that, but I powered on—"if I die, I don't want you to go through your life without happiness, without love."

He still wasn't moving. I thought for sure he'd say something. When he didn't, I said, "Time won't ever be on your side, Quinten. Don't let it slip away."

"It isn't on anyone's side, Matilda. What I had with her . . . what I could have had . . ." He inhaled and held it like he was sorting through the possibilities of unattainable tomorrows. "That's gone." Then he walked out of the room.

I'd never seen my brother give up fighting for something he wanted before. He was so determined to save my life that he was willing to go through with a half-cooked plan to travel back in time for me.

But for himself, for Gloria and whatever they had once been and might still be, he was just letting it all go.

I rubbed at my face with both hands. "I will never understand people," I said into my palms. "If you love someone, if you want to be with them, if they make your life better, and you want to make their lives better, then you stand up and do what must be done to get on with it."

I pulled my hands away and studied Abraham in the low light. Still asleep, or what appeared to be sleep. Pale and bruised. I didn't know the details of how he had gotten shot, but from the short time I'd known him, I figured he'd done something stupid and loyal and noble.

"That's a surefire way to get a target on your head," I said, leaning one arm on the side of the bed, careful to keep it outside the blanket and out of danger of touching him. "Did you stand up for your friend Robert Twelfth? Or did you just get in the way of some stupid revenge between Houses?"

Abraham, being unconscious, didn't say anything.

"Who shot you?"

I sat there in the silence while my thoughts chased questions with no answers, then finally crossed my arms and closed my eyes. It would be dawn soon, and we'd have to be moving on before the Houses tracked us down.

But I had decided if it was the last thing I did, Quinten was going to survive this. He was going to live a life, a long life, without worrying about his little sister anymore.

I just wasn't sure how I was going to make that happen yet.

8

Do you remember me? I still remember you.
You changed my life. You gave me life.
*   —from the diary of E. N. D.*

Abraham grunted, the deep, painful sound of waking up hurting.

I opened my eyes and sat forward, reaching out to touch him, then snatching my hand away.

Maybe an hour had passed since I'd closed my eyes. I could hear the faint sound of heavier traffic moving past the building.

"You're all right, Abraham," I said. "You're with friends. But you've been injured. It would be best if you didn't move much."

He exhaled and stilled. His chest wasn't rising, and I am not ashamed to say I had myself a little moment of panic. Then he curled his fingers into a loose fist and very carefully inhaled.

At the top of the inhale, he opened his eyes.

It was done so purposefully, by rote, as if he had been

flat on his back, hurting and dying many, many times before.

From the experiments done over the years on the galvanized, I knew he probably *had* done this many, many
times.

He blinked once and exhaled slowly, sweat beading
across his forehead and running a line down his temple
to the scruff of his jaw.

"Can I get you something?" I asked. "Water?"

"Let me see you," he rasped.

He hadn't turned his head. It occurred to me maybe
he couldn't.

I braced one hand on the side of the table and leaned
in until he could see my face.

"Hi."

He blinked a couple times and swallowed. Then his
eyes seemed to settle on me.

"Beautiful," he whispered.

"Oh, now. Don't go wasting your air on that. You were
terribly injured, and me and my brother, Quinten, dragged
you out of the gathering before things got worse."

I was ducking the big stuff: Oscar's death, Robert accusing Abraham of killing Slater Orange. But I always
thought it nicer to sort of ease into telling someone they
had a price on their head and were likely to die before
the fruit in their kitchen went bad.

"Where are we?" he said.

"San Diego. At a doctor's who's good at staying quiet.
Quinten patched you up, but you lost a lot of blood. How
are you feeling?"

"Swell." One corner of his mouth slipped up into a
lopsided smile, but turned into a grimace again.

"Are you hurting?" I asked.

He widened his eyes.

"Right, dumb question. But you know, galvanized can't usually feel pain, or much pain, so I just thought ... it's not like you to be hurting, and yet ..." I was rambling, nervous, and worried about him. This was no time to get fluttery about being around him. I didn't know why he could feel this pain when normally he shouldn't be able to.

Was it a result of the Shelley dust or the thread and jelly Quinten had used to string him back together?

Whatever it was, I'd handled plenty of wounded and hurt people and beasts before. I'd handled a wounded Abraham just a couple days ago.

I didn't know why now it seemed so crazy and out of my control for him to be lying beneath me on a doctor's table, in pain.

Apparently love did weird things to a girl's practical decision-making skills.

"I'm going to get you a little water," I said, because he needed it, and I needed a second to clear my head. "I'm sure your mouth feels like something fell over dead in it."

"Don't." He swallowed and lifted his hand, reaching toward me.

There was no way I was going to touch him and cause more pain.

"Stay," he said.

"Don't stay?"

"Stay," he said.

I gathered up a corner of the blanket and, with it covering my hand, I took his hand.

He closed his eyes for a moment, his fingers curving

around mine. I thought he'd gone back to sleep, but a couple minutes later he said. "What day?"

"We've been on the run for just over twenty-four hours."

"Oscar?" he asked after another long pause.

I squeezed his hand a little and didn't say anything.

He opened his eyes, and they skipped sideways before focusing on me again. His eyes were glassy, fevered, the hazel of them gone red, the whites of them bloodshot. "What happened?"

"Things got pretty bad. We can go over it when you're feeling better."

"Tell me. All of it," he said. Then: "Please."

I so didn't want to do this.

I did it anyway.

"You were summoned by Slater, Head of House Orange, so you dropped me off and went to attend him. You didn't come back. Not in time to go with us to the gathering. I was so worried." I paused, pulled my shoulders back just a bit. I hadn't expected to be so relieved I could talk to him again. But that relief was mixed up in the sorrow and fear of losing him.

Memories, images flashed behind my eyes.

He had been falling apart. Legs, arms, organs, as if his body refused to carry his spirit, his soul anymore. He had been dying.

"Tilly?" he asked.

I cleared my throat and used the back of my other hand to whisk away the hair that slipped across my face.

"We went to the gathering in Hong Kong without you. But I had made a deal..." I'd promised never to speak of it. Under threat that if I did, people I loved would die. Well, Reeves Silver would have to be pretty quick to kill us before time wiped us out first.

"... I made a deal with Reeves Silver. In exchange for him getting my brother out of his captivity with House Orange, I'd stand aside at the gathering and let things play out. I didn't know." I shook my head. "I didn't know his plan was for Helen Eleventh to shoot Oscar. I truly didn't know."

"Is he dead?" His voice broke over the last word.

"Yes," I whispered.

He closed his eyes, lines of pain spreading from the corners and hooking on either side of his mouth. He wasn't breathing again, and I didn't know if it was from the pain in his pulverized body or the pain in his heart.

He'd been like a father to Oscar, and a son. He'd known him for all of Oscar's life, and had stood by the Head of House Gray's side as Oscar stepped into ruling and made decisions that were far better for the people he ruled than the previous House Gray leaders.

It was a lot to lose. A friend. A lifetime.

When Abraham took his next breath, it caught in his throat and he coughed to clear it, a sound too close to a sob.

"I'm sorry, Abraham," I said. "I am so, so sorry."

One more breath, on a soft groan, and then he bent his elbows, getting them beneath him so he could lever up into a half-sitting position,

"No, no. Not a good idea," I said. "You should rest. Wait for the doctor to check on you. You should hold still."

"I should turn myself in," he ground out as he pushed

all the way up to sitting. "I have failed my house. I have failed my people. I have failed Oscar."

"You had nothing to do with him being murdered. You were dying when he fell."

"It is my job." Here he stopped and glared at me, anger fueling his words. "Keeping him safe, keeping him alive is my *job*. I failed. There are consequences I must accept. Punishment."

"Really?" I pulled my hand away from him, not because I was worried I'd make him hurt. I knew grief wasn't easy for any of us. It made us do strange things. But we had no time for a martyr.

"You want to tell me how putting your head on a chopping block is going to bring Oscar back to life?" I asked. "How causing yourself pain will take away the pain of him dying? It won't work. That never works. Death is death, Abraham."

"Not for me," he growled.

"Death is death for us all. Oscar, me, you. All of us."

"Galvanized don't die."

"Galvanized *do* die," I said. "It just takes us a lot longer to dig our graves."

He was breathing hard. Frankly, I was impressed with his ability to remain sitting. Maybe it was the mix of pain, grief, and anger that was giving him the strength to fight his wounds.

"No," he said, "galvanized *don't* die. What we do is pay our debts. Head of my House falls, I am there to carry the burden, to take the blame. If necessary, to ensure peace among the Houses with my life."

"This isn't like when you drew up the treaty between House Brown and the other Houses," I said. "You can't throw yourself on this landmine and end this war. Sacrifice isn't going to work."

"You don't understand. If I don't stand and accept this blame, all the Houses could be in danger. Even House Brown."

"Did you shoot him? Did you shoot Slater Orange?"

"No."

"Then you're not the one who brought blame on the galvanized. And it is already too late to fix that. Helen Eleventh shot Oscar. Helen is a galvanized. She killed a head of a House. *She* broke the treaty, not you. She should bear the burden, the blame. Not you. But that water's so far under the bridge it's nothing but ocean all the way down."

"Helen?" he asked, apparently just now paying attention to what I'd told him a few minutes ago. "No. Oh, dear God, no."

I didn't say anything. I didn't want to rub salt in his various wounds. I just wanted him to understand the situation. He was a smart man. It didn't take him long to work out the consequences of a galvanized—not him, but Helen—killing a head of House.

It was the end of peace between the Houses.

It was the end of galvanized being considered free.

It was the end of House Brown being . . . well, anything at all.

I'd be surprised if we got through another day before all the Houses joined to declare martial law. Then House Brown people would be dragged and tagged, thrown into service for whichever House got their hands on them.

Their land and their children would be taken away, their lives and freedom destroyed.

"So, do you understand what I'm telling you? The situation that we are in?" I asked.

"Yes," he said. "Yes. I understand." He planted both hands firmly on each side of his thighs, elbows locked. I think they were the only thing keeping him upright. He swayed just a bit each time he inhaled and exhaled.

"You are injured," I said. "That's something else you need to understand. You were falling apart into pieces. I don't think sitting is a good idea."

"I'll be fine."

"You were shot. With Shelley dust."

He tipped his head up and peered at me through the wave of his bangs. "I know. I was there."

I couldn't help it. A little swell of delight hit my heart. There was my sharp-witted man.

"Who did it?" I asked. "Who shot you, and why? Was it Slater Orange? You told me only heads of Houses carry that dust."

"Was Robert Twelfth at the gathering?" he asked, avoiding all my questions.

"Yes. You were there too. Don't you remember him being there?"

"I was . . . injured. Out of my mind . . . hallucinating. I have only vague impressions of what happened."

"What happened was your best friend, Robert Twelfth, accused you of murdering Slater Orange, and all hell broke loose."

"How . . . convenient," he grunted. "He's not Robert."

"I know. Robert's body, but the mind of Slater Orange."

He scowled at that. "You know?"

"My brother was a part of it. He was forced to transfer Slater's thoughts and personality into Robert's galvanized body."

Abraham's face went stone still, and even through all that pain I could see the dark anger coiling within him. "He killed my friend?"

Ah, hell. I had not thought that through.

"I suppose that's the way of it, yes." I could apologize, I could explain that it was Slater who forced Quinten to do what he did, but I knew it wouldn't change the reality we were boot-deep in the middle of: my brother had, effectively, killed Abraham's best friend.

He pushed off the table, grunting as his feet hit the floor, then lost one knee so that he had to catch himself on the side of the table.

I didn't rush up to help him, although every instinct in me wanted to. He was hurting, grieving, pissed as hell, and the best thing I could do was let him work through all that to get his feet under him. Both literally and figuratively.

"Where is he?" he asked.

The blankets fell away, and I had a feeling he didn't know he was standing there in nothing but his undershorts. The bruising on his body was immense, spread out like the hand of some giant had slapped and punched him until he was black and blue and red all over.

Most of his old stitches were dissolved, and new thin silver thread whipped through the bloody gashes across his thighs, ankles, stomach. Bullet lines crossed from each shoulder down to his hips, across that swollen gash in his stomach. More stitches tracked around his biceps, wrists, neck, and face.

I'd seen him mostly naked when he'd been wounded

at my house, but he'd also been basically healthy then. Now his body raged against the poison pouring through his veins.

"Where is who?" I asked.

"Your brother?"

"Upstairs. Good luck climbing on those legs."

His jaw clenched, and so did the one hand that wasn't braced against the table. Then he very deliberately pulled himself up, shoulders squared, feet spread, head high. Like a gladiator ready to face down a lion even though he was the one who was about to become dinner. "Where. Is. He?"

"Okay, let me just explain one more time exactly how this is going down," I said, planting my fists on my hips. "You are half dead. You owe being half-alive enough to stand here and demand things from me to my brother.

"My brother stitched you together. You were in pieces—literally in pieces—and he mended you. My brother, with the assistance of a doctor, gave you those tubes in your chest you're currently ignoring that are pushing chemicals through you to neutralize the Shelley dust that was eating away your insides. Quinten did that. Quinten *fixed* you. And if you want to keep on being fixed and mended so that you can stand on your feet just like this and face down your real enemies, you will not be stupid enough to try to storm off and kill my brother."

"I didn't say . . ." He grunted and leaned into the table again, both hands holding him up this time.

"Give me your word, Abraham Vail. Tell me you're not going to hurt him."

"I won't kill him," he gritted through clenched teeth.

"Or hurt him."

"I gave you my promise."

"Yeah, and I watched you cut off a man's ear because you didn't like his tone of voice. Promise me you won't injure my brother."

Again the long inhale, the long exhale as he braced himself to accept this new restriction. "I will not injure him."

"All right. Good. We agree you'll wait here for Quinten to come see you. And you'll talk to him then?"

"Yes."

"Do you want any help back onto that table before you rip the tubes out of your chest, or are you angry enough to do it on your own?"

He shook his head and swore in that language I didn't know. *Russian?* He hoisted himself back onto the table with a groan and shifted so that he was on his back, breathing hard, with a wet catch at the bottom of each breath that worried me to no end.

I bent, picked up the blanket, gave it a shake, and spread it over him. "That was a stupid thing to do. Wear yourself out like that."

"I'm not worn-out," he said, his eyes closed, his words barely comprehensible.

"Think you can drink some water?"

"Yes."

"I'll be right back." I walked off to the kitchen, found a cup and filled it half full with water. I checked to see if there were straws but didn't find any. Well, we'd manage.

I strolled back into the room and took a moment to pull on my boots and lace them. Dawn was breaking, and I knew we'd need to be out of here soon.

If Abraham could move. If we had to carry him, we weren't going to get very far very fast.

"Are you still awake?" I asked quietly when I reached the side of the table.

"Mostly," he said.

"They didn't have a straw, so you'll need to sit up a bit to drink."

He opened his eyes, turned his head to look at me. Frowned. "Where is the doctor?"

"In bed, I think. Why? Did you break something, pull something?"

"I hurt."

Coming from anyone else, I'd tell him of course he hurt. He was only just recently falling to pieces. But the thing about galvanized—well, all galvanized except me—was that they were mostly numb, and had been mostly numb for over three hundred years.

The only time when they'd been able to feel was when I touched them.

I'd thought it was a strange thing that contact with me could restore their nerves, their sense of touch, but we hadn't really had time or resources to puzzle out why exactly that had happened.

And while there were still a hundred variables that could disprove my assumptions, there was one thing linking Abraham and me right now. One thing that tied us both together.

The thread.

I studied his arm outside the blanket and the thin but impossibly strong thread that held his muscle, bone, and skin together. It wasn't something you could buy off a shelf. There was only one place in the world where it was made: in my father's lab back on our property.

He called it *Filum Vitae*. Life thread.

"Is it bad?" I asked.

"Yes. Better now that I'm holding still." He gave me a small smile, so I didn't bring up the fact that I'd been telling him to hold still ever since he woke up.

"Let's try this water; then I'll get Quinten."

His eyebrows dove at my brother's name and that deep anger roiled in him again, but he held my gaze and nodded.

He might not like my brother, might not like what my brother had done, and I didn't blame him for that. But right now he was going to hold to his promise and put his issues with my brother to the side.

"How about I help you lift your head so you can drink?" I placed the cup on the other table near the head of where he lay and pressed my lips together, steeling myself for the pain I was about to bring to him through my touch.

"Are you ready?" I asked.

"No," he said, "but I'm thirsty. Tastes like something fell over dead in my mouth."

I smiled. So he had been listening. Good to know. "Let's see what we can do about that."

He lifted his head and I slid my hand down the back of his shoulders, bracing to prop him up a bit.

He grunted but his breathing hadn't changed.

I tipped the cup to his lips and he drained it in three deep gulps.

"More?" I asked, helping to ease him back down.

"No. It's enough."

I drew my hand away and he closed his eyes.

"Did I . . . was it worse when I was touching you?" I asked.

"No," he said, that one word drawn and drowsy. "I miss . . . feeling. Touch. I miss . . . you."

The next breath he took in was deep and slow. He was asleep. Just like that.

I stood there, my pulse pounding too hard, trying not to weigh his words on the scale of my heart but failing miserably.

He said he missed touch, I told myself. Maybe he meant he missed that I could make him feel touch. He'd been galvanized for three hundred years. Anyone would crave contact.

He said he missed me.

"Okay," I said quietly. "You get some sleep. If we need to flee for our lives, I'll wake you up. In the meantime, I'm going to cook breakfast."

I waited for a minute to see if he had heard me. His face was fully, completely relaxed. He was sleeping or unconscious. Standing up and proving his point had taken a lot out of him. I just hoped it wasn't too much.

9

*I regret many things. But not living. This life
has been good to me.*
                        —from the diary of E. N. D.

Someone was in the kitchen; I could hear them moving around. The scent of fresh-brewed coffee, eggs, and toast filled the air and made my mouth water.

I peeked in through the door before opening it fully. Gloria stood at the stove. She had changed into jeans and a long, soft golden sweater, and pulled her hair back into a single ponytail with a gold band. Most people wore the color of their house. Since she was a doctor, it only made sense that she would wear white for the House that controlled medical. But she made her legitimate credits selling books and merchandise, which meant she had to be claimed by the House she reported her income to.

The soft gold meant she was claimed by House Gold, Money. The House that handled credit, monies, and the transfers and tracking of such.

"Morning," I said quietly as I entered.

She glanced over her shoulder. "Good morning, Matilda. How do you like your eggs?"

"Cooked," I said. "I'm not picky. Can I help?"

"I think I have it under control. Coffee? Tea?"

I pulled a mug out of the cupboard. "Tea, thanks." She went back to stirring the eggs while I poured hot water from the kettle into a strainer of leaves.

"Abraham woke up." I leaned my back against the counter and blew the steam off my mug, my hands wrapped around it.

"Was he aware of his surroundings?"

"Yes. I'm pretty sure he was."

"Did he speak? Did he track your movements?" She pulled a plate off a stack near her and filled it with eggs, and toast that had been grilling in what smelled like garlic and butter. "Fruit is on the table," she said.

I took the plate. "Thanks." It might have been only a few hours since I last ate, but this constant threat of death was hungry business. "Abraham got off the table."

"Oh?"

"He had some idea that he could go kick my brother's ass."

"What?" She turned, spatula poised in one hand, a look somewhere between anger and confusion on her face. "What could he possibly be angry at Quin for?"

Quin. I hadn't heard anyone call my brother that since my parents had died. It was his nickname, but after our parents were killed, he'd insisted I should use his full name at all times. I never minded, and always supposed his nickname reminded him too much of his time with Mom and Dad.

"Quin?" I said. "He lets you call him that?"

"Quinten," she corrected herself absently. "Why is Abraham angry at Quinten?"

"Mostly because my brother killed his best friend."

At her startled look, I added, "It's complicated, and it wasn't done on purpose. This mess . . . the Houses, the gathering. It's just . . ."

"Complicated," she agreed.

I nodded and took my plate and tea to the table. Another sip of tea sent across my tongue a burst of sweet mint leaves that reminded me of spring blooms and rain. I closed my eyes for a moment, losing myself to that sensation.

"I'm impressed he was on his feet," she said after a bit.

"Once you meet him, you won't be. Stubborn as a rock. Tough as a rock too—diamond. Annoyingly pigheaded when wounded." I dug into my food before it got cold. So good. Then I plucked an orange the size of a grapefruit out of the fruit bowl.

"Why did you save him at the gathering and bring him with you?" she asked.

"Abraham?" I stuck my thumbnail into the orange skin and a burst of ripe juices filled the air with citrus perfume. "He was dying and falsely accused of murder."

"So you saved him out of a sense of justice?"

Her back was still turned to me, but from the way she said that, she was fishing for something. "That's a nice sweater," I said. "Gold."

Yes, I was basically asking her if she was spying on me for House Gold. It was rude of me, but I'd recently discovered my farmhand had been a spy for House Silver for two years, and the woman I'd trusted enough to let care for my grandmother while I was gone also worked for House Silver.

It wasn't so strange to think the good doctor, and maybe girlfriend of my brother, might be working for another interest on the side.

"It makes the customers comfortable," she said. "They'd rather see a woman working for House Money than the rebellious House Brown. And I can't let just anyone know I am a doctor. The Houses have eyes. You know my heart is House Brown, Matilda." She smiled over her shoulder. "I'm opening the shop in an hour or so and I didn't want to have to change."

"I know. Sorry for accusing you, it's just been—"

"Complicated," she said again. "No apology needed. I just didn't know if Abraham had some other kind of hold over you. Blackmail or something you couldn't see a way out of."

"No," I said. "Nothing like that." I popped a section of orange in my mouth. The explosion of sweet juice was enough to make me moan in pleasure. "Oh, my devils, this orange is good."

She turned off the burners and set a lid over the food to keep it warm. "They still grow fresh out here. I forget you can't get them this ripe back East." She carried her cup of tea and plate with a single slice of toast over to sit across from me.

"I take it your brother never told you about us," she said.

I shook my head. "He's always been private about private matters. Especially when I was younger. And then he was gone for a year at a time. I always felt like he was unpacking one bag while packing another. We didn't get a lot of chances to catch up. Do you . . . care for him?"

She took her time finishing a bite of toast, then sat back as if the breakfast was flavorless, which I knew very well it wasn't.

"I do," she said. "I have. Very much. But he's changed. Life has changed him."

"Life changes us all."

She sipped tea. "He thinks he can change the world, Matilda. Not with some vague, random campaign or pipe-dream notion. He thinks he alone has his finger on the pulse of the world. And with one press he can change the rhythm of its heart."

From the sound of it, he hadn't told her exactly what he planned to do: control time. I wondered why he wouldn't want her to know his plans.

But as I'd said, private is private for him.

"He's always aimed high with his goals," I said.

"I'm not sure."

"Of his aim?"

"That the world needs to be changed," she said.

I ate the last of half the orange, then separated the sections of the remaining fruit while I thought about that. "You don't think things could be better for people?"

"I do think some things could be better. But it seems that what actually happens when someone manages to change the world is that things are just different. The head of House Gray is dead. Another member of that family will rise to take his place. Things will be different. But it won't really change. The world won't change.

House Gray will still be House Gray. House Brown will still have no voice to fight for people's rights.

"But Quinten can't see that. He's trying to sweep starlight with a broom. Nothing he does . . . nothing any of us does, no matter how great or small, will ever leave a lasting impact. It's just . . . impossible."

I popped another slice of orange into my mouth and brushed my fingers on my pants. "I see that you've never met my brother. There is no impossible thing that he isn't determined to conquer. Doesn't matter how long it takes him to figure it out, doesn't matter what or who he has to give up to get it done. Home. Family. Sister. Girlfriend." I paused at that, and let that truth hang between us. "When Quinten's caught up in an idea, he rides it like a demon into the pits of hell."

"I know he's determined," she said. "That doesn't mean he's right."

"He hasn't been wrong yet. Not when he saved my life when he was only thirteen. Not when he stood up as the go-to in House Brown, creating a better communication system, and I would go so far as to say: not in this."

"You think he can change our world? Make it better?"

"I'd bet my life on it. I guess I have."

She took a bite of toast and nodded slightly.

"He cares for you too," I said.

She sighed. "I haven't seen him in five years. That's a long time without contact in a caring relationship."

"Even if for three years of that he was being held prisoner?"

"I'm not angry that he didn't contact me then. I wouldn't expect him to find a way to get me a message in that situation, but it's . . ." She bit her bottom lip, then picked up her tea and took another sip.

I'd finished off all of my orange and moved on to the rest of the eggs and toast. She had seasoned the eggs with fresh basil, and it was delicious.

"Complicated?" I said.

She nodded. "Complicated."

"Still, if there's something worth fighting for, it's worth fighting for, isn't it?" I asked. "Maybe what you and Quinten had was just a passing thing. Two people in the right place and the right time for companionship. I understand that. I understand lonely. But I've known my brother all my life and have seen him go through his infatuations with women."

I waited for her to ask.

Finally, she did. "And?"

"And I've never seen him so soul broken over not being with you."

The kitchen door swung open and we both glanced up.

Quinten stood there. He'd taken a shower, combed his curls into order, and taken the time to shave. He wore the same clothes as yesterday because none of us had a spare pair on us, but he'd tucked his shirt into his slacks, buttoned his vest, rolled up his sleeves, as pressed and presentable as one could hope for under the circumstances.

"Good morning," he said more to Gloria than to me.

"Morning," I answered anyway. "You didn't tell me Gloria was such an amazing cook. You have to try these eggs." I pointed my fork toward the pan on the stove.

"Basil?" he asked, eyes on her alone.

Boy had it bad for the woman.

"Fresh from our—*the* garden," Gloria said, blushing over her verbal misstep.

He smiled just a bit and walked over to the stove. "How are the plants doing?" he asked as he dished out his meal.

"Well," she said. "Very well. I've expanded the garden. The neighbors don't mind when it comes time to harvest."

"Good," he said. "That's good. That garden always held such . . . promise."

"Yes, it did," she said. "But that was a long time ago."

He turned with his plate and coffee, his features carefully schooled. "It was, wasn't it?" He hesitated a moment, then sat next to me. He started eating without saying anything more, his head bent, gaze fastened on his plate.

She watched him while she drank her tea and tried not to appear like she was watching him.

I rolled my eyes, which she caught and gave me half a smile for. "Would you like some privacy to talk?" I asked. "I'm about finished anyway."

"No," Quinten said with a hint of panic. "It's fine for you to be here. Take your time. Stay."

Gloria's gaze shifted over to me and she blinked once slowly.

I opened my eyes in a "can you believe this guy?" expression, and Gloria raised one eyebrow in agreement.

From that, I assumed she wouldn't mind a little private-talk time.

"Abraham woke up." I pushed away from the table and took my dishes to the sink, rinsing them before leaving them in the sink for proper washing.

"Oh?" Quinten sounded happy for the change of subject. "Did he seem lucid?"

"Yes. Also, he hates you for what you did to Robert."

Quinten paused with a forkful of eggs dangling near his mouth. He set the fork down on the plate and sat up straight, stiff, his fingertips bent around the edge of the table.

"I see," he said.

"He just doesn't understand," I said. "I know you didn't do it on purpose. You had no intention or desire to hurt Robert. You were forced. I told him so, but he's injured and not thinking things through very clearly."

"Don't," he said. "Just . . . don't, Matilda. There is no excuse for what I did. I chose my life over another's."

"You chose my life too. And the life of . . ." I almost said "all the galvanized," but his eyes flicked up to me, pleading me to stop. "The life of many over the few. You aren't the first man in history who has had to make that choice."

If he hadn't told Gloria about his plan to travel in time—which I could only assume was true, since she hadn't brought it up—I could also guess he hadn't told her that all the galvanized would be dead in a few days. Maybe he didn't want to leave her with information that would get her killed if our trail was tracked here.

And I guess it was that—the look of panic and love on his face, the need to keep Gloria safe even as his own life was very likely about to end—that did it to me.

I made a choice. A hard choice. Probably a stupid choice.

But it was my choice.

If it was the last thing I did—and, hey, less than two

days left to breathe here, so last-minute was pretty much my middle name—I was going to make sure I was the one who went back in time to fix this mess.

Alone.

Quinten wasn't the only Case who could save the world.

10

I try not to say your name anymore. They remember you with sorrow. I will always remember you with joy.

—from the diary of E. N. D.

"I just thought I'd warn you," I told Quinten. "About Abraham. He knows you're the one who sewed him up again, and I think he's grateful for that. Truly. But . . . well, he's not grateful for everything you've had to do."

"I wouldn't expect it to be otherwise," he said quietly. "How are you feeling, Tilly?"

The way he said it told me he was worried. Probably wondering if this time-mending event was going to harm me slowly or kill me fast. Wondering if there would be signs or symptoms I would suffer the closer I came to death.

"I'm good. A little tired, but too jumpy to sleep. I'm going to go splash some water on my face and pull my hair back. Don't check in on Abraham until I come back down, okay?"

"I think we can handle him." Quinten sipped the last of his coffee, still not looking at Gloria.

"Just because he's injured doesn't mean he's not strong as a dozen men," I reminded him. "Also, he's in a lot of pain. Pain he can feel."

"Really? Huh." Quinten scooped eggs on his toast. "Hurry, then. I'd like to check on him as soon as possible."

And with that, I had officially given them an excuse for a little alone time to talk.

Gloria mouthed *Thank you*, and I nodded. Maybe Quinten didn't think they needed private time, but it looked like she had other ideas.

Plus, I had something I needed to do: find Grandma's journal.

Quinten was a hell of a researcher, but I'd always been our go-to person when it came to hacking into tightly locked data vaults. If Slater Orange had Grandma's journal, I was certain he must have recorded those faded old paper pages in some fashion. It would be beyond foolish to have only one fragile copy of the information. And Slater Orange was not stupid.

Quinten said he scoured the House histories for the info and hadn't found it.

Which meant Slater must have had some idea of what my brilliant brother was searching for. And if he knew, he wouldn't have put the information anywhere Quinten would expect it to be.

So where would he have stowed it?

I jogged up the stairs, not bothering to be quiet. If Neds weren't up yet, too bad. It was past time for sleeping.

"Morning!" I called out. But Neds was not in his bed, which had been made up as if he'd never been there.

I crossed the room, pressed my palm against the blanket. No heat. He'd been up for a while, then. I wondered where he'd gotten off to.

I checked the bathroom. Empty.

I used the facilities and then splashed cool water on my face and grimaced at my hair. Something would have to be done about it. I twisted it along my temples and braided it back in one thick rope that rested between my shoulder blades.

That style gave my cheekbones an edge and made my brown eyes wider. While I wanted my hair out of my way, the problem with braiding it back was that my stitches showed. I didn't need to draw more attention to myself.

So I went back out into the sleeping area, looking for cloth I could use to hide my stitches. Finally found something that might have been a scarf or table runner. The rough cloth was a simple weave in an olive green, but wide enough and long enough it should do fine.

I took a minute in front of the mirror again, wrapping the cloth over my head like a hood, then down around my neck, where I looped it a couple times before tying it in a knot and letting the ends hang loosely over my chest.

I didn't have gloves to hide the stitches on my hands, but there was an easy fix for that: pockets.

I cleaned the brush, making sure to flush all the strands of hair down the toilet. I knew I couldn't get rid of all the DNA evidence of us being here, but I could do the basics, including a quick mop of the floor with more dampened tissue and running the shower for a minute or so to clear the trap. Gloria said the room was set up this way for other people who had stopped by to be tended to by her, so there was a good chance any trackable evidence we were leaving behind would be covered, mixed, muddled by the people who had come before us and would come after us.

Our beds were all made and I did one last search for any personal items left behind.

Not that we really had anything to leave behind. I shifted the strap of the duffel hanging across my chest and started down the stairs. I had hoped Neds would have shown back up. I needed access to a computer and wasn't going to risk Gloria's safety by using hers.

Neds leaned at the bottom of the stairwell, one boot propped on the first step. "You done getting prettied up?" Left Ned asked.

"Where were you?" I asked. "Did you eat?"

"Just headed that way," Right Ned said. "Went out when you and Abraham were arguing. Had to secure us a means of transportation."

"You heard me and Abraham arguing?"

"Yes," Right Ned said.

"You didn't think you should step in on that?"

"Why, Tilly," Left Ned said with a smile that meant he'd just spotted himself a sucker. "Did you need us to ride to your rescue? Was that man who's only held together by a string and a prayer too much for a sweet thing like you to handle?"

"Shut up," Right Ned and I both said at the same time.

I gave Right Ned a grin, and he grinned back at me.

"He might have fallen and hurt himself is all I meant," I said. "My hands aren't the best for catching him."

"He'd survive," Left Ned said.

"How's he doing?" Right Ned asked.

"Sleeping, last I saw. I need a favor."

They held up their hands in a "go on" gesture.

"I want you to cover for me while I go out and find a computer."

"Pretty sure Gloria has a computer here," Left Ned said.

"Why?" Right Ned asked. "What are you doing, Tilly?"

"It's just something I want to check on. We need some information Quinten couldn't get ahold of, and I have a couple ideas where it might be found. But I don't want to use Gloria's lines. She's already in enough trouble, housing us."

"How not-legal is this?" Right Ned asked.

"I'd think the most not-legal," I said.

They were still a moment, and I wondered, not for the first time, if they could hear each other's thoughts. I'd asked them once, and they'd given me innocent smiles and spun a tale about how they always knew what the other was thinking, and then proceeded to prove it to me by declaring what thoughts the other was thinking. Which, of course, they swore was true.

Liars.

Still, I knew Neds had a way of seeing visions when he touched a person. It was an odd skill that he didn't like to talk about much. It was possible those boys had other skills they didn't like to talk about much.

Or it could be just that they had spent every breathing minute together and had an innate sense of each other.

"I'll go with you," Right Ned said.

"No," I said. "That's not what I'm asking."

"Sure, but I know where you can patch a link," Right

Ned said. "It's not far. Also, I have the car and the keys, and I'm going with you."

"When will you learn not to argue with us, Matilda Case?" Left Ned asked.

Crap.

"Okay, fine." I started down the stairs. "Let's do it fast, before Quinten comes looking for me."

We snuck out past the kitchen, then through the medical room, the storage room, and out the door we'd come through just hours ago. It was morning now, the sun pulling up from the east and catching the still-foggy world all aglow.

I was grateful for the cover the fog offered, but kept my scarf up and head down, just in case there were cameras on us. Neds and I got into the van. Then he drove us down the main street for half a block, took a jag between buildings, rattled slowly through a couple tight alleys, and parked.

He moved into the back of the van next to me, both of us hidden from sight, and pulled a palm-sized screen out of his pocket.

"Seriously? You had it on you the whole time?" I asked.

"Just since I went out this morning," Right Ned said, entering a set of codes I'd never seen before. "You said you didn't want to use Gloria's line. So." He shrugged.

"What's that all about?" I asked, pointing at the code.

"Trust." Right Ned handed me the screen. "Me trusting you. And you trusting me. I've linked you in to a very, very private line. Only one other person I know can access this. Which she will. And when she does, she'll have questions."

"What? Why did you do that? I don't need to answer questions. I have my own back-line servers."

"Yeah, we've seen them," Left Ned said.

"No matter how secure you think your lines are, these are even more so," Right Ned added. "Get on it, Matilda," he said. "You won't have much time."

"Who, exactly," I asked as I accessed back routes and bounced off so many signals, I'd be lost in the noise, "are you trusting our lives to?"

"Someone worth the trust," Right Ned said.

"I sort of hate you making assumptions for me, Ned," I said, furiously streaming contact points. "Placing my trust without permission."

"Are you accusing a man of betrayal before breakfast?" Left Ned asked. "Thought you gave folk the benefit of the doubt before you kicked them to the curb."

"Don't turn my words on me. You were the one who said I was too trusting. So?" I prompted. "Who is she?"

"Someone who does business strictly beneath House notice. Way, way beneath," Left Ned said.

"She owes me a favor," Right Ned said.

"She owes both of us more than that," Left Ned said.

I was surprised to hear sadness in his tone. Left Ned wasn't the sort of man who had time for sentiments or regret. So whoever this *she* was, they had history with her.

Seemed to be going around lately.

I hated knowing that someone else could see what I was doing. Could maybe even guess who I was and what I was looking for. Which only made me want to work faster.

"She won't trace it, won't track you," Right Ned said,

correctly interpreting my scowl as my fingers flew over the screen. "This is more off the record than anything else in the modern world. Safer than . . . anything we know."

"I do not like having to take your word for that," I said, "but it's not like I have time left to be fussy."

I didn't have time left to search through much data for what I was looking for either. So I focused my crawlers in one place: Robert Twelfth's private, locked files.

If Slater had planned to have himself implanted into Robert's body, he would have hidden away information that only Robert, the galvanized—who would actually become Slater—could access. And if he thought Grandma's journal was important enough to keep away from Quinten, I had a good feeling he would have thought it was important enough to keep away from everyone else.

I launched my precoded crawlers and cut them free so they wouldn't be tracked back to this line. It wasn't the fastest way to get into someone's files, but I should have some kind of result in the next eight hours or so.

"That's it," I said. "Done." I handed Neds the screen.

He put in another string of code, then shut the thing off and tucked it back in his pocket.

The whole thing had taken us fifteen minutes, tops. Drive included.

"Did you get what you wanted?" He crawled back up to the driver's seat and got us on the road back to Gloria's place.

"I certainly hope so," I said. "Did you find some way to get us across country?"

"Yes," Right Ned said. "It won't be comfortable, but it will work."

"I don't care about comfort," I said as he parked the

van back in the lot again. "I care about fast, and how close we can get to the farm."

"Fast won't be too much of a problem," Right Ned said. "Close is going to be the kicker."

The fog was burning off under the heat of the sun. Neds and I walked back to the door. I wondered how he'd gotten in and out of the locked door on his own today. Then he pulled out an electronically coded key and slipped it in the lock.

We stepped inside the shipping and receiving room and shut the door behind us, the illegal scrubbers and locks engaging with a deep hum.

"Did you steal that key from Gloria?" I asked.

"A little bit, yeah," Right Ned said.

"Naw, we were just borrowing it," Left Ned said.

I shook my head as we headed into the medical area. "And you think I'm trouble."

"I know you're trouble," Right Ned said.

I grinned back at him. "Maybe a little bit. I'm going to see if I can wake Abraham. Is there room for Abraham to be transported on the stretcher if he needs it?"

"Won't need it," Abraham said.

He sat on the table, the tubes removed, which I was sure Gloria and Quinten were going to be thrilled about. The bruising was still all shades of horror, but the swelling, over all of him, seemed to be a little less.

"I'd rather not travel naked, though." He waved one hand toward the blanket across his hips. "Boots too, if we have them."

"We'll find something," I said. "You're . . . looking better than earlier." I tried to sound cheerful, but it came out a little thin.

"How long has it been?"

"Since you and I were talking? Just over an hour," I said. "You look a day better, at least."

"That is a good sign." Quinten walked into the room from the kitchen area. He had his authoritative-genius attitude buttoned in place, and breezed through the room like he had all the answers.

Abraham's eyes flicked up to weigh and measure him, and then his gaze slipped to me. Darkness and anger roiled behind his eyes and hardened his silence into a killing thing ready to strike.

I tipped my chin up just a bit in warning. We had a deal. No harming my brother. And if he broke his word . . . well, he was going to hate what I was willing to do to stop him.

"It means the solutions were strong enough to reverse the effects of the Shelley dust," Quinten went on as if his well-being hadn't just been on the chopping block.

Abraham raised one eyebrow, still holding my gaze. A sort of "you owe me" stare, then he turned his attention back to Quinten.

"I understand I owe you my current state of health," Abraham said in a clipped tone. "I thank you for your efforts. From here forward, I would prefer, and you would most certainly *benefit*, from keeping your hands and your attentions to yourself."

Such formal words. But said with enough of a primal snarl behind them that even my occasionally oblivious brother paused in walking any nearer to the man.

"He needs to check your wounds," I said.

Abraham didn't look away from Quinten. "Does he?" It was a threat, a challenge.

My brother was no stranger to looking his own death right in the eyes.

"Yes," Quinten said. "I do. If you are coming with us, as my sister insists, then you need to move under your own power. I want to look over those wounds. Treat them if I can."

"For your sister?"

"For all of us, Abraham Seventh," Quinten said stiffly. "We are only as strong as our weakest member, and right now that member is you."

"What we also are," I said, cutting off Abraham's reply, "is in a hurry. We need to be going as soon as possible."

Abraham glowered at me. I crossed my arms and stared right back, unimpressed. Quinten stepped up near enough to study Abraham's stitches and joins.

Abraham made good on his promise and largely ignored Quinten while he did other doctorly things, like asking him to breathe while he listened to his lungs through a stethoscope.

Gloria joined in the examination, and they made Abraham lie down so they could drape that diagnostic film over him again.

"Could you find him some clothes?" I asked Neds.

"And miss the explosion he's about to let off?" Left Ned said.

"He's not going to explode. But he's going to draw attention if he's walking around naked—don't you think?"

"Yes," Right Ned said. "We do think. Which is why we already found him some duds. Nothing fancy, but it will get him through the streets and past the cameras."

"If our luck holds," Left Ned said. "Which it won't."

"Which it will," Right Ned said.

"Won't," Left Ned replied.

"Where are the clothes?" I interrupted. When those two got caught up in petty arguments, they snipped at each other for days. I already had a headache; I didn't need two more.

"Hold on." Neds walked out of the room and came back a few seconds later. "You want to throw them at the angry lion, or shall I?" Right Ned asked.

"I'll do it." I took the pile of clothes out of his one hand and the pair of well-worn boots out of the other. He wasn't kidding; they weren't fancy. They were ragged enough, a beggar wouldn't wear them.

Great. I drew them up to my nose and took a hesitant sniff. A little musty, like they'd been in storage for a long time, but otherwise they didn't smell too bad. "So, how's the patient doing?" I asked with my cheerful firmly in place as I walked up to the table.

"He's improved greatly," Gloria said, handing Quinten a hypodermic needle, which Quinten jabbed into the side of Abraham's neck.

Abraham winced but otherwise didn't show that he was in pain.

I wondered why he was hiding his pain. Maybe so Quinten wouldn't know he could feel. Maybe so Gloria wouldn't be aware of it either. But I'd already told them that he had sensation.

"Do you need to tend the shop?" I asked Gloria. "You said you'd need to open it soon, right?"

"I unlocked the doors and set the sign," she said. "There's a camera in the front. I'll know if anyone comes in. I don't get a lot of early traffic. However . . ." She nodded toward the second hallway that led off in the opposite direction of the stairs and attic.

"First door on the right is my feed. Could you keep an eye on it for me?"

At my hesitance, Quinten said, "It's fine, Matilda. Abraham will be on his feet in under five minutes. Just give us a moment. You can put the clothes down there."

Gloria wheeled a cart over to the table. On it was a machine that seemed to have a lot to do with electricity. The paddles and clamps attached to it seemed to have a lot to do with pain.

"Are you okay with them?" I asked Abraham.

He was breathing slowly again, staring at the ceiling, his hands clenched loosely in fists. He knew how to bear the kind of pain he was in. Had probably done it many times before.

"It won't take long," he said, so, yes, he must have done this many times before. He knew what they were doing, even though I didn't. "You shouldn't stay," he said. "I'm fine."

It wasn't until the Neds walked me out of the room that I realized all of them had wanted me out of there.

"Why?" I spun on my heel, and Neds nearly ran right into me.

"A little warning?" Left Ned snapped, poking a finger in my shoulder.

"Why what?" Right Ned asked, gesturing me toward the feed room.

"Why are you all trying to get me out of there? What are they going to do to him?"

The distinctly mechanical whine of a battery charging with electricity pierced the edge of my hearing.

A heartbeat later, Abraham made a sound I'd never heard out of a person before. It was a choked-off cry of raw pain that was oddly soft.

"What are they doing to him?" I said again.

The whine started up again, and Abraham cursed quietly. I could hear Gloria's voice, comforting, professional. Abraham pulled another long breath.

"The Shelley dust dissolved the connection in some of the parts that make him up," Right Ned said. He blocked my pathway out of the room. "On the inside and the outside. Stitches alone aren't enough to fuse all those bits back together again. That out there is standard repair for galvanized. You should know that, Tilly."

"I haven't had to be . . . put back together again since I was first made," I said.

Abraham yelled. His pain ended on a hard sob, and I wanted to run to him, comfort him, shoulder the pain with him.

"Galvanized don't usually feel pain. He shouldn't be feeling this. The thread, my thread, is in him now. He can feel that. He feels all of it."

"Well, that sucks for him," Left Ned said. "They gave him a shot—the one in his neck—so he won't remember most of this. And as far as I know all the galvanized feel this kind of mending with or without your thread. Whatever nerves are still working are going through hell right now."

"Get out of my way, Harris," I said.

Both of them shook their heads.

"Best not," Left Ned said. "Matilda, it's hard on anyone to watch. For some reason you like Abraham. Let your brother spare you seeing him inflict that kind of pain on him."

Left Ned was not the sort of man who was given to dispensing wisdom or comfort. It was surprising enough, it drew my attention away from the next wounded-beast cry from the other room.

"Let's just do our part right now," Right Ned said. "We said we'd watch for Gloria's customers. It won't take them long to get this done."

He gently turned me and I walked the rest of the way into the room, wishing there was something else I could do. But stopping Quinten and Gloria from fixing Abraham was exactly the opposite of what we needed most right now. And I knew if I went out there, I would tell them to stop.

I couldn't stand the sound of his agony.

"I didn't know," I said as Neds stood in front of the door, closing it partly behind him, maybe trying to block the sound or just trying to keep me from bolting past him. "About the procedure. Quinten had to do that to me once too, didn't he?"

"I suppose he did," Right Ned said.

Quinten had been only thirteen and I'd been eight. I couldn't imagine what kind of horror that had been for him.

Mom and Dad said he'd sat awake by my bed for days after he'd put me in this body. None of them knew if the procedure he'd invented to place one person's memories, thoughts, and personality into another person's mind would work. They could have ended up losing me. They could have ended up with the original girl as a daughter. Or they could have ended up with us both dead.

Dad had been furious at Quinten. So had Mom. I didn't remember that part, but Grandma had told me about it once, in her faltering, forgetful way.

Still, there had been no cure for my illness. The chance Quinten had taken to save me could have killed me, but I would have been dead anyway.

I remember he was there when I woke up. I remember how glad I was to see him smile.

"Oh, shit," Right Ned breathed.

I shook out of my thoughts. I'd been standing there for a good minute or three, staring at the screens but not really seeing them.

I focused on them now. The cameras were trained on the front door to Gloria's shop. It was open. A man walked in. The man was dressed in black—boots, gloves, and hood—a long coat almost covering all the weapons he was carrying.

Shit.

"We have to go," Left Ned said. "Now. Right now. We have to run."

He pushed me out the door and was right behind me as we sprinted to the treatment room.

"Who is that?" I asked. "Ned?"

"Domek."

"Who?" I asked.

"Assassin, hunter, killer of all things," Right Ned said. "Killer of us if we don't get the hell out of here. Now."

"If he's that good of an assassin, why did he just stroll into a shop rigged with surveillance?"

"Because he doesn't care if we see him coming," Left Ned said. "Hell, he might prefer it that way. Hope we'll run scared and make mistakes. He is that good. And if we don't run, we're gonna be that dead."

11

*I'm happy. You should know that. As long as
the Houses leave us alone, I know everything's
going to be all right.*
                    —*from the diary of E. N. D.*

Abraham was sitting on the exam table, covered in
sweat, his hair finger-combed off his forehead. He
had on pants and boots. Quinten was tying off a knot in
a bandage he'd wrapped over both Abraham's shoulders
and down around his chest and stomach.

Gloria looked up from where she was putting things
away on a shelf.

"We've been made," Left Ned said. "In the shop.
Domek. Assassin. Run. Now. You want to get out of here
quick, Gloria. He's armed."

"Domek?" Abraham's head snapped up and his eyes
cleared. "Are you sure?"

*Everyone seemed to know about this assassin except
for me.*

"More than sure," Left Ned said.

"How long until he can get back here?" Quinten

asked as he quickly shoved medical supplies into a duffel Gloria tossed to him.

"Can't get in from the front," Gloria said. "Did he come into the shop?"

"Yes." Neds cased the room and stuffed his pockets with jars of pills.

"He'll discover there's no access to this part of the building in five minutes or less," she said. "How quickly he gets in here depends on how much firepower he's packing."

I jogged over to Abraham and helped him into a flannel shirt and jacket.

His hands trembled. He was kicking off an awful lot of heat even though he was shivering.

Fever.

"Can you stand?" I asked as I helped him up off the table. "Can you run?"

His feet touched the ground and his eyes tightened. He hissed air between his teeth, and I looked around for the stretcher.

"I'm fine," he gasped, one arm pressed against his stomach. "Let's move."

"Are there any other ways out of here besides the parking lot?" Right Ned asked.

"Basement," Gloria said, pulling a coat off a hook and slipping into it. "This way." She ran toward the hall Neds and I had just come in from.

"Hurry," Quinten said, throwing the duffel over his shoulder and following Gloria.

Abraham took one step, then another. From the way his body stiffened against each movement, I knew it hurt like hell.

If he was already feeling everything, then I didn't see how me touching him could make it worse. "Here," I said, sliding my arm around his back and drawing his arm over my shoulder. "Lean if you need it."

He leaned.

I helped him take the next few steps, and wanted to scream for how slow we were moving. But with each step his body seemed to come back to itself; muscles and joints and nerves seemed to remember how to move as one whole.

And then he seemed to remember how to move smoothly and quickly, until we were walking at a fairly fast pace.

But we were not running. We were nowhere near running capabilities.

"Faster, faster," Left Ned chanted behind us.

Gloria and Quinten dragged a heavy cabinet away from the end of the hall and shoved it up against one wall. Gloria crouched down and pressed a button in the floorboards. A hatch popped up, and she pushed it to one side, where it slid seamlessly into the floor itself.

"Watch your step." She started down a ladder, Quinten hurrying after her.

I looked up at Abraham. This wasn't going to be pretty.

He scowled at the ladder. "Go," he said, pulling his arm away from me.

"I won't leave you."

"Down. I'll be right behind you."

I didn't waste any more time arguing. I sat and slipped my boots to the first rung, then scurried down as fast as I could.

Not a lot of light at the bottom of the ladder. It smelled of damp and mold and rot. I took a few steps away from the ladder. The ground beneath me felt like hard-packed dirt.

"What's taking them so long?" Quinten whispered from the shadows to my right.

Abraham's boot, first one, then the other, pressed against the ladder rungs. He climbed down methodically, but not nearly as slowly as I'd expected.

Neds scrambled down almost on top of him.

As soon as Neds' heads cleared the floor above us, the hatch closed, *snick*ing into place, then sealing with a *thud* of metal sucking down vacuum tight.

The darkness was complete now.

"This way," Gloria said. She shook something and a soft yellow glow appeared in her palm.

I heard Quinten shake something too, and then the little packet strapped to the back of his hand glowed.

"Do you need assistance?" he asked Abraham.

Abraham was leaning against the ladder, still breathing hard. Sweat caught in small droplets at the ends of the hair over his eyes, and his clothes were soaked with it. He looked like he'd just run a marathon, not walked down a single hallway and a single ladder.

"Go," I said to Quinten. "We'll catch up."

Abraham pushed away from the ladder. "We'll keep up," he said.

Neds, probably Left Ned, swore softly. He stepped over to Abraham and wrapped an arm around him.

I came up on the other side and did the same. I'd expected Abraham to argue, but from how much he was leaning on us both, I didn't think he had the air for it.

"Don't like ladders?" I asked as we moved forward over the hard, uneven dirt.

Abraham breathed for a bit, as if just trying to keep his lungs and feet moving at the same time was taking all his concentration.

"Most. Repairs," he said, one word on each exhale. "Days. To recover. Coordination. Difficult."

"It's coming back to you pretty quickly," I said.

"Wouldn't hurt to step it up a bit, though," Left Ned said.

The glow of Quinten's and Gloria's lights bobbed ahead of us faster than we could keep up.

"Think you can?" I asked Abraham.

Instead of wasting breath, he just put a little more effort into walking. He had longer legs than either Neds or me, but I wished he was moving at about twice the speed.

"Do you think Domek will find the hatch?" I asked Neds.

"Yes," Right Ned said.

"How long?"

"Hopefully not before we're out of this tunnel," Left Ned said. "We're fish in a barrel down here."

"Where do you think this empties out?"

"No idea," Right Ned said.

Abraham was doing what he could to stay breathing and moving. Even wounded, fevered, weak, and hurting, he didn't complain.

"Hold up here," Gloria said from ahead of us. "I'll see if we can cross."

"Just a little more," I said to Abraham. We finally caught up to Quinten where the tunnel widened a bit.

The walls were a rough mix of dirt and bricks, the ceiling supported by wooden beams. Gloria's light skipped ahead, casting yellow over more bricks and more beams; then she took a sharp right and was gone.

"Let's lean for a second," I suggested. Neds and I guided Abraham to the wall and leaned against it.

We were all sweating and breathing a little hard. Abraham closed his eyes and tipped his head back, trying to get his breathing under control.

Quinten squinted at the shadows that filled the tunnel where Gloria had been moments before. Then he dug in the duffel over his shoulder and pulled out a soft canteen. "It's water," he said, offering it to me. "He should drink as much as he can."

I took the container, a waterproof fabric with a hard nozzle and cap at the top. I unscrewed the lid and held it up for Abraham. "You should drink," I said. "Doctor's orders."

It took him a moment, but he opened his eyes and tipped his head down again. He shifted and pulled his arm from around my shoulders, then did the same with Neds.

He locked his knees to hold himself up against the wall and held out his hand for the water.

I gave the canteen to him and he drank several long, deep swallows. He pulled it away from his mouth, paused to get his breath again, then drank more.

While he repeated this, his breathing getting better and better after each time he drank, I studied the tunnel, trying to set its location in my head.

"Do you have any idea where we are?" I asked Quinten.

"Other than under the city? No. She's told me she had a way to get out if she was ever discovered by a House."

"I think I love her a little for that," I said.

He smiled, the shadow and light carving into his profile as if he were made of wax. "There's a lot about her to love."

I walked the short distance to my brother and leaned in close. "I need to talk to you about Abraham. Now. In private."

"Wait here," he said to Neds and Abraham. "We'll walk partway down the tunnel, to watch for Gloria."

Before Neds could argue, Quinten took my wrist. We strode about halfway to the junction Gloria had taken to the right.

"What?" he whispered.

"He feels pain. Ever since he first woke up, he's had sensation," I said. "I told you that. I think it's the thread you used on him. My thread. And the scale jelly. Whatever it is, he can feel now."

Quinten frowned and glanced back over his shoulder, then back at me. "He seemed to handle the procedure normally. We administered the block before we did it."

"I'm sure. How painful would that procedure be on a normal human?"

"It would be excruciating." Quinten wiped at his mouth with his nonglowing hand. "He shouldn't be walking. Matilda, we need to find a safe place to leave him. He won't be able to keep up. Running will only do more damage to him."

"I won't hold you up," Abraham said. He walked on his own toward us. I had to admit, he seemed to be carrying himself better.

Neds followed behind him. I couldn't see their expressions in the darkness, but Right Ned shook his head.

Abraham appeared calm, confident, and collected.

Yeah, I'd seen him put on that act before. I knew he was weak, wounded, and hurting.

"If you care for your well-being," Quinten said, "you'll allow us to find a safe place for you so you can recover fully."

"There's a price on my head," Abraham said. "There is no safe place for me."

"Then if you care at all about my *sister's* life," Quinten said, "you will put her safety before yours and leave this group."

"Hey, now," I said. "Stop it. Both of you. Fighting isn't going to help anything."

I may as well have been scolding shadows.

Abraham advanced on Quinten and glowered down on him. "I care very much about your sister's life. Do you understand me, Quinten Case? I know what you've done to make her. I know what you've done to keep her. I know what you've done to hide her. But she is no longer your secret to own. The Houses know about her; the world knows about her. And they know about you. If you think you can outrun those who rule this world, you are an idiot."

"She was safe until *you* put her in danger," Quinten snapped. "She would have stayed safe if *you* hadn't stepped into our lives. I blame you, Abraham Seventh, for all the damage done to her. All the damage done to my family."

"Hey," I warned again. "We've done plenty on our own to damage our family."

"I will tell you this only once, Mr. Case," Abraham said in a low growl. "You will regret choosing me as your enemy."

What? No one was choosing enemies here.

"Enough!" I pushed my way between them, grabbed the sleeves of their jackets, and physically pulled them apart.

Yes, I'm strong enough to do that. "We are all going to get along—do you both understand that? I do not care one bit about who thinks they have or haven't done enough to keep me safe. For one thing, keeping me safe is *my* job. I will not be argued over like I'm a fragile knick-knack someone dropped and chipped.

"Right this second, I could wrestle you *both* to the ground and make you cry uncle, so do not even *think* of testing how serious I am about this. We travel together. Period. We keep the hate, the blame, and the anger where it should be kept: against the Houses who have apparently sent an assassin to kill us. Our enemies are not in this tunnel. Not yet.

"We're all in, all the way together. Are we gold on that?"

Neither of them said anything, their gazes locked, hands in fists.

"Do not make me knock you both out and drag you through this tunnel. Are we gold?" I shoved back my sleeves so I'd have better reach to wrestle them.

"We're gold," Abraham said, still staring at Quinten.

"Fine," Quinten said. "We travel together. If Abraham falls, we all fall. That should be a familiar refrain to you, Abraham Seventh, now that all the galvanized are falling because of your actions."

Abraham lifted his head and it was a massive, obvious effort to force himself to take a couple steps away. I noted it put him out of strangling range, which was pretty much what it looked like he wanted to do to my brother.

"Uncalled-for," I said to Quinten, stepping up and placing my hand over his racing heart. "Look at me."

He finally did, and some of the caged-animal wildness left his eyes. Quinten had been out of captivity for just over a day. It was no wonder he was running a little close to the other side of sanity.

"Slater Orange is the one who started this," I said. "And Helen Eleventh. You know that. You do. We're going to fix it. All of it. The entire world. But right now the only thing we can do is get through this tunnel and get back to the property."

Quinten swallowed and nodded, lifting his hand to touch my arm. "I know." Then, quieter, "I'm sorry."

I smiled, hoping he could see it in the low light. "We're gold."

"Property? Your property?" Abraham asked. Abraham wasn't stupid. He knew Quinten had been held by Slater. I supposed he even has some ideas of what Slater may have done to him.

"Yes, our property," Quinten said.

"Why?" Abraham asked me.

Quinten answered him. "Because if we don't, the time anomaly that has given the galvanized such a long life will end, killing all galvanized instantly."

Abraham was silent for a moment. Just a few hours ago, I'd told him his friend Oscar Gray was dead. Just a few hours ago, he'd found out my brother had killed his friend Robert Twelfth. And now he was being told his own death was days away.

The bad news just kept coming.

"What time anomaly?" he asked with far more calm than I was feeling. I kept glancing back in the shadows behind us, expecting Domek to be there with a gun.

So far the shadows were just shadows.

"Wings of Mercury experiment," Quinten said. "It was our great-great-and-greater-grandfather's experiment. And, according to the notes I've compiled, the break in time he triggered is going to mend. In just over two days. I think I can stop it."

"How?"

But there was no time for an answer. A blast ricocheted through the tunnel. *A bomb?*

"Go." Left Ned grabbed Abraham's arm, pushing him to move past us down the tunnel. "Domek must have blown the hatch. He'll be on us."

I jogged after them, caught up, and took Abraham's other side.

Abraham was supporting more of his own weight and his breathing was steady. He'd gotten enough water and rest back there that we could sprint for it.

So we ran.

Down to the end of the tunnel. Hard right following where Gloria had gone.

Could be a dead end.

Could be a trap.

Could be Gloria had been captured and we were running to our doom.

Could be none of that mattered because Domek was

behind us, and he would kill us deader than dead if he caught us.

A light ahead of us descend in a single dull-yellow beam from the ceiling. That light showed a shaft leading upward at the end of the tunnel.

"Hurry!" Gloria pulled a cage door to one side and waved us in behind it. "Where's Quinten?"

I ducked out from under Abraham's arm, leaving him to lean against the back of the cage—maybe an elevator— and peered through the darkness and dust behind us for Quinten.

I couldn't see him, but the light he carried arced and then hit the ground. He'd thrown it away. I didn't know why.

"Quinten!" I got three steps into the dust toward him when a hand shot out and grabbed my wrist.

"Run, run, run!" Quinten said.

We hauled it into the elevator. Gloria worked the controls. It was an old freight lift, mechanics and gears, pulleys and chain. It clattered and rumbled, starting up.

"Did you see him?" I asked Quinten.

"Cover your ears," he said.

Which was a weird answer, but then it all clicked. He had a lot of different medical compounds and chemicals in that bag he'd packed. If he didn't have something that was already a bomb, he was sure to have packed something that could pretty quickly become a bomb.

I covered my ears.

The blast hit, sound and impact simultaneously pounding over us. Dust and rock smothered out the air, stung my eyes, and covered us in grit. I prayed the mechanics on the lift would withstand it. I prayed that Domek wouldn't withstand it.

The elevator shuddered like an animal that had just had its jugular cut.

It slowed but kept rising, grinding and shrieking as it cranked up and up.

Quinten was saying something, but I couldn't hear him after that blast. Gloria shook her head, pointed at her ear, then pressed her fingers over her lips. Quinten shut up.

Neds and Abraham were covered in a thick layer of dust. I supposed we all were. They had seen Gloria's signal and weren't talking either.

The elevator hopped to a stop. I hoped we were at the top and not dangling somewhere between.

Gloria pulled the cage door open and stepped through it. We were in a concrete enclosure lit by a dull bulb on the wall, a single steel door directly opposite us. "This is it," she said. I didn't know how loud she was talking, but I wouldn't have understood her if I hadn't been watching her lips.

She took a second to bat the dust off her shoulders, head, face, and hands while we all stepped out of the elevator, Abraham under his own power.

"Which wire do I cut?" I asked.

Quinten flicked a look at me, then at the elevator gears that were exposed. He pointed. "That should work."

I reached over, wrapped my hand around the cable chain, and pulled.

Not as easy as it looked, but I am an uncommonly strong woman. It finally gave under my insistence.

"It won't stop him," Left Ned said. "He'll keep coming until we're dead."

"Just trying to buy us some time," I said as we hurried over to where Gloria was picking the lock on the steel door.

"No key?" I asked.

"Never had one," she said.

"Let me." Right Ned flicked a ready-all out of one pocket and a slim knife out of the other.

Gloria moved aside, and Neds got busy with the lock. Right Ned gave a little "Aha," and had it sprung in less than three seconds.

"Three seconds? You're getting rusty, Harris," I said.

"Want me to reset it so you can give it a try?"

"There's no time for squabbling, children," Quinten said.

Neds stepped back and pulled his jacket hood up, so that at the casual glance you wouldn't suppose he had two heads.

I adjusted my scarf and took a look at Abraham. He had his hands in his pockets, and with the dust and scruff, even the stitches on his face were difficult to see unless a person got close enough.

Quinten and Gloria left their heads bare, which was a good move. Five people all hooded up might be more than a little suspicious.

Gloria opened the door and we all stepped through.

The light wind and clear, sunny day made me want to gulp down big lungfuls of the cleanness of it. I'm not claustrophobic, but that run through the tunnels had my shoulders creeping up.

The elevator had deposited us in an alley between

two buildings, one that must be a restaurant, from the smell of hot oil and fish that was coming from it. The other looked shut down for renovations.

Right or left? Left was darker, leading to a narrow cross street and another jag of alleys. *Safer in shadows.* Right was light, a busy street, maybe a park beyond it. Vulnerable and exposed.

Abraham strode off to the right, to the light.

"Where are you going?" I asked, jogging after him and catching his sleeve.

He paused and shifted a little woodenly to look down at me. Those wounds of his were giving him zero flexibility. He still radiated heat from that fever and was sweating hard. "I know who can throw him off our trail."

"Not that way," Quinten said. "Every camera in the city and sky will see us out in the open."

"Domek will expect us to hide," Abraham answered. "He'll chase us down the darkest alley he can find, and it will become our graves."

"The cameras will give us away," Gloria said. "To the Houses. More assassins."

"I know someone who will help us with that," he said. "Cameras shouldn't be a problem for him. Hurry. Domek will find a way out of that tunnel, even if he has to climb the elevator shaft to do it."

I let go of Abraham's sleeve. "Who?" I asked following him. "Who do you know who can help with the cameras?"

But by then he was at the end of the alley and striding out into full and open daylight.

12

Quinten is leaving for the summer, but no one will tell me where he's going. I don't know if he's coming back.

—from the diary of E. N. D.

We couldn't stand here waiting for Domek to storm out of the tunnel, guns a-blazing. But walking into the sunlight—the open, public world—felt a lot like painting CATCH ME across my back while standing naked in the middle of the road.

I didn't want to follow Abraham out into that sunlight. But I didn't want to lose him either.

"Matilda," Quinten said. "Don't."

Too late. I pulled back my shoulders and stepped, as casually as I could, from between the buildings.

To my surprise, there were no gunshots. No automatic armed forces out there ready to cuff me and throw me in jail. No one even looked my way.

It was a nice day on a nice-enough street in the middle of the city. A patch of green beneath scant tree cover created a small park across the street. People in vehicles and on foot went about their business as people always did: getting where they were going in the world without ever really looking around at it.

But no matter how nice the day or city was, the street and sidewalk and buildings all had some kind of surveillance built into them.

We were, right this moment, being recorded.

I spotted Abraham striding down the sidewalk to my right. He stopped in front of an advertising screen that scrolled across a narrow section of the building jutting out onto the sidewalk.

I heard the others exit the alley behind me.

"Stupid, stupid," one of the Neds, Left Ned, I thought, was muttering.

"Take it easy and stroll," I suggested, not looking back at him. He came up and matched my pace.

The sidewalk wasn't all that crowded at this time of day, and the few people who passed us wove by without even slowing. I did my best not to stare at each of them, wondering if they were gunmen hired by the Houses or if they were signaling our location to people who were.

"What the hell is he doing?" Right Ned asked.

"Something smart, I hope."

"Doesn't look smart from here," Left Ned said. "Looks like he's . . . ah, shee-it. He's calling out."

He was right. Abraham held his left hand in the center of his chest, palm outward and said, "Whiskey echo lima tango Oscar November, 1880 Vail. Link."

We stopped about ten feet away from him. It sounded like a nonsense string of words, but something seemed familiar about it too.

Then it came to me: he was using old—very old—

military alphabet phonetic. And I realized what he'd just spelled out.

"Crap," I whispered.

"What?" Right Ned asked.

I shook my head and I chewed on my bottom lip, waiting for the sirens, waiting for Domek to round the corner behind us or for someone to open fire from one of the never-ending streams of cars moving past us.

I waited for the answer to Abraham's message.

The screen filled with bright yellow, and a location just down the block and across the street flashed across it. It happened so quickly, I would have missed it if I'd blinked.

Abraham turned toward me. "Follow at a distance." He started down the block.

I glanced at Quinten. He was stock-still, his hand in Gloria's, as if they were two people in love out for a stroll. Which might actually be true.

But they were also two people who were on the run from the law.

"Did you get that?" I asked him.

"I did. Thoughts?"

He was asking me if we were going to follow Abraham and put our lives in the hands of the man he'd just contacted. "Better than going back the way we came."

"Go," Quinten said.

So we went, following Abraham, Quinten and Gloria walking far enough behind us, it didn't look like we were all traveling together.

My heart revved too high, pounded too hard. Every loud sound made me want to duck; every second we were out in the open, I expected bullets to start firing.

I hated this. Hated being exposed.

Abraham crossed the street through a narrow gap in traffic. Neds and I stopped on the corner, waiting for traffic to clear.

"Really would like to know what the hell we're doing," Right Ned said. "Who did he contact?"

"Welton," I said.

"Damn," Right Ned said.

Welton was the head of House Yellow, Technology. When I'd been around him, he had seemed to be a friend to not only his galvanized, Foster First, but to all the galvanized, who treated Welton like a younger, annoying sibling.

"Do you think bringing a head of House into this is a good idea?" Left Ned asked.

"No. But this wasn't my idea. If any of the heads of Houses can be trusted, it might be Welton."

"None of the heads of Houses can be trusted," Right Ned said.

Yeah, I was worried about that too.

"I don't mind putting my money where my mouth is," Left Ned said. "And I promised I'd see this through with you to the end. But that man of yours just gambled with my life. With all our lives."

"With whatever we have left of them," I said. "We're all gambling. Time isn't really something we have to spare, you know. We have to take some risks."

"Do you believe Quinten about the time thing?" Right Ned asked. "That he can fix it so you don't die?"

"You know my brother," I said.

He snorted. Right. He didn't know my brother. They hadn't met before yesterday.

"Yes," I said. "He thinks he can make it so that I won't die when time heals."

"Do *you* think he can?"

I shook my head and wished the traffic would open up so we could get across the damn street. "I don't know. If we don't get caught. If Domek doesn't shoot us down. If we can get home with the intel we need? Maybe."

"Intel?" Left Ned asked.

"What I was looking for earlier this morning. We need to confirm the calculation of the experiment. Quinten thinks Grandma had it written in her journal, which was taken when our parents died. I'm trying to track down a copy of it."

"Your drifty-minded grandmother? He thinks something in her lost journal is going to be a fix-all? That is . . . shit. Finding it in time . . . that's impossible," Right Ned said.

"I know. But if there really is only one last place the calculation was written down, I can only assume someone would have wanted to make a copy of it somewhere."

He reached out and took my hand. I was standing on his left, and so it was his left hand that took mine. Right Ned controlled that side of the body, while Left Ned controlled the other side.

"We'll make it work," Right Ned said softly.

Neds had a way of seeing things, visions when they touched a person, me included. Right Ned had never made me ashamed of what I was made of or what he'd seen of me when he'd touched me. Just the same, contact with the Harris brothers was a very rare thing. Which made his gesture all the more endearing.

I squeezed his fingers and let go of his hand. "Yes, we will," I said. "Come hell or hinterlands."

Traffic finally broke and we jogged to the other side of the street.

"Just make me a promise," I said once we were on the sidewalk again.

"Another one?" Left Ned asked.

"Please."

Right Ned peered over at me from beneath his hood. His eyes, blue as spring, were clouded with worry. "All right. What?"

"If things don't go our way," I said.

"They will," he insisted.

"But if they don't." I waited to make sure he wouldn't argue.

He nodded.

"If they don't," I continued, "I want you to take over leading House Brown."

"Whoa," Left Ned said as if all the air had been pushed out of his lungs.

"Are you listening to the nonsense that is coming out of your mouth, Matilda Case?" Right Ned asked.

"I am. And I am serious." I took a chance and shot a look back the way we came. I couldn't see Domek in the people there. Didn't see an armed man wearing all black in the shadows. Was it possible he hadn't found a way out of the tunnel yet? I thought he was the best of the best. We couldn't be that hard to track.

"You've proved that you know how to stay below radar," I said. "You know a lot of people who are willing to help others—"

"If by *willing* you mean 'can be bribed,'" Left Ned said.

"—and I know you care about people being free. People like Sadie and Corb. People like me and my brother and Gloria. Please. Promise me you'll take on the communication hub at the farm and try to keep House Brown safe from the other Houses."

"I make it a point not to make deals with delusional people," Right Ned said. "For one thing, we're going to make it through this. *You* are going to make it through this. Brilliant brother has a plan, and all that."

"Then make the promise," I said. "Tell me you'll take over House Brown if anything goes wrong. Since you know it's all going to go fine, what do you have to lose?"

We were striding along a little faster. Abraham was a ways ahead of us and had picked up the pace a bit. Neds shifted his wide shoulders so both of him could look at me.

"Matilda," Right Ned said. His eyes were sad. So were Left Ned's. "Don't make me promise that."

"House Brown needs a man like you," I said. "Both of you."

"Fine," Left Ned said, "I promise." His voice was a little rough around what sounded suspiciously like emotions. "Now will you shut up about it?"

Right Ned just gave me a sad smile. "I promise."

"Good," I said. "I like knowing it will be in good hands."

Abraham had stopped in a loading area in the shadow of a building. He had his arms crossed over his chest. We walked up to him.

"Welton Yellow?" Left Ned demanded in a low whisper. "For hell's sake, how is that going to do any good? We already have one killer on our asses, in case you forgot."

"What was your plan to get out of the city?" Abraham asked coolly.

I would have bought the stone-cold act Abraham was putting on if he wasn't sweating so badly. His color had gone off too, or maybe it was just the coating of dust, but he looked greener around the edges, with dark, purple-bruised shadows, as if everything under his skin was leaking and bleeding.

"The old freight lines," Right Ned said. "Substations. I know a guy. He can get us to Kansas. There's a woman there who can get us within a couple miles of the farm."

"Freight lines?" Quinten asked as he and Gloria closed in behind us.

"From back before the Restructure?" Gloria asked. "Those haven't been in service for more than a hundred years."

"They haven't been in service for the Houses," Right Ned said. "Not even for House Brown. But they work. Things get shipped. Private sorts of things."

"Black market?" Abraham asked. "That's all reported to House Silver."

Neds made a so-so gesture with his hand. "People skim, people barter, people get what they want if they try hard enough. I got us passage."

"How do you even know about this?" I asked. "House Brown could have used those connections once or twice over the past few years."

Quinten's eyebrows shot up and he leaned back just a bit, maybe surprised that his little sister would be willing to deal dirty. Yeah, well, times had been hard and it had fallen on my shoulders to care for not only our farm and family, but also any of the House Brown people who had emergency needs.

And everyone has emergency needs.

"Like I said," Right Ned repeated, "I know people. Not the kind of people you want to invite around for tea."

"Unless your life depends on it?" Abraham asked.

"Pretty much. Folk who run this rail aren't here to do you any favors. Money talks. Trade too, if you've got something worth trading. Like those medical supplies." He nodded toward Quinten's duffel.

"We'll have plenty to trade," Gloria said. "Were we supposed to meet someone?"

"We?" Quinten turned toward her. "Not you. You're staying here."

"No, I'm not," she said.

"She can't stay here," I said. "They know she helped us. There was a killer in her shop. Who, by some miracle, hasn't found us yet. Is that making anyone else jumpy?"

"Welton," Abraham said. "He set up a few diversions for Domek. False leads and trackers."

"You'll be in more danger if you travel with us," Quinten was saying to Gloria.

I turned to her. "Do you have anyplace where you can drop out of sight?"

She shook her head. "If all of you weren't right here with me, I'd be calling out to your place, asking you if you knew someone in House Brown who would let me hide out with them."

I nodded, turned back to my brother. "She stays with us until we can find her a safer place to be."

He threw both his hands in the air, then spun away from her direct stare and paced two or three steps away and back. "This is a terrible, terrible choice," he said.

"It's my terrible choice to make," she said.

"Where's the entry to the freight line?" Abraham asked.

"Down a couple streets near the old library," Right Ned said.

"There's nothing near the old library," Gloria said.

"There's a hidden entry to the freight line."

"I don't like this," Quinten said.

"None of us like it," Gloria answered. "But all of us are doing it."

"So, what are we waiting for?" I asked.

Abraham was still standing with his arms crossed over his chest. He uncrossed his arms and ran his right hand back through his hair. It was a very purposeful thing to do. A signal.

A loud pop echoed out down the street. Then another and another in quick succession. Six, a dozen.

I bolted into the shadows, searching the street. So did everyone else except Abraham. "Gunfire?" I asked.

Abraham hadn't moved. "Power overload on old wires," he said. "House Yellow really ought to have taken care of it years ago. Cameras, traffic control, and backup systems will be out for days. Streets are going to be a mess. Satellite feeds broken. Tracking anyone and anything will be impossible."

He grinned and it was a wicked sight. "We're as invisible as the head of House Technology can make us. Let's go."

"This way." Gloria took the lead, since she knew the quickest way to the old library.

We jogged through the rising confusion that wasn't quite chaos yet, but would be soon.

"This is it," Gloria said.

Ahead of us was a building that must have once been made of brick but was mudded over with multiple layers of concrete, all of which had fallen off in clumps. The state of disrepair was echoed by busted windows and copious graffiti. It looked like a building-devouring blight had hit the thing and eaten it from the inside out.

A tall concrete barrier rolled off from our right, and separated us from the empty plaza in front of the old library.

The place seemed to be abandoned. No movement. Not even any sleeping transients.

That was weird.

"Are you sure?" Quinten asked.

"Yes," Gloria said.

"Where's your contact, Ned?" Quinten asked.

Neds stood just in front of me and to the side a bit. So I saw when he suddenly stiffened. "Shee-it," Left Ned breathed.

Too late. Too late to run. Too late to hide.

Domek stepped out from behind a column of that dilapidated building and opened fire.

13

I'm afraid, but then, everyone is afraid lately.
There are rumors of the plague returning.
              —from the diary of E. N. D.

Chaos.

We dove for cover behind the concrete wall. The barrier was old and wouldn't last long under the heavy artillery he was unloading.

Shit.

"Does he have anyone with him?" Quinten yelled over the gunfire.

"Does he need to?" Left Ned answered as bullets chipped holes through the top of the wall we were huddled behind. Concrete scattered over us in a rain of rocks and sand.

We couldn't stay here. We couldn't call for help. Even if there was someone out there who would help us without turning us in, Welton had shut down the city and all modes of communication.

There had to be a way out of this.

I unzipped my duffel and pulled out my revolver.

"You have a gun?" Quinten asked.

"No one ever searches the girl." I squat-walked to the edge of the wall. "Knife? Mirror? Screen?"

Gloria dug through her duffel and handed me a palm-sized mirror. I pressed my back against the wall with the mirror aimed over my shoulder so I could get a line on Domek.

Another barrage of bullets rained down around us, lasting for at least a minute this time.

Holy hell, that was a lot of bullets.

But I'd gotten a look at him before I'd had to tuck back behind the barrier.

Domek stood out in the open of what had been the library's plaza, like an idiot who underestimated that one of us would be armed, and two of us were galvanized.

"He has an automatic weapon," I said.

"Old news," Right Ned said.

"And he's in the open," I went on. "Nothing for cover." I checked the chamber of my gun for bullets.

"Revolver's not going to do you any good." Left Ned said.

"If my aim's clean, it only takes one bullet to end this." I pulled up the mirror again to locate him. Then leaned out, took aim, fired.

But the wind shifted, my hand shook, and I was pretty sure I didn't do anything more than make him aware that we were not going to go with him peacefully.

Not that he'd asked us to put our weapons down or go with him, peacefully or otherwise. Weren't hired guns for the Houses supposed to tell us to come out with our hands in the air or something? Or had he skipped basic etiquette class in assassin school?

"Got any bombs left?" Left Ned asked Quinten.

Quinten nodded. "One."

Abraham leaned forward a bit. "I'll toss the bomb and draw his fire," he said. "All the rest of you run into the building."

"Like hell, you'll draw his fire," I said.

"If some of us are to survive, some of us will have to make sacrifices," Abraham said.

Hadn't we just gone over the *no* of this back at Gloria's?

"All of us are going to survive," I said. "*None* of us are going to make sacrifices."

A hard hail of gunfire shattered the air overhead.

"Sonofabitch," Left Ned said. "We need to move."

"We need a plan," Quinten said.

Then Domek decided to join the conversation. "Quinten Case," he yelled. "Surrender yourself and the others will be unharmed."

Quinten? We all stared at him.

I'd thought Domek was after Abraham, who was accused of murder. Who would have sent an assassin out looking for my brother?

Quinten's back was pressed against the wall. Even through the tunnel dust, sweat, and concrete debris that covered him, he went pale. His clever blue eyes ticked over to me, wide with fear; then a decision narrowed them. I shook my head.

"No," I said, "Whatever you just thought of? No. Nobody sacrifices themselves."

"A distraction," Quinten said. "You could run for the station."

"Like he won't shoot us in the back?" I said. "We do

not trust people who are shooting at us. C'mon. That's survival 101, Quinten."

"He said he wants me," he said.

"He'll have to go through me to get to you," I said. "If you walk out there, I will do mad, foolish things to save you. You know I will. And you know I can survive a hell of a lot of hits before I go down. Let's not go willingly into that nightmare, okay?"

He shook his head. "Matilda . . ."

"No."

"She ain't budging," Right Ned said. "So your surrender's out. What else you got, Tilly?"

No support from satellite, phone, or any other connection. Local law was tied up with a million problems from the blown grid, so no cavalry to come riding to the rescue.

We had one gun against a heavily armed, highly trained killer who was just playing with us.

"How far is it to the station entry?" I asked Neds.

"Should be right behind Killer Man there," Right Ned said. "The actual entry to the station is inside the building."

I tipped the mirror to get another look at the distance to the door. "Okay. Fifty yards. There's another concrete half wall about ten yards from the door."

"I'll give you to the count of three," Domek yelled into the relative silence. "Then you will all come out with your hands where I can see them."

"Options?" I asked.

"Quinten throws the bomb," Abraham said. "You and I take out Domek."

"With one revolver?" I asked.

"With brute strength."

Abraham was terribly wounded. Even so, we were both galvanized and frighteningly strong. "Rush him?" I asked.

He pointed to a rusted blue industrial Dumpster that stood on broken skids about half the distance between us and Domek. Concrete and scrap metal filled it. "I am in the mood to throw that at his head."

"Shee-it," Left Ned said. "Can you?"

The thing must weigh a couple thousand pounds. "Okay," I said. "Let's do it."

"What?" Quinten said. "No."

"Three . . ." Domek yelled.

"Yes." I handed Quinten my gun. "Bullets won't kill us unless he gets in a very lucky head shot, which isn't likely after a bomb blast and us crushing him under a Dumpster. Give Neds the bomb."

"Why Neds?" Quinten was talking, but that didn't mean he wasn't also moving. He quickly dug the glass vial out of his duffel and handed it to Neds.

"I know the arm he has on him, and, no offense, brother, but you haven't been working the farm for three years. Ned," I said, "chuck it and make it count. If he goes up in pieces, I'm not going to cry any tears."

Right Ned took the corked glass vial from Quinten. "Do unto others, I always say. And that man is out to see us dead."

"Two . . ."

"What happens after the bomb?" Gloria asked.

"You, Quinten, and Neds run for that building and get inside fast," I said. "Use the half wall there for cover if you need to."

"But what about you and Abraham?" she asked.

"We'll be okay," I said. "And we'll be right behind you. Ready?"

"One!" Domek yelled. He didn't even wait a second longer before he starting shooting again, blowing through chunks of concrete.

"Jee-zus!" Right Ned pulled a Glock out of his pocket.

"You had a gun?" Quinten yelled.

Neds leaned out and unloaded the clip, then cocked back and threw the bomb, whipping it full force.

A blast of white-hot fire shook the ground and buildings around us.

"Go, go, go!" I yelled, even though I couldn't hear my own voice.

They bolted for the building. Abraham and I ran to the Dumpster.

But Domek recovered too quickly.

The bullets came fast and hard. One hit my thigh, another my arm.

I yelled and slammed up behind the Dumpster, breathing hard.

"For shit's sake!" I said. "I think we made him mad."

"You're bleeding," Abraham said.

I wiped the pain sweat out of my eyes, my hands shaking with adrenaline. "So are you." I nodded to his gut, which was seeping red through his crappy secondhand clothes. "Ready?"

His eyes hardened and he nodded. "Lift. Throw. On three. One . . ."

I crouched, my hands under the edge of the metal. If the thing hadn't been tilted on broken skids, there would have been no way to get leverage.

Use your legs, I said to myself. I exhaled, prepping mind and body for the lift. *Just like a bale of hay. A really big, really heavy bale of hay.*

"Two," he said.

I inhaled.

"Three!"

We both stood, balancing the massive weight of the thing between us as we used our upward momentum to heave the Dumpster up and out.

It should have been impossible.

But, then, we were a little impossible ourselves.

Concrete and metal thundered across the plaza as the Dumpster tipped too far over in midair, scattering part of its load before it landed in a ground-pounding thump right on top of Domek. The stink of rust, oil, sour water, and garbage rained down around us as the impact shot debris into the air.

"Go!" Abraham yelled.

I turned and starting running toward the library.

But Abraham was striding the other way, toward the Dumpster, toward the fallen, buried Domek.

Had he lost his mind?

Abraham bent and picked up a hundred-pound chunk of concrete one-handed and threw it like a skipping stone at the mess of debris over Domek.

He was cursing in that language I didn't know, his body filled with a rage it couldn't contain, every movement power and pain and violence.

I took a step toward him.

"Go!" he yelled again.

A flash of metal moving in that pile of debris caught my eye.

"Abraham!" I yelled. Too late.

A spattering of bullets fired out from the garbage. Abraham jerked back as they hit, riddling him.

I ran for him, not thinking that I was running into the fire, not caring that the bullets would tear through me next. I couldn't die, *we* couldn't die unless Domek blasted our brains out of our heads. And I wasn't going to let that happen.

I didn't know how Abraham was still standing, but he yelled in that language, bent, grabbed spine-breaking chunks of metal and rock and heaved them at the gunman.

Abraham was anger, violence, hatred. Unstoppable. Galvanized.

The bullets paused.

I grabbed his free arm, determined to get him the hell out of there before they started up again.

He pivoted on me, eyes burning red, scorched by pain and fury.

"Move!" I yelled.

He seemed to come to his senses. We ran, pounding toward the building, three steps, six.

Bullets hissed into the ground beside us, tracking our path. In less than a minute, we'd be nothing but holes and lead shot.

But we didn't get that minute.

A cannon blasted out overhead, followed by gunfire that screamed with guided ammunition, target guaranteed. *Shit. Tracers.* If someone wanted us dead, this would do it.

Searing, spitting bullets rattled out like World War End. Far more than Neds or Quinten could lay down. Far more than Domek had on him.

Abraham and I ducked and rolled behind that low concrete wall not far from the library door. None of the others were here. I hoped they'd made it into the building.

"You will stand down," a new voice bellowed over a bullhorn during a short interval in the holy-shit chorus. "Throw all weapons on the ground. Now."

"Do you see him?" I asked.

Abraham scanned the sky and the roof of the abandoned library. "No."

"Is this making sense to you?" I asked.

"No."

The only thing I could come up with was either a House had just stepped in to stop our killer and capture us, or Ned's contact we were supposed to meet here had a lot of illegal tracer firepower and a bullhorn.

Then I didn't have time to ponder. The distinctive *plink* of metal canisters hitting the ground rattled across the plaza.

Not just canisters; tear gas. Dozens of them.

Damn it.

Domek went back to shooting, but the bullets weren't coming our way. I didn't care who was on whose side now. We just needed to get out of here.

Abraham was on his feet, pulling me up.

I ran through the cover of tear gas rising to fill the air, went blind by the time I'd taken ten steps, and had to feel my way along the side of the building.

Wandering blind in the line of fire was going to get me dead. Any minute now.

Then hands reached out pulled me into a space with no wind and a hell of a lot less smoke. I heard a door shut behind me.

"Here," Quinten's voice said, "put this over your face."

We must be inside the library. "Abraham?" I croaked.

"He's here," Gloria said.

So we all must have made it inside the library. Hurray for our team.

Quinten dropped a damp cloth in my hands and I pressed it over my face, taking in several breaths of the sour-grape and chemical solution. Whatever he'd drenched the cloth with did an amazing job at stopping the burning in my eyes, nose, and throat.

The voice on the bullhorn outside was still yelling demands. Another volley of bullets rattled out. If Domek wasn't dead, he would be soon. Tracers always hit their mark, and if not, some clever weapons designers had rigged them to act as impact explosives.

Right on cue I heard the *pock-thoom* of the mini explosives triggering.

"Is this everyone?" a man's voice I didn't recognize asked.

"This is us, Slip," Right Ned said.

"One extra will cost you extra," the man said.

"Of course," Right Ned said.

I squeezed my eyes tight and rubbed the cloth carefully over both eyes, then my mouth and nose. My vision was a little foggy, but the basics of the situation were easy enough to see. We were in the burned and gutted library. Abraham had planted both shoulders against the wall and was scowling, silent, as he drew the cloth away from his eyes. Gloria handed him a new cloth, which he pressed against the wound on his stomach. He wasn't just bleeding. He was bleeding badly.

"Pay before party, Harris," Slip said.

Slip was medium height and build, strung together with the ropy muscles of someone who spent too much time in salt water. He stood with his back toward the interior of the building, facing Neds, who were ahead of me to my right.

Slip's shoulder-length hair was dry and sun bleached, his weathered tan skin carved with wrinkles at his forehead and eyes. He wore a sleeveless hoodie and pants with plenty of pockets down the outside of the legs. He also had on a thigh holster, a full quiver and crossbow across his back, and a pinched expression of suspicion on his face.

Ned reached into his jacket pocket and pulled out a bottle of pills. "Antibiotics, full strength."

Gloria's eyes went wide. I guess she hadn't realized exactly what Ned had taken off her shelf. Antibiotics were rare and valuable. But, then, the pills were paying for her passage, so maybe she was paying for herself.

Neds tossed the medicine to Slip. He shook the bottle without looking at it.

Voice on the bullhorn outside laughed and cussed. There was only intermittent gunfire, then a lot of silence.

"This isn't enough," Slip said. "One of you stays behind."

"We all travel together." Left Ned pulled an even bigger bottle out of his other pocket. "Painkillers." He held it up. "This bottle squares our debt."

"How many pills?"

Left Ned shook the bottle. It sounded full.

The man curled two fingers in a "give it over" gesture.

"We're square," Right Ned repeated, still holding the

bottle. "Full passage for her and for the rest of us. To Kansas."

Slip opened the bottle in his hand, sniffed the antibiotics, then dumped one out and pressed it against his tongue. He nodded before dropping the pill back in the bottle.

"Along with that"—he nodded at the painkillers in Neds' hand—"we're square."

Neds tossed him the painkillers, and Slip jammed both bottles away in a bag that hung at his belt.

"While I'd like to say I want to know all your names," Slip said, raising his voice like he'd suddenly become our tour guide, "I don't. You can call me Slip. If you want a ride on my boat, walk this way."

He gave us each a quick up and down, as if setting the details of us to memory just in case we became worth turning in for a ransom.

When he looked at me, his eyebrows quirked down just a notch. I didn't know what he saw in me. I saw in him a man who knew the profit he could make off anything that fell into his hands.

We weren't people to him. We were cargo.

I didn't like him. Nor did I trust him.

The door behind us swung open, and I spun toward it.

"Whoo, that's good times!" A tall, lanky, dark-skinned man with an autotracer cannon slung over his shoulder and a bullhorn in one hand strolled in. "I do love breaking out one of these babies." He grinned at us, then tossed the bullhorn to Slip.

"This here's Lucky," Slip said by way of introduction.

"Is he dead?" I asked Lucky.

"The assassin? Not if he's a fast runner and can find a

doctor quick. Well, and a bomb technician." Lucky sauntered across the floor, heading toward the far side of the library. "Might have annoyed him enough for him to call in backup, though."

Slip followed the other man and gestured for us to do so. "I usually charge extra for taking out an agent of House Black," Slip said, "but Domek out there is a personal annoyance—"

"Always up our asses," Lucky said.

"So we are more than happy to kick his shit for free. But a few bullets and toxic gas won't stop him. We move now."

Slip pressed his hand into a wall that I didn't think had a scanner in it. I was wrong.

The wall opened, swinging on silent tracks, and I briefly noted the inside was fitted with shelves that still had books on them.

A tiled staircase with inset lights took us under the library. Slip led the way, and Lucky brought up the back. After a second long flight of stairs, we stood in a tunnel that was about as different from our escape route out of Gloria's place as I could imagine.

The entire underground station had the look of lost splendor. Ceilings were worked with glass and metal. Spirals of cast iron and stained glass created cathedral arcs that bloomed like petals of stunning flowers down the length of the place. A second-story railing and walkway ringed the station, doors and rooms dark behind that walkway.

The air smelled of salt, oil, and a meaty stagnancy. We appeared to be the only people here, which I supposed made sense if hardly anyone knew about the place.

A lowered rail ran down the length of the tunnel. On it was a train: a round-cornered rectangular, dull silver engine connected to a string of identical cars that gave it the appearance of a blind, subterranean caterpillar.

I thought this train, with boarded-up windows across the twelve boxcars, might have been originally designed to take people to and from work in the city. In about the mid-2100s it would have been part of the cross-country multicity work lines that connected the subrails. Not every line had been completed back then, but it had still been a strong secondary transportation system, though it was a people mover more than a freight mover.

Then the aboveground speed tubes had been tested and built. Since they were four times as fast as anything else over or under land, all the funding for the substations was funneled into the tubes. Freight moved quicker on tube, and so did people.

It was no surprise Gloria thought this system was defunct. Everyone thought it had been defunct for more than a hundred years.

The train that waited on that track appeared clean and well maintained. Bluish light poured out through the open doors.

"I hope you don't mind tight quarters," Slip said, walking toward the train. "Well," he pivoted on his heel, half bent with his hands up, not quite in apology and not quite a bow, "you really don't have a choice, do you?"

Lucky opened the door to one of the train cars.

Quinten strolled up to it like a rich man inspecting insufficient accommodations. He stepped onto the train, and Gloria followed.

That left Abraham, Neds, and me all standing outside.

Lucky braced his arm across the doorway. It wasn't enough to stop any of us if we wanted to get on board. Bones were easy to break. But we waited.

Slip's gaze took me in again, boot to head, stopping just briefly on the bullet wounds in my thigh that hurt like a bitch, and the matching bullet wounds in my arm that hurt like a bitch.

Then he gave Abraham the same inspection. Abraham was bleeding too. Worse than I was.

But Abraham didn't show that he felt pain, if he did indeed feel it. His feet were spread wide in case he had to fight, arms crossed loosely over his chest as if Slip and Lucky wouldn't be worth his time to fight. He radiated a "do not fuck with me" attitude, his eyes burning red.

"You didn't tell me you'd have two stitches with you," Slip said to Neds.

"What do you care?" Right Ned asked.

"They're galvanized," Slip said.

"And you're the king of the black-market rats. Are you telling me there's cargo too hot for you?"

"Both their eyes are red." Slip said.

Our eyes were red? I supposed they might be. When I'd first met Abraham, his eyes had been red with the pain he could not feel from a gut wound. My eyes turned red when I was in pain too, and, like I said, those bullet holes hurt like a bitch.

"So?" Left Ned said.

"You know what they say: 'Eyes of red, you'll soon be dead,'" Slip said. "If that's true, then the ride stops here."

"I'll tell you what," Right Ned said. "I'll give you a piece of free advice: your life will be a whole lot easier and much, much longer, if you don't give these two any reason to find out if that old saying is true."

"The woman's bleeding," he said.

Wow. It had been . . . never since I'd been so completely ignored and dismissed from a conversation.

Abraham had made a point of explaining to me that galvanized did not have human rights, that we were essentially not considered human. But I'd lived out on the farm all my life with my family. I'd never been treated like a thing that couldn't talk for itself.

"We'll take care of her," Right Ned said.

Slip gave me one hungry look.

Lucky chuckled. "I'll plug her holes for her."

Abraham moved so fast, I could barely track him. He was beside me, then past me, on top of Lucky and pounding his head, then ribs, so hard, I heard bones crack.

Lucky crumpled like a wet tissue.

And Slip grabbed for his gun.

14

*News is not good. Some think the ferals carry
the disease. We have no cure.*
                           —from the diary of E. N. D.

"I wouldn't do it, pal," Left Ned said, his Glock already in his hand. "All those stories about galvanized strength aren't stories. She'd kill you a hundred times over before you'd ever even hurt her enough to stop her. And your friend there already pissed off the other one."

Abraham slammed his fist into Lucky's head one last time, then stood and turned toward Slip, flexing his bloody hands into fists.

"Do you really want both of them angry?" Left Ned continued. "They'll crush your train like an empty can, pull off the tracks, and beat you to death with them before they'd break a sweat. You saw what they did with that Dumpster out there."

Abraham, wisely, wasn't moving in on Slip yet. Wisely, because I didn't think Abraham needed more bullets in him, and I was pretty sure if we killed Slip we'd have to find new transportation across the country.

Slip snarled, and then his mouth curled into a false smile. "I'm sure we all want the same outcome here," he said to Neds, though his gaze returned to Abraham again and again, as if expecting him to attack.

"You keep those stitches quiet, out of sight, and the hell away from me," he said. "If I find either of them loose or rough-handling my employees, I will put a bullet in *your* head." He smiled again at Neds. "Both of them."

"We won't be trouble if you don't make us trouble," Right Ned said.

Slip walked over to Lucky and kicked him. "Pick yourself up."

To my surprise, Lucky moaned and dragged himself up on his feet.

Abraham must have been holding back.

Or too wounded to kill him quick.

"You get us to Kansas," Right Ned said, "and we'll be gone." He gestured for Abraham and me to follow him into the train car. Abraham didn't look at me, but he shifted as if to cover our retreat, glaring at Slip and Lucky. I followed Neds.

The inside of the train was a lot smaller than I'd hoped. The back half was filled with unmarked crates stacked almost up to the ceiling. I had no idea what was in them. The front half of the car had a couple cots folded and leaning up against the wall, plus two folded chairs and a wooden bench.

It smelled like pears and cedar, which was a lot better than I'd been expecting it to smell.

Abraham finally stepped into the train behind us.

The doors sealed and locked with an electrical whine. Even if we wanted to get out, we couldn't. Well, we could try crushing the train like an empty can, but I didn't think either Abraham or I had that in us right at the moment, no matter what Neds had said.

"He's an ass," I observed to no one in particular. The bullets in my thigh, arm, and maybe one in my hip were really starting to hurt now.

Quinten and Gloria were setting up a cot in the back of the car.

"Anyone claiming this chair?" I picked up a chair made mostly of plastic and set it with the back against one wall. That left room for another cot on the side and the rest of the chairs to be set up in the remaining middle space.

I lowered myself into the chair and cussed. "This has been a crappy day."

"We're not dead," Right Ned noted.

"Yet," Left Ned added.

"Gold star for optimism," I said.

"Matilda?" Quinten straightened and stepped over to me. "Let me look at your wounds."

"I'm fine," I lied.

"Let me make sure of that."

Abraham moved to the back of the train car, the width of him taking all the spare room of the place as he passed by. He settled onto the cot with a grunt.

"Abraham is much worse—" I started.

"Gloria is tending him." Quinten knelt in front of me and shrugged out of his duffel. "I'll check on him after I tend you." From the very steady, very calm tone of his voice, I could tell he was trying not to sound very worried.

"How much blood am I leaking?"

"Enough," he said.

I glanced down at my leg.

Wow, that was a lot of blood.

"What do you have in your duffel?" He asked. "Bandages or any other supplies?"

"There's not much, but you're welcome to it." I sat forward to pull the strap off over my head and instantly regretted the decision. That shot arm was really starting to hurt.

"I got it." Quinten drew the strap over my head. I tried not to be a baby about how much it hurt when he jostled my arm, and bit my bottom lip to keep from making any sound.

"Thigh and arm?" he asked. "Anywhere else?"

"Hip? Unless it's just sympathy pain."

He frowned at the side of my hip. "Good news," he said as he set my duffel on the floor and dug through it. "It's not sympathy pain."

In the bag was wool that used to be a scarf my grandmother had knit for me. That scarf had given me the spare seconds I needed to escape, literally, when I pulled the stitches out of it, since Grandma knit it from the wool the pocket sheep on our farm provide—wool that gathers up little bits of spare time.

Other than that, I thought the duffel had a couple spools of *Filum Vitae*—thread we'd almost used up patching Abraham—plus whatever was left of the scale jelly that helped wounded stitched people and critters, some needles, a shirt or two, and the remaining cloth and jewels from that dress I'd worn at the gathering.

"Oh." He paused in his digging, something in his hand, but his hand was still in the duffel so I couldn't see what he'd found.

"Need any help?" Gloria stood next to him.

Quinten didn't seem to hear her.

"Hey, bro," I said, nudging his bent knee with my good foot. "Something wrong?" I would have gotten more worked up and worried about his current nonreaction, but blood loss was making me sleepy. "Stab yourself on my pocketknife?"

"No," he said. "No. It's fine."

I thought I heard the very soft chiming of bells as he removed his hand from the duffel. Maybe it was my imagination. Or that blood-loss thing that was going on.

"You need to get out of your pants," Quinten said.

Well, that woke me up.

"And your jacket. Shirt too, if it's long-sleeved."

"Just how naked do you need me to be?"

"It's not like I haven't seen you before," he said, threading the *Filum Vitae* through a hooked darning needle.

"Sure, when we were kids," I said.

"You don't have to be naked," he said. Was he smiling? *He'd better not be smiling.* "I just need to get to your wounds. Drop your drawers."

I gave him a look and a sigh, but neither had any effect on him. Gloria also wasn't on my side. She was busy laying out what we had that they could use for mending. A scalpel, a bottle of powder, and a pair of needle-nose pliers.

Oh, this was going to be just a bucket of fun.

And I was going to do it mostly naked.

Neat.

The run-and-almost-die sweat I'd worked up was drying now, a salty, cool layer that made me shiver at any shift in the car's stale air.

Or maybe it was just that my body was suddenly aware that I was shot and hurting.

"Want me to give you a hand?" Quinten asked. "With the buttons and . . . stuff?"

"No, I got it. Just give me some room."

He moved the supplies out of the way, and Gloria stood on one side of me. I grabbed hold of the floor-to-ceiling metal pole with my good right hand, then hauled up onto my feet.

Pain shot through me. Everything went white for a second, and then hot razors flayed my thigh up to my butt, back, and shoulder.

Shit and shinola. I should never have sat down. Standing hurt.

My hands were shaking pretty hard and I was full-body sweating again. I worked the button on my pants with my functioning hand and tucked my thumb into my waistband, pushing my pants down. Well, pushing half of my pants down halfway. I reached across to do the same on my left hip.

But Gloria was in front of me now. I thought she might even be talking to me, though I wasn't hearing anything but my own breathing and the thumping in my head.

How much blood was too much to lose?

She put her cool hand over the back of mine, and it was such a marvelous, comforting sensation. "Let me help. It will be quicker."

Her pretty brown eyes crinkled at the corners with a smile. "Us girls have to stick together," she said.

I stared over her shoulder at the others in the car. Neds had his back turned, his arms crossed over his chest as he leaned one hip and shoulder against the side of the car. Abraham sat on the cot, his head against the crates behind him, his eyes burning red. He was staring at me with unspoken anger. Or at least I thought it was anger. It was certainly pointed and hot.

He blinked his eyes slowly, watching me, intense with a different kind of heat.

Okay, maybe not anger.

Quinten stood near Gloria and me, the jar of scale jelly already open in his hand. I knew how much that jelly would numb the wounds, and suddenly couldn't get out of my clothes fast enough.

"Here." Gloria took my hand and placed it back on the pole. "Hold on."

I held on. She shucked my pants down around my ankles, leaving me in my panties and boots. I groaned as the material ripped away from the bullet wounds. It hurt more on the back of my thigh than the front because the exit wound was a bigger mess.

I stared straight ahead, which meant I was looking at Abraham. Neither of us broke eye contact for several heartbeats. There was a lot we had to say to each other in that gaze. Some of it was along the lines of *Why the hell did you run into the gunfire for me?* And the answer, from both of us, was, *I'd do it again.*

When I thought I could actually breathe evenly, Abraham's gaze slid down to my bust, my stomach, my thighs, and my boots, then slowly retraced the path. When he looked back up at my eyes, he raised his eyebrow in a "you look good out of your pants" sort of expression.

Much to my surprise, low on blood and hurting like a brawler, I could still blush.

". . . going to take off your jacket now," Gloria said. "I'll do it quick, but it's going to hurt."

I just locked the knee that was working best and held on to the pole.

Pain rattled through me, and I was not quiet about it. A whimper ripped out of my throat and I squeezed my eyes tight, trying to get my breathing under control as Quinten worked to clean and stitch my wounds.

I wasn't usually so noisy about being hurt, but these wounds *hurt*. What was taking Quinten so long? It felt like he had been poking and prodding for hours.

Hands reached out from behind me, wide and hot. Heated arms wrapped around my ribs, and that same heat pressed against my back, anchoring me, holding me. Strong.

"It's almost over," Abraham said. "They're almost done. Just breathe."

Abraham's voice in my ear. Low and soft like a lover reading poetry. His words held me up, becoming air for my lungs, peace for my mind. A lifeline I could hold on to while the pain of Quinten digging in my wounds, cleaning and sewing and binding, rolled over me.

I was aware of the pain. But I was also aware of Abraham's arms around me, steady and unyielding. The pushing beat of his heart on my back, his words soothing. I didn't want him to let go of me, and had to fight the desire to just turn in his arms and hold him.

It had been a really bad past few days. He'd almost died. More than once.

I hadn't had a chance to tell him I'd thought I was going to lose him, and what that had done to me.

"That's it," Quinten said. "Let's get her to the cot."

Cot? I'd be happy if they let me sit.

"Do you need help?" Quinten asked.

"I've got her," Abraham said.

"Me," I said, but it came out a whisper. I cleared my throat. "I've got me," I said, only marginally louder.

They weren't listening.

"Just lean if you need to," Abraham said. Funny, hadn't I been the one telling him that just a few . . . what was it . . . hours ago?

He shifted his grip, hands replacing his arms, and I made a small, disappointed sound when he pulled his body fully away from me, letting the cold wash between us.

I didn't dare let go of the pole to wipe the sweat out of my eyes. I was in bad enough shape, the entire room seemed to be rocking.

Abraham took a step and I did too, but the floor wasn't where I expected it to be and my foot came down wrong.

Abraham caught me up before I stumbled. I opted to take him up on the leaning offer and pressed the side of my face into his chest, inhaling the copper and smoke and leather scent of him. We walked the rest of the way to the cot, and then he helped lower me onto it. I didn't moan or cry, because the worst of the pain was gone.

My cot was rocking too. Just how bad a shape did a couple of bullets leave me in?

"Now," Quinten said, easing past Abraham so he could pull a chair up by my cot. He settled into the chair just like he had for months when I'd been little and dying. "I need you to listen to me, Til. The bullets went all the way through, which is better than being lodged in there. We cauterized the wounds and slathered them with jelly. I've sewn them up and wrapped your thigh and dressed your hip. Your arm is in worse shape than your leg. It's in a sling for now. That sparkly gray dress of yours is really coming in handy."

"The room's rocking," I said.

"We're on a train," he said. "A moving train. We have about three hours before our first stop. I want you to sleep. I'll be right here if you need anything."

I wanted water, but I knew we didn't have any. Quinten brushed stray strands of hair away from my face, a familiar gesture.

Maybe it wasn't the best sibling bond, him tending to me when I was wounded, but it was comforting. I knew if there was anything at all that could be done to make me feel better, Quinten would do it. And if he said sleep was the best idea right now, then I believed him.

Abraham had been coaxed over to the other cot, where Gloria convinced him to lie back so she could finish looking over his wounds.

Looked like we were both going to get some sleep.

I stared at the curved ceiling, where old fluorescent tubes shone hard white light against patches of paint that may have once held color but had been scraped and scuffed so that only squares of different sorts of dirt were left behind.

The rocking of the train should be soothing, but it kept me awake. Awake meant I started thinking through what we were going to do.

No matter how I stacked it, we had too little on our side. I still needed to find Grandma's journal. At the next stop I'd get off the train and see if I could patch into a secure line. If there was any luck left to me at all, my crawlers would have found information on where and how Robert Twelfth's information was stored, and hopefully her journal would be there.

We had a handful of medical supplies, almost no valuables to hock, maybe one head of one House looking out for us. The train would get us only halfway across the distance we needed to travel.

Against us was the world and every ticking minute. So, yeah, things didn't look all that great.

Still, if I had to spend my last days with anyone on this planet, Quinten would be the top of my list. So would Abraham and Neds, but for different reasons. I thought if I had enough time, I might get to really like Gloria. She had been nice so far, and plenty levelheaded under some pretty extreme stress. Plus, she liked my brother, which was nice.

Since I'd sort of been the reason that she'd just lost her home, I wished I had a chance to make things up to her before I . . .

Well, before whatever was going to happen happened to me.

The only other person I wished I could be with before I died was Grandma. Just thinking of her wandering our old house, unaware that Boston Sue, our neighbor and spy for House Silver, wasn't watching after her out of the goodness of her heart made me angry.

I had trusted Bo to keep my grandma safe when I left to the city. But instead of keeping her safe, Bo was just another kind of danger. I didn't know what Reeves Silver might want Bo to do with Grandma, but it wouldn't be good.

A hand reached out and rested on my ankle. Abraham's hand.

I knew I wasn't the only one who had made mistakes. I knew I wasn't the only one who wished things could be different.

But right now, in this speeding train, there wasn't anything more any of us could do to fix any of it.

15

We've helped House Brown where we can.
Quinten doesn't want me to leave the farm.
                                   —from the diary of E. N. D.

I heard Quinten's and Gloria's voices over the low rumble of the tracks passing beneath us. Neds were sleeping in a chair. I would have thought Abraham was sleeping too, except he moved on the cot where he was resting often enough that I knew he was just as uncomfortable as I was.

The scale jelly did its work and cut my pain in half; I'm sure it had helped him too. I was healing, but neither of us would be better for days.

"What did he say?" I asked.

Only Abraham was close enough to hear me, since Quinten was sitting with Gloria a ways off.

"Who?" he asked.

"Welton."

Abraham paused, maybe thinking about what he should tell me, maybe thinking there might be a camera on us here too.

I heard him shift, boots scraping across the hard floor, then grunt as he pushed up and took a couple steps, his hand catching hold of the bars above his head. He stood above me, looking down, one arm up, the other crossed over his stomach as if moving had fired the pain in him.

"We didn't talk." He dropped down into the chair by the head of the bed that Quinten had left empty.

"Do you think he's hunting us down?"

"Welton? Undoubtedly."

I tried to imagine what Welton Yellow would do with us once he found us. Help us again or turn us over to House Black? I didn't know.

"It was nice of him to blow out the cameras," I said. "Wish he would have done something more about Domek."

"If I'd known . . ." he said.

I rolled my head to the side and looked at him. Gods, he was a handsome man. "Yes?"

He folded his hands together, unfolded them, placed them on his knees, then drew them back together. Every movement was discomfort, uncertainty. I'd never seen him like this, so unsure. But, then, his entire world had gone inside out recently; he had every right to be a little off his footing.

I held my good hand out to him. He tipped his head, then took my hand. "If you knew what?" I asked.

"If I knew that finding you on your farm and bringing you into House Gray would have meant this—Oscar dead, you injured, running from all the Houses, no credit to our names, riding the black market—I wouldn't have come to find you."

I thought that over. "Someone else would have. That

message my mom sent was meant to be found. Someone wanted me to be found. And even if no one had come out to my farm, I would have walked into the cities on my own eventually. I had a brother to rescue, remember?"

"You would have ended up in such a mess if you'd tried to find him on your own."

"As opposed to this sweet situation?" I smiled slightly. "Someone was bound to screw up my life. I'm just glad it was you."

He exhaled on a soft laugh. "Thank you?"

"You're welcome," I said.

He gently rubbed his thumb over the back of my hand, thoughtful.

"How bad is it?" I asked. "Feeling?"

"The pain isn't more than I can endure. But it's foreign." His gaze took in the crates behind my cot, the walls, floor. "It's like I've been a blind man. And now I can see. Even pleasant sensations are strange. Jarring."

"Maybe you just haven't had the right pleasant sensations yet," I said.

His gaze snapped back to my face. He raised one eyebrow and studied the innocent look I was probably not pulling off.

"What, exactly, are you suggesting, Matilda Case?" he asked.

I wasn't expecting the man to take me in a passionate embrace. As a matter of fact, I'd stab him if he jostled me too hard right now.

But a little tenderness didn't seem like too much to ask. "Maybe a kiss before the end of the world? Seems like we've both earned it."

His wide shoulders and chest pulled up, but he tipped

his head down so he could better study me. I liked the look in his eyes. It was steady and intense, but there was a hesitance, a question there.

"I want to kiss you," I said clearly, just in case he hadn't gotten the hint.

His breathing shortened for several breaths before he seemed to notice and get his lungs back to normal.

"In front of your brother?"

I glanced past him. Quinten was leaning toward Gloria, lost in conversation. "I think I'm the least of his concerns at the moment. Neds are sleeping. And also?" I added. "It's just a kiss. I'm not nearly well enough for anything more than that. Although now that I think about it, maybe it's you we should worry about."

"Why?"

"The one other time you kissed me, you drove off and got yourself shot and framed for murder."

He took a moment to survey the train car. "Might be a little more difficult to do either of those things here."

"Don't bet on it." I grinned. "My brother you've been arguing with? Very short temper and lots of capacity for revenge."

"Noted," he said, one arm braced above my head, the other still holding my hand. "But I'm not worried about your brother. I'm worried about you."

Now it was my turn to breathe a little funny. He rested his forehead briefly on mine. "You make me want so many things," he said, pulling back, his gaze lingering on my lips before slipping back up to my eyes.

"We could start a list," I said, uncertain of what to do with the sudden heat his words caught in me. "Just to make sure we remember to cover all the bases."

"Do you have a pen?" he asked.

"Not on me. Think we should probably just move on to the kissing."

"Yes," he said. "We should." He finally lowered his face to mine.

His lips pressed against mine with heat and hunger that made me want him even more. He was gentle, catching my bottom lip with a slow stroke of his tongue and sending shivers of pleasure to war with the pain in my body.

I opened my mouth, wanting more of him. He exhaled, slanting his mouth against mine and setting off warm, rolling waves of electricity that radiated from my chest and pooled with a hot weight below my stomach.

I pulled back and he waited there, inches away from me, his eyes roiling with sorrow and need and regret.

"No guns. No murder?" I whispered.

"So far so good," he said.

"I think we're going to be okay," I said, the truth of that, the hope of that, echoing behind my words.

"So do I."

He gently pressed his mouth over mine again, a promise of comforting things we wanted to give to each other, but knew we couldn't have.

Things we might never have time for. But we had time for this moment, this kiss.

We finally pulled apart. He leaned back in his chair. I worked on sitting, but twisted my arm a little too much and caught my breath. I paused, then sat the rest of the way, resting my back against the crates behind me.

Quinten glanced over at me, and I gave him a reassuring smile. His gaze ticked to Abraham, and he frowned as if seeing something new in him. Maybe seeing the man I loved.

"If things were different . . ." Abraham said in what sounded like the beginning of another apology.

I couldn't handle that. I couldn't hear how sorry he was for things that were not his fault.

"You know what I'd do differently if I had the chance?" I interrupted him.

He pressed his lips together, and I couldn't help but watch him bite his bottom lip before releasing it. All I could think of was those lips on mine, and that tongue exploring . . . well, more of me than just my mouth.

When I finally looked back up into his eyes he quirked an eyebrow at me, as if he had caught me thinking dirty thoughts and approved.

Which he had.

"What would you do?" he asked.

"I'd have taken you to my bed when I first had a chance, and never let you go."

His small smile curved upward. "Now I really wish things had been different. If we were both still working for House Gray, if Oscar wasn't dead . . ." He looked away for a second, as if finding a place to stash that pain. "Well, wouldn't that have been something?"

And there it was. We both wanted this. Wanted more. For however long we had left, we'd have each other.

Ned yawned noisily and stretched in his chair. Left Ned took stock of everyone, and Right Ned rubbed at his eyes, still yawning.

"This is it," Left Ned said. "First stop."

I hadn't felt any change in the engine. The only way he

would know that a stop was coming up was if he had ridden this line before.

As if on cue, the train's engine geared down and the forward momentum changed quickly enough that I grabbed hold of the side of the cot so as not to get pushed out of it. Brakes squealed and then the lights flickered.

After what felt like a short forever, the sense of motion slowed, slowed, then stopped completely. It was strange to suddenly be so still. My legs vibrated with memory of the sway and motion.

Neds pushed up off the cot and rolled the kinks out of his shoulders. He paced over to the door, bent, and looked out it. "This is Callaway Station. We won't be here more than five minutes."

"Help me up?" I asked Abraham.

He did so, both of us doing what we could to work around our various wounds. Standing wasn't as painful as I'd expected, though I was still a little light-headed, probably from blood loss and no food.

Quinten stood too, and walked over to me. Gloria stayed where she was.

"How are you feeling?" Quinten asked.

"Good," I said. "Better. Did you give me a pain-killer?"

"Last one. And the jelly should still be working. I'll want to reapply it on both of you—"

"I'm fine," Abraham said.

"On both of you," Quinten repeated in his kind but doctorly voice. "First Gloria and I are going to go out for supplies."

"Take my duffel," I said. "Use anything you need for barter." I brushed my hand over my hair, catching at my braid and throwing it back behind my shoulders. The scarf over my head was gone. "And reload the gun before you go out," I said, "I think there might be a couple bullets in the bottom of the bag."

"Already done," Quinten said.

My brother might not have been a farm boy for the past few years, but he was a born and bred scrapper who had been making his own way, off grid, through life. He knew that when going into unknown situations like this, the presence of a firearm was a necessity.

"What supplies can we find here?" Quinten asked Neds.

"What do you want?" Left Ned asked.

"Water, medicine, bullets," Gloria said. "In that order, I think."

"Water's doable," Right Ned said. "Medicine will take you too long to find, and there's no knowing it won't just be repackaged rat poison. Bullets won't be easy either."

"What do you think we should look for here?" she asked.

"Water. Food," Right Ned said. "Cloth that can be used for bandages. Maybe clothing, so they're not walking around bloody." He pointed at Abraham and me.

"Wouldn't hurt to look for a low-tech walkie-talkie. We could use a way to keep track of each other if we get separated and when we get close enough to the farm."

"We'll look for that," Quinten said. "Good thinking, Mr. Harris."

What Quinten wasn't saying was that it was good thinking for someone he knew only as a farmhand. Neds was much more than he appeared to be.

"Anything else we should know?" Quinten asked.

"This isn't like the station in San Diego," Left Ned said. "Lots of people here, which means lots of eyes in this place. Lots of ears listening in. So don't talk more than you need to, don't use each other's names, and don't do anything to draw attention to yourself. If anyone asks, say you're on a trip to visit your aunt in Schenectady."

"Schenectady?" Gloria asked.

"It's code for *none of your damn business*," Left Ned said.

The train door opened and Slip stuck his head in the room. "You've got four minutes."

Quinten and Gloria shouldered the duffels and pushed past Slip into what sounded like a crowded, echoing station.

I needed to get out there too, to tap into the network and see if I could get any kind of bead on Grandma's journal. But like Neds had pointed out, I was covered in blood. I figured even in an "aunt in Schenectady" kind of crowd, I'd stand out.

"You," Slip said to Neds. "I have a proposition for you."

"Blow off," Right Ned said. "You got your fare."

Slip leaned toward Ned, but slid a look over at me and Abraham. "Did myself some reading. And seeing as how there's money on the table—a lot of money—I want you to know I can set up an arrangement that would be very beneficial to both of us."

Yep. He'd just so much as said he would split the ransom on our heads if Neds would let him turn us in. Jackass.

Before Neds could say anything, Abraham strolled their way. The man was six foot four and had the shoulders of an ox. He turned on Slip and cracked his blood-caked knuckles in a fist against his palm, first one hand, then the other.

He didn't say anything. He didn't have to. He loomed over Slip, every inch of him a threat.

Slip worked the odds on his chances of surviving a fight with the grim and bloodstained galvanized who didn't look like he had a lot to lose. Then Slip's smile was back, even though his eyes narrowed with anger.

"Do you have a problem with me, *stitch*?" he asked Abraham.

"Bad move, Slip," Right Ned said calmly.

Abraham shrugged one shoulder. Then grabbed Slip by the neck so fast, even I jerked.

He pounded Slip up against the nearest wall and leaned on him a little, his face inches away from the other man's.

"Do you know what I was before House Gray took me in, little man?" Abraham asked.

Slip had enough sense in his head to save what breath he was getting past Abraham's hand for filling his lungs, not words.

"A killer," Abraham said. "Hundreds of years. Oceans of blood. Now there is no House to claim me. To tell me how civilized I should pretend to be. And I'm asking myself how, exactly, I want to behave. You are making my decision dangerously easy. If you want to stay alive, do not cross me."

He pushed off Slip's neck and leaned away.

Slip coughed and choked, his hand sliding up to his neck, his face red. "Off. Get off my train!" he yelled hoarsely.

"Not happening," Right Ned said. "We're paid and clear. If you toss us now, I'll go straight to Sallyo."

If he had looked angry just a moment ago, now all the color slicked out of his face.

"I'm sure she'd love to know what happened to that load of narcotics you said you never received," Left Ned said.

Slip stared at Neds for an extended moment, swallowing against the pain in his throat. "I don't know what you're accusing me of."

"Yes," Right Ned said, "you do. Skimming off the top of House Silver shipments can't go unnoticed forever."

"So let's boil this pot dry," Left Ned said. "Sallyo is expecting us in Kansas and will come looking for us if we don't show. We ride your rails, we get off in Kansas, and we get out of your way. You won't make any convenient deals concerning our welfare, and I won't tip off a woman who'd be happy to blast this little train line of yours to smithereens and spit on your corpse. Agreed?"

Slip gave us all one last look, then stormed out of the car.

16

*Everyone's angry. There are more rumors
about the Houses plotting war. I'm afraid of
what will happen if the rumors are true.*
                    —from the diary of E. N. D.

"You just run with the nicest people, don't you, Ned?"
I asked.

"I've made it a point to know how to swim in any
river," Right Ned said.

I supposed that spoke to the practical nature of living
in this world as a man who wasn't put together like most
other men. A man whose worth might be used or discarded at a whim and whose physical difference could
tag him as an oddity or make him completely invisible as
a human being.

"Give me your link," I said.

Right Ned looked over at Abraham, who leaned one
shoulder on the metal pole that reached ceiling to floor
near the open door.

"We have—what—three minutes?" I said. "I need to
check in."

"Check in on what?" Abraham asked.

"I'm hacking into some private files."

"Hush. Away from the door," Right Ned said.

I moved farther back into the train car, and he followed, pulling out the screen and unlocking it before handing it to me.

Left Ned just sighed and shook his head.

"Whose private files?" Abraham asked as he shifted his position so he could keep watch out the door.

"Robert Twelfth's."

"What?" Right Ned said.

Abraham was silent, but the look he threw my way was anger and pain. "Why?" he asked.

My fingers were already flying over the screen. If the last crawler I'd sent out hadn't found a way into the records, I'd try another route. We needed that journal.

"Because I think Slater Orange is the kind of man who plans everything. He planned his own death. He planned for Quinten to implant him into Robert Twelfth's body. He planned to frame you for murder. And I think he planned to keep as much leverage as possible over people who would be useful to him."

"You think your brother's useful to him?" Right Ned asked.

"Domek wasn't asking for anyone else to come out with his hands up," I said. "My guess? Slater was behind the assassin, not House Black. But even if I'm wrong about that, someone wants my brother alive."

"Which of Robert's files are you looking for?" Abraham asked.

"A copy of my grandmother's journal. Quinten thinks it has the formula we need in it so we can alter the Wings of Mercury experiment. Which, if he's correct, means you and I don't die."

That sat in the silence between us for a moment. Hope was a strange thing, often more phoenix than butterfly.

"Do you think Robert—I mean, Slater—knows how important that journal is?" Right Ned asked.

"You think he made a copy," Abraham said, putting it together.

"Yes," I answered both of them. "How much time do I have left?"

"About a minute and a half," Left Ned said.

The crawler had run into a roadblock that was slowing it down and making it impossible to navigate the routes I'd sent it on. I tagged into some secondary access routes. *Robert's files must have a weakness.* And I was going to find it.

The crawler chewed through data, exploiting every angle.

Then the screen froze.

"Shit," I said.

"What?" Right Ned asked.

Quinten stepped through the door with Gloria on his heels. "What are you doing?"

"I'm screwed." My heart was pounding hard and sweat that had nothing to do with pain washed over me. I'd been caught.

"How screwed?" Left Ned asked.

"Someone froze my search," I said, madly tapping through abort options.

"What?" Left Ned said.

"I thought you said this thing was so secure no one in the world could hack it," I said, panic raising my voice.

"Shhh. It is." Neds stepped over to me.

I was doing what I could to abort the search, to back out, to bail completely. But nothing was working. Someone had their sights on me, and there was nothing I could do to hide.

"You're hacking?" Quinten asked. "What are you hacking into?"

"Does it have our location?" Gloria asked. "Should we throw the screen out the door before they get a lock?"

"No," Right and Left Ned said at the same time. "Doesn't matter if it's with us or not—whoever wanted to find us just did."

"Shit," Gloria breathed, echoing my thoughts.

"They're uploading a file," I said.

"Can you tell what it is?" Quinten asked.

"Or who sent it?" Right Ned asked.

The train engines fired up, a deep roar of combustion and gears. The door sealed and the engine rumbled up to an even louder growl.

"No," I said. "There's nothing . . . wait. Crap." I turned the screen so they could see it.

The screen had gone a flat yellow, with a circle of what looked like runes in the center.

"Is that's House Yellow's seal?" Gloria asked.

I glanced over at Abraham, who was holding on to the bar above his head, and adjusted the screen so he could see it better.

"Is it?" I asked him.

The train jerked, brakes releasing. We were under way again, the clacking, rocking motion a little too much for my standing abilities. I sat on the cot, and everyone else, including Abraham, pulled a chair close.

He held out his hand and I gave him the screen.

"Well?" I asked.

Abraham studied the screen. "It is House Yellow's seal," he said. "I see two outcomes."

"What?" Quinten asked, pulling open his duffel.

"This is from Welton Yellow and it will be a secure communication."

"Or?" I asked.

"Or it's triggered so that when I enter a code, our location will be sent to every satellite and tower in range."

"Or that ass Slip could have set up a bomb and that's the trigger," Left Ned offered.

"A third possibility," Abraham agreed.

We all stared at the thin rectangular screen propped on Abraham's knee. No one moved to touch it.

"Maybe we should take a moment and think on it," Quinten said. "We brought food."

After another pause, Left Ned spoke up. "I never did want to die on an empty stomach. Hand over the grub."

Before any of us could argue, Gloria pulled out three soft canteens of water, and I realized just how thirsty I was. We passed those around while Quinten retrieved a cloth-wrapped bundle.

"Sandwiches." He handed us all flat bread stuffed with meat, cheese, and grilled vegetables. They smelled delicious, and I suddenly felt like I hadn't eaten in days, not just hours.

"This looks good." I gave back the water to Gloria and held out my hand for a sandwich.

We each took our share. Abraham left the screen on his knee while we ate. We tried not to stare at it, but it was clear we all wanted to know what that message held.

I finished the last bite of my food and wiped my fingers on the least-bloody part of the hem of my shirt. I hoped Quinten and Gloria had found some clothing for us, but right now, being bloody wasn't what I was worried about.

"Whatever it is," I said, "I think we should just face it. Deal with it now."

Abraham nodded, and so did Gloria.

"Neds?" I asked.

"I say we open it. Find out who's gonna be in our way," Left Ned said.

Abraham wiped his hand over the scruff on his chin and scratched at the edge of his jaw.

Then he pressed his thumb into the corner of the device and drew a line between the runes, creating a secondary, ghostly symbol.

The screen instantly lit up. Abraham's eyes flickered over the information playing out there, then tapped something into it. Another pause, and he finally looked away from it to the rest of us.

"It appears to be secure. Compliments of Welton Yellow. It's a recorded message."

I held out my palm and he gave me the screen. I propped my good arm along my knee, screen faceup and angled so all of us could get a clear view.

I pressed the little play icon. Welton Yellow appeared on the screen.

His heavy-lidded eyes made him look like a sleepy cat. His hair was parted in the middle and combed down straight so it fell just above his dark eyes. His skin was iron-deficient white. He wore a T-shirt, the edge of which showed an image of an octopus with a piece of candy in seven tentacles and a gun in the eighth.

He sat forward a bit, adjusted something, then leaned back. Welton might look like a man with no ambition, but that wasn't true. He was easily a match for my brother's brilliance and was the youngest person ever to take over the position of head of House—in his case, the house that ruled technology.

"This won't be traced, so you don't have to worry. Matilda, you little devil, you. Digging around in files you have no right to be digging in. I do hope you found what you wanted. But if not, you'll see I've cleared a path for you. Be quick about it. You're welcome.

"Abraham, you have no idea the amazing shit storm you touched off. It's . . ." He shook his head and then chuckled. "Oh, it is *so* good. Well, not good. But all the simmering, nice-nice backstabbing and bribery rules the Houses have been playing by for the past decade or so—gone. It is bare-knuckled business going on right now. You should have seen John Black when he stopped in to try to arrest Foster. It was . . . well, I'll get to that. Most of the business the Houses are focused on is how to hunt you down and kill you."

"Tell us something we don't know," Left Ned muttered.

I shushed him.

"Here are the basics: House Blue and House Red are locked in a struggle of who can yell the loudest and make the other Houses follow them. Hollis Gray has stepped up to take over House Gray, and he's siding with House Red, who, if you asked me, is the House that put the hit on Oscar Gray to get Hollis into that position, though only the devil knows why.

"Speaking of the devil, Reeves Silver claims his galvanized, Helen, killed Oscar Gray without his knowledge. Reeves, as we all know, is full of shit. He has a bet on every side of the board and deals in the works with every House. I'm sure he'll come out of this on the rising tide, no matter what fresh hell we land in.

"House Orange . . . that's a little more troubling." He paused. "They say you walked into Slater Orange's bedroom and shot him in the head, Abe. If you did indeed do that, let me be the first person to thank you. Slater was a power-hungry, masochistic prick and the world is a better place without him.

"But I gotta tell you, buddy: killing a head of a House wasn't your smartest move. House Black has issued orders to lock up all the galvanized until you turn yourself in. You know John Black and Oscar were close. He's taking his death at Helen's hands as you might expect: guns and grenades and assassins. Domek, interestingly enough, wasn't his hire. I believe House Orange put that hit on you, which means your galvanized buddy, Robert, is out for your blood. You might want to cross him off your Christmas-card list.

"The rest of the Houses are waiting for John Black to bring you in. Alive or dead-ish—they don't care. Most of them—Green, White, Violet—are waiting to see where the more powerful Houses align before setting their allegiances in the matter. Gideon Violet intends to keep Clara, his galvanized, under lock and key himself. He considers her innocent until your sin is declared a burden to be borne by all galvanized. And I don't think any of the Houses have the balls to argue with House Religion about its moral stance."

He laughed again, then clapped his hands together

once. "Priceless. All right. So what you really need to know is that House Orange's galvanized, Robert, is acting as head of that House, with Reeves Silver's backing. It is a *very* strange coincidence that all the likely inheritors of House Orange died in the past three years or so. There's a poor ten-year-old kid who has the most direct bloodline tie to the recently deceased Slater Orange, but because of his age, it puts into motion a lot of archaic rules of House succession that will take months to sort out.

"Robert seems to have learned very well from Slater over the years, which is a pity. I always liked Robert, and it's a shame to see his temporary moment of power turning him into a dick.

"Kansas, which is where I assume you are going, will be tricky. I've done what I can from my side to scramble data on your whereabouts. John Black will fry my nuts if he ever finds out what I did to half his scout team.

"Anyway, I want you to know something. I'm stepping down from head of House Yellow. I'm going to put my cousin Libra in my place, which should set off another bout of confusion among the Houses. Really wish I could be here to see it, but, you know." He shrugged one thin shoulder. "I'll have to catch it on the newsreels."

"What else?" He stared at the ceiling for a moment, ticking off fingers one at a time. "Houses. John, Robert, Reeves, Gideon, me . . ." He was silent a second. "Oh yes. I think there's something going on with the basic physics of the world. Time, specifically. The instruments in some of my . . . research centers—"

Quinten snorted.

I threw him a look. He just shook his head and pointed at the screen.

"—are kicking off readings that are very exciting. And odd. If Quinten Case is still with you, tell him I owe him a bottle of booze. He was right."

Everyone looked over at Quinten, who was frowning at the screen.

"So, this isn't *good-bye*," Welton said. "This is just a short farewell. I'll do what I can on my side to clear your way before I leave my station here. That is, assuming I am right about where your path is leading you. Oh, who are we kidding? I'm always right." He waggled his eyebrows. "Until we meet again: good luck, and for fuck's sake, delete this message."

The screen went blank. I stared at it, then hit DELETE. The screen reset to the original display, except for a line of numbers rolling across the bottom.

"There's something wrong with time?" Gloria asked.

Quinten nodded. "Very wrong."

"Out with it," Left Ned said. "What does Welton know?"

"I spent a year with House Yellow." Quinten pressed his fingertips against his mouth, as if thinking through his time there.

"Welton Yellow wanted to know where my research was taking me. I never told him what I was looking for. I keep all my notes in my head. There is no paper trail, and I always vary my research with other random searches and reading. So, it was . . . impressive when he asked me what project I was really working on. Even more impressive when he guessed it was the Wings of Mercury experiment."

"The rumors and history of that experiment are a hobby of his," Abraham said. "He's been fascinated by it for years."

"So," I asked, "what did he mean when he said you're right?"

"I assume he means that I'm right about the time event closing in." Quinten dug two fingers into his shirt pocket and pulled out the pocketwatch Reeves Silver had given me as proof that my brother was alive. It was an old family heirloom handed down from elder Case men to younger Case men.

He thumbed the edge of it and held the watch carefully while twisting the cover. He turned it toward us. The face of the watch was not a watch at all. It was a disk of softly glowing liquid in which five arcs were slowly converging on a central point.

I'd seen something very similar to that down in the basement of our farmhouse.

"That's like the timetable you set up, isn't it?" I asked.

"It is."

"Is it counting down the seconds we have left?" I asked.

"Roughly," he said.

"Is this any more accurate?" I turned the screen. A long line of numbers counted down there, while a second, shorter set of numbers counted up. I was no math genius, but even I could see that both those numbers were aiming toward a zero point.

"Welton," Quinten breathed. "He really is . . . thorough, isn't he? May I?"

I handed him the screen.

"What, exactly, are you hacking into?" Gloria asked.

Everyone looked over at me. I shrugged and regretted it. My arm still hurt.

"Matilda." Quinten pulled his gaze away from the screen. "Who were you hacking?"

"Robert Twelfth."

Quinten straightened, and I could see his Adam's apple bob as he swallowed. "Why?" he breathed.

I almost shrugged again but caught myself. "You implanted Slater Orange into Robert's mind," I said as evenly as I could. Even so, Abraham's shoulders tightened and he clenched both hands into fists.

"He forced you to do it," I said, "but he must have been planning it for a long time. At least as long as he held you prisoner. You told me he had Grandma's journal."

"I think he lied about that," Quinten said.

"Or maybe not," I said. "I think he's thought this through. All the possibilities of his immortality and how to keep it. Now that he's wearing the body of Robert Twelfth, he might not have access into Slater Orange's most personal, valuable files."

"You think he copied it." Quinten perked up a little, his eyes shifting, as if he could read something in my gaze.

"I would have. Wouldn't you?" I said simply.

"Yes," Quinten agreed. "I would have." He handed me the screen. "Welton said to be quick."

"Right." I opened the screen again, and was amazed to get a signal. "Let's see what's what." I tapped back into my crawler and whistled. "Nice." I didn't know how Welton had opened up a channel straight into Robert's files, but I wasn't going to sit around enjoying the scenery. I set the crawler on a new route, sending it straight into the depth of Robert's files.

"How long?" Gloria asked.

"Until what?" I said.

"Until you find the copy?"

I glanced at the estimation of data that would need to be crunched and felt my stomach drop. Robert Twelfth had massive archives of data. Massive. Which I suppose wasn't all that surprising, as he was more than three hundred years old.

I scrubbed my way out, leaving the crawler inside the archives, doing its work.

"I'll need a few hours," I said. "Or more. But I'll find it. I'll find it in time."

Abraham stood, his arm pressed over his stomach, and stepped over to lie down on his cot.

Quinten was watching me. I don't think he believed me either.

"Want to make a bet on it, brother?" I asked with a smile I did not feel.

He just shook his head. "No. I believe you."

"Good. Because I'm not wrong. So," I said, "does anyone know what Welton meant about Kansas? Sallyo's waiting for us there, right?" I asked Neds.

"Sallyo?" Gloria asked, startled. "You aren't really taking us to her, are you?"

Left Ned shrugged. "We need fast and we need discreet. Sallyo does both."

"Why does everyone jump when that woman's name is mentioned?" I asked.

"She's practically a legend," Gloria said.

"What kind of legend?" I asked.

"You haven't heard of her?" she asked.

"No."

"She's been supplying House Brown with drugs while undercutting House Silver—and any other House, every chance she got—for years," Gloria said.

"There's another thing I would like to have known," I said, giving Neds a look.

"Can't believe there's a person who hasn't heard of her," Left Ned muttered. "It's not my problem you're uninformed."

"She does everything necessary to keep her deals quiet," Gloria said.

Right Ned was holding my gaze. I could guess just exactly what *everything necessary* meant.

"She kills the people who talk?" I asked.

"No," Right Ned said. "Killing's too kind for her. One strike and your nearest dearest get their throats slit and eyes scooped out. And the rest of them are sent to your doorstep in little brown boxes tied up with string."

"Lovely." I took the water and swallowed some down. "So, why does she owe you favors, Neds Harris?"

Gloria was quiet, eating the last bit of the bread from her sandwich and watching Neds.

"We have ... history," Left Ned said, an echo of sorrow in his voice that I'd never heard before.

I raised my eyebrows, waiting for the rest of that story, but neither of them spoke. From the look in Right Ned's soft blue eyes, I knew there was something more wrapped up in that favor. Regret. Maybe loneliness.

I wanted to ask him more, ask him what his relationship to Sallyo really was, but this train car was neither the place nor the time for me to be digging in my friend's painful past.

Neds stood and made a noisy spectacle of stretching. "I'm gonna get some shut-eye," Left Ned said, dropping back down into the chair by the wall. "Oh, and just to bring everyone up to speed, Slip will likely try to kill us when we set foot off his train."

Terrific. As if we didn't have enough problems.

"What other supplies did you get?" I asked Quinten, who was rummaging through the duffel.

"Some painkillers for you." He handed me a bottle. "Take three. Also bandages and blankets." He held up several silver rectangles about the size of a deck of cards. "That's all we had time for. I'm sorry we couldn't find any clothes for you or Abraham."

"No, that's fine. That's a lot," I said, "especially the painkillers. Are you sure they're okay?"

"Yes."

I popped three in my mouth, swallowed them down. "How did you pay for everything?"

He stopped rummaging, glanced up at me and then away. "The charm bracelet."

I suddenly knew why he had paused when looking through the duffel earlier. That had been Mom's bracelet. I'd packed it for my trip to House Gray, maybe as a memento, maybe as a valuable item I could barter with.

Quinten hadn't seen it in years. I'd found it in Grandma's things only a couple years ago.

"Pure silver, some nice little diamonds, and the heart charm was a nice-sized ruby," he said, as if listing quality real estate. "Unmarked. Easy to break up or melt down. Valuable."

"Quinten, I'm sorry."

"No. It was smart of you to pack it." He finally looked over at me. There was old, familiar pain in his expression. "Besides, she would have been proud of how practical you were," he said. "You know how she wasn't one for frippery."

"True," I said. Although I suppose that made the charm bracelet all the more rare and sentimental. It was one of the only pieces of jewelry she ever wore, and she was always delighted when Dad found or made an new charm for it.

"Maybe you should get some rest," I said, squeezing his arm gently.

"I'm not the one who was shot," he said. "Give me the screen. I'll let you know if anything pings."

I hesitated.

"You might be a better hacker, but it doesn't take any special skill to stare at a screen," he said with a wry smile.

"You'll wake me?" I asked, holding out the screen but not letting it go yet.

"Yes."

"Promise."

"I swear by all my swearables." He said it with a straight face, but it was something we used to say to each other as children.

"You'd better." I let go of the screen.

He settled back in his chair, his foot propped on the duffel.

"Matilda?" Abraham said softly from where he'd been lying on the cot.

He shifted onto his side, his back against the wall. That opened up a sliver of room on the cot next to him. He lay there, his hand in that empty space, offering it to me.

End of the world, right? A girl who was running out of time shouldn't waste a single moment.

I walked over and lay on my good side, my back

pressed against him, his arms wrapped around me. It felt safe. Warm.

"Do you think we'll make it home in time?" I asked him quietly.

"Yes," he lied.

It was nice of him.

I closed my eyes, inhaled the smoke and spice scent of him, and wished this, right here, would last forever.

17

*I don't care what the others said. This is my
fight too.*

—from the diary of E. N. D.

Abraham and I stood shoulder to shoulder, waiting
for the door to open. Abraham carried my revolver
with our remaining bullets, and I had two little glass bottles full of something Quinten told me not to shake too
hard.

The latch clacked and the seal popped. Then the door
slid to one side.

Slip stepped back a pace and narrowed his eyes at
Abraham and me. The bruise from Abraham throwing
him against the wall was black and red and spread up
over his jaw and cheek and down beneath his collar.

"Don't get in our way," I suggested.

He paused, his hand on the gun in his thigh holster.
That was such a bad choice.

"Back down now, while you're still breathing," Abraham said.

Slip's eyes were wide with anger.

"Get out," he croaked. Sounded like his throat was nothing but raw meat on the inside. "Get the hell off my train."

I stepped out first, scanning the platform. If there were assassins staring us down, I'd never spot them in the throng of people crowding the place.

Abraham stepped out next, and then Neds followed, with Quinten and Gloria behind him.

"If I ever see you again," Slip said to Neds, "I will kill you."

Ned reached out and patted Slip on the shoulder as he walked past him. "I can't say it's been good doing business with you, Slip."

Slip pushed out from under his hand and stormed off, yelling at someone from his crew.

So far, it didn't appear that he had turned us in for the reward on our heads. That was something, at least.

The station at San Diego had been a faded beauty, but the station here had long gone to seed. Patchwork and cobbled, the walls were covered in faded canvas posters, behind which we could see brick, metal, concrete, and rotted wood. The staircases that lead upward on either end of the platform were missing several steps and looked like they'd tumble down if a hard breeze hit them.

Not that there was any breeze down here. There was hardly any air. The place stank of sweat and sewage and fish, the air so hot and damp, I wanted to spit out each breath to get rid of the taste.

And while San Diego had been silent and Callaway Station had been busy, this place was packed with people—nothing but jostling crowd as far as the eye could see.

The small bubble of space that our little good-bye with Slip had afforded us collapsed in on us, and I felt like I'd just been swallowed whole by sheer mass of humanity around me.

"Do you have any idea where we're supposed to be?" I asked Neds, trying to keep up with him and not get separated.

"Yes," Right Ned said. He pushed through the crowd, one hand out to sort of warn oncoming people to move out of his way.

My bad shoulder was bumped, jostled, and wrenched back by people squeezing by in the other direction. I clenched my teeth against the pain. My leg started shaking after we'd traveled only a few yards.

This underground rail obviously wasn't a secret like the one in San Diego. My guess was the line in California was mostly used for smuggling, since it was so close to a port. Whereas this landlocked station was just a cheap, if crowded and slow, way for people to get across the country.

I counted twelve different rail lines as we shoved our way through the river of people. That was a lot of trains taking people to a lot of places. I wondered which one we'd be getting on.

Neds turned a corner and then we were walking along a very thin platform with a railway ten feet or more below us. One shove to the side and someone would be in for a bone-cracking fall.

Of course, we weren't the only people trying to navigate the narrow one-way walkway like it was a spacious two-way highway.

To complicate it all were the bags, boxes, and baskets everyone was carrying.

Neds took it all in stride, literally. But, then, he used to run with the circus. I suppose heavy crowds and deadly drops were just every other Thursday for him.

The walkway bent again to the right, moving away from the rail. A very thin metal-and-wood bridge was built out over this section of the rail. On the other end of that very thin wood-and-metal bridge was a separate wing of the station. The two-story structure on the other side was made of windows and doors. The top story had a matched set of guards standing on the balcony, sniper rifles casually resting in their hands.

No one was walking that way. As a matter of fact, people were going to extreme measures to not so much as brush an elbow on the railing of the bridge. Everyone knew that the bridge didn't belong to them, and so they pretended it wasn't there.

Except for Neds. He strode right on across the bridge like he was coming home for supper.

"Son of a bitch," I mumbled.

Yes, I trusted Neds. But I had a bad feeling about this whole Sallyo thing.

Even Quinten hesitated before he and Gloria followed. Abraham brought up the rear.

Neds stopped on the other side of the bridge and held up both his hands so the guard above could get a good look at him. I'm sure they had already scoped and scanned us all. If they had any inclination to want us dead, they were in the perfect position to either turn us in to the Houses or pick us all off nice and clean.

The door opened.

A woman dressed in black stepped out. "This way," she said.

We went that way into the building.

Correction: into the office. A very clean and modern office space, the white walls covered by security screens that showed every corner of the station and a collection of old route maps. No extra chairs, just an expansive cast-iron desk with paper logbooks and other files spread out across it.

It was cool here. A light, pleasant breeze perfumed with a hint of gardenia wafted through the air, making the stench of the station behind us a faint memory.

In front of that desk were two pyramids of stacked little brown boxes tied up with string.

Behind that desk sat a woman. Her skin was the same light almond of my skin, but that's where our similarity ended. Her jet-black hair was shaved up off her ears and spiky on top. A cascade of jewels fastened around the top of her ear and ended in what looked like a set of snake fangs at her earlobe.

Her tailored jacket was gray with wedges of white and brown slicing through it, sharpening her curves. Her face was triangular, a small mouth and chin widening to incredible kohl-lined eyes that were a golden green, the pupils slitted like a snake's.

First impression? She was the boss, and she wasn't afraid to kill people until they understood that.

Second impression? She had something for Neds.

A slight movement of her lips, a minute widening of her pupils, gave away a world of history between them. They'd been close. Maybe lovers. Maybe more.

"I didn't think you'd come," she said, her voice a soothing alto.

"If I had any other choice, I wouldn't have brought

this to your doorstep," Left Ned said. "I just want that said."

Then Right Ned said, "It's good to see you, Sal."

She sat very still, but I could see the jewels on her ears trembling to the beat of her rushing heart. She might look cool on the outside, but there was a storm of emotions rolling through her.

I didn't know if that storm was blowing from fury or sorrow.

She nodded once. "This wipes our debt," she said softly.

"I understand," Right Ned said.

"And you?" she asked Left Ned.

This woman must really have known them a while. In my experience, most people thought of the Neds as one man. That Neds thought the same thoughts and spoke the same opinions.

Nothing could be farther from the truth. Those men were two very different people, so much so that sometimes I wondered how each could stand the other.

But Sallyo, for that's who this must be, understood that, which meant she had an intimate knowledge of the Harris boys.

"I understand," Left Ned said.

"There are rules to this deal." She stood up from behind her desk. I'd put her at several inches shorter than me, even in those heavy-heeled boots.

"You will be blindfolded."

Quinten made an annoyed sound, which she completely ignored.

"And if you make one more noise, you will also be gagged. You will be allowed to keep your weapons. Once on my transport, you will be locked in your quarters. It will take two hours to arrive at your destination. We will have your quarters under guard, locked, and wired. You will not send or receive data of any kind. Complete technological blackout conditions.

"When you have reached your destination, you will be blindfolded and taken to a drop point. Do not speak. Do not argue. Count yourself lucky this man has claim to a favor from me. Do not think I am unaware of what and who each of you are. Do not think I am unaware of what each of you has done." Here her eyes flicked to Abraham, who regarded her with a soldier's boredom.

"If I ever see any of you again, I will kill you, no questions asked, no hesitation."

We sure were hearing that a lot lately.

She didn't do anything to signal anyone, but suddenly the room was filled with a dozen guards, her people, carrying guns and black hoods.

There were enough people that one person could throw a hood over each of our heads and there would still be plenty more people with guns in the room.

The woman who walked up to me was yellow-haired and brown-eyed. She paused in front of me, probably a little startled by my eyes, which I assumed were red, since I was still hurting.

Eyes of red, you'll soon be dead.

I just nodded, and she snapped out of it.

She dropped the hood over my head and tugged on a string around my neck. It was snug but I could breathe.

Darkness. The cloth smelled like cedar and whiskey and dust. Even with my eyes open, my eyelashes scraping the cloth, I couldn't see a damn thing. I couldn't hear very well either.

So this was more than just a blinding hood. They'd rigged up some sound buffering in the thread composition; might even have had them wired to tune out sound on command.

The idea of the hood being wired brought other, more gruesome ideas of what it could be used for.

I did not like putting my head in Sallyo's hands. A bullet to the temple would end this trip awfully quickly for any of us.

But Neds could be trusted. He'd promised he could be trusted. He'd promised that he wasn't a spy for House Silver too, which had been a lie. But he'd promised he hadn't been spying for a long time.

He'd even promised he'd take over House Brown if I died.

Whether it was smart or not, I believed him.

"Move," someone—I think the woman who had hooded me—said. She grabbed my bad arm, and I grunted in pain.

Was that it? Was that enough of a noise that Sallyo would kill me, kill us?

"She's injured," Right Ned said. "Take her other arm."

How did he know what had just happened? The only way he could have seen that was if he wasn't wearing a hood.

Did that mean he wasn't going with us? Did that mean that he'd just sold us out?

A strong hand gripped my other arm and forced me to walk.

I could hear the scuff of footsteps from the others around me, so I knew we weren't being separated, but I didn't hear Neds' footsteps. No, what I heard was his voice, barely above a whisper, as he said something halting and tender, and was hushed by Sallyo.

Then a door shut behind us and it was impossible to hear anything through the damn black hood.

I went up a bridge or plank or ramp and then down something similar, and was told to stand still. Something rumbled, maybe a door on tracks. I was led along a space that echoed loudly enough I could hear all our footsteps almost clearly, unless that was a trick of the hood, and then there was a blast of cold. I held my breath on a gasp as we pushed through the cold quickly, and then there was more walking.

I have a good sense of direction. You grow up in the scrub, you keep your whereabouts about you. But I didn't have any idea where the hell I was in relation to where I had just been.

I did not like it.

Finally, we stopped and the woman's hand left my arm. Fingers fumbled against my neck. The string released, and I took a deep breath even though it hadn't been restricting my breathing. Then the hood was pulled free.

We were in a room decorated like a nicely appointed study.

A quick check showed me we'd all made it. The last guard was removing the hood from Abraham. Neds were here too, sitting on the plush couch and watching mostly me.

Any other day, I'd make myself comfortable, and there was plenty of room to do so. Three couches; several wide, stuffed chairs; a wall with shelves that held books; and another that seemed to have a window that looked out over the ocean, a selection of alcohol and chemical delights below it.

Thick carpet at our feet. The guards exited through a door that I didn't think was carved rosewood, as it appeared to be.

There were a lot of visual tricks going on in this room. The door locked, bolted, and sealed.

"We can talk now," Right Ned said.

"Where the hell is this?" Quinten asked. But Neds were still watching me.

"It's mostly hologram, isn't it? The window, the door?" Right Ned nodded slightly.

"We're in a speed tube, aren't we?" I asked, putting it all together. It was the only manner of transportation that wasn't a plane that could fling us across half of the country in two hours. I was certain this was not a plane compartment.

"Speed tube?" Abraham asked. "Those are all owned and closely guarded and regulated by the Houses. There are no other speed tubes."

"None that the Houses know about," Right Ned said. "Sallyo will go to extreme measures to make sure it stays that way. Breathe a word of this to anyone, ever, and she will know. And then she will kill you, everyone you love, and anyone you've been in contact with for the past ten years."

"Little brown boxes," I said.

"Tied up with string," Right Ned said.

"That seems . . . excessive," Quinten noted as he paced the parameter of the room.

"She'll follow through on it," Left Ned said.

"I'm sure she would." Quinten opened a crystal decanter, smelled the amber contents, and replaced the stopper.

I sat down on the couch next to Neds while the others continued to look around the place. "You were lovers?" I asked.

Neds were silent a minute. I waited him out.

"There are some things a man doesn't want to share," Left Ned said.

"She was ... when we knew her we were young," Right Ned said.

"You don't have to tell the woman our life story," Left Ned said.

"We were in the same institution together," Right Ned said, ignoring him. "You know the places where they send babies so different from other babies it's assumed they won't survive?"

"But she's not ..." I stopped. Her eyes had been snake-pupiled. And I knew Neds said touching a person let him see things about them, visions and such that were always true, whether or not the person knew them to be so. Maybe she had a hidden ability like that.

"She is different, isn't she? A mutant?"

"Lord," Left Ned muttered.

He nodded. "Some of us were found to be ... useful. Houses got interested in our potential. And so we were used."

"Hold on. Have you been working for House Silver all your life?" I asked.

"No. But when a House wanted to know something about someone, a thing only I could know ... I was bought. Many times."

"And Sallyo?"

"Don't bother asking," Left Ned said. "What she can do, what she is, that's personal and it's hers to tell."

"Sallyo bought out my contract," Right Ned said. "Found a loophole I could drop through and out of sight. So I did. Met Sadie and Corb. We ran with the circus for four years."

"Do you still love her?" I asked again.

"Time changes everyone, Matilda," Right Ned said quietly. "Time changes everything. Sallyo and I have said our good-byes. Our final good-bye. I hope you will leave it at that. All of you," he said, raising his voice to the rest of our group. "Please."

I could count on my hand how many times Ned had asked anyone please.

He hadn't just cashed in a favor when he'd brought us here; he'd cashed in a lifetime.

I did him the kindness of not touching him and also of dropping the subject.

"Thanks for getting us this far," I said.

"Thank me when we get back to the farm alive." Left Ned closed his eyes, and Right Ned just gave me a small shrug.

I got up, pulled the screen out of my duffel, and paced with it in the palm of my hand.

"Sallyo said no sending or receiving data," Abraham said.

He had settled down on a love seat, his feet up on a footstool, a book in one hand.

"I know." I paced over to him, restless, paced away, then back.

He set the book on his knee, watching me.

I finally stopped near him and leaned against the wall. I tucked the screen away in my duffel. It was no use to us now anyway.

Quinten had decided on a liquor to pour and was filling five tumblers. Gloria sat on the couch. She had taken off her shoes and was now pulling off her socks to shake the bits of concrete debris out of them.

"Do you remember the Wings of Mercury experiment?" I asked Abraham. "Do you have any recollection of that day, of the moment time broke?"

"I don't know," he said on a sigh. "I remember the last day I was human." He sat forward and removed his jacket, taking the time to fold it even though it was filthy, and laying it across the arm of the love seat. "I'd been detained by the sheriff who didn't like me spending time with his sister. It was raining—hard—and he'd been drinking harder. Accusing me of things . . ." He shook his head. "He was a gun looking for a target, and I was right there behind bars, making him angry. He came over waving his pistol at me, and I knew I wasn't going to be walking out of that jail cell. Ever." He paused, his gaze distant. "You never forget the first man you kill," he said softly. "His name was Virgil Milne. We struggled for the gun, the bars between us. I got the draw. He got shot."

"Neds saw that," I said. "Back on the farm when he first touched you. He saw you behind bars. Warned me that you were trouble, and I shouldn't go following you around."

Abraham grunted and looked over at Neds, who were sitting with their fingers laced together in their lap, lost in their own thoughts. Since each of them operated one side of the body, this was the position I'd seen them unconsciously take when they wanted comfort.

"Did he see anything more?" Abraham asked.

"A girl?" I said.

"Yes," he said, his words slow, as if dredging the water of deep memories. "There was a girl in the doorway, wearing a dress and boots. She was soaked and muddy, as if she'd been running through the rain. . . .

"I'd never seen her before," he continued. "But there were always families coming through town, settling in while they looked for a fortune, then moving on.

"She knew my name. Told me we had to run. Had to stop . . . something. Then there was this sound. Greater than a bell, louder than metal breaking. It thickened the air until I could hear the ringing in my bones, my teeth. A ringing that filled the jail with the scent of lightning and taste of copper. It was the strangest thing."

"Did you see anything else?" Quinten asked from across the room. "A flash of light? Sudden darkness?"

"No. There was that sound, that great, infinite bell. . . . Then . . . then I woke on an operating table, and it was twenty years later."

Quinten picked up three of the tumblers. Took the first over to Neds. Right Ned accepted it with a nod.

"Do any of the other galvanized remember that day?" Quinten asked, bringing the tumblers to us.

"They all do, in some manner or other," Abraham said. "Under the circumstances, I wish I remembered more." He took the tumbler from Quinten, frowned at the liquid, sniffed it, then tossed it back in one shot.

"Do you remember what time it was?" Quinten asked, giving me my glass.

I sniffed it too. *Brandy,* I thought. I took a sip. Hot, strong, with the smoke of burnt cherries on the back of my tongue. Yep. Brandy.

"It was a few hours after dawn, I think." Abraham

rubbed at his jaw and scratched at the stubble there. "Maybe closer to noon."

"Was there a bell that usually rang out in town at that time?" Quinten walked back to the liquor cabinet and took the last two tumblers with him. He eased down onto the couch next to Gloria. She accepted a glass, tapped the edge of it against his, and took a drink.

Quinten just held the glass in one hand and rubbed at his forehead with the other. He looked dog tired.

"No," Abraham said. "There was a church bell for service on Sundays and for emergencies. A school bell rang in the morning. But this bell, this sound . . . it resonated in everything."

"No mills, factories, mines using bells for shift changes?" Quinten asked. He raised the glass to his lips, drank down half the brandy.

Abraham shook his head again. "Noon whistle for the factories and mills. Train whistle when it came in and out of town, but not a bell. And not a bell that was so . . ."

"Unworldly?" Quinten offered.

"Yes. I said it was ringing, but it wasn't a metal-on-metal sound, not a wooden sound. It was more like. . . ." He paused again. "All these years, all the things I've seen, and I don't have a way to describe it. If Earth were a bell, the whole world made of a material that would resonate, it sounded like that. As if something had hit the whole world so hard, it gave out a single, endless peal."

"You're not far off on that image, really." Quinten finished his drink, then leaned his head back on the couch and closed his eyes. "Something hit *time* so hard, it cracked. And we are going to see it glued back together properly."

Abraham offered no comment. I didn't think he entirely believed my brother.

I didn't blame him. The longer I thought about all this, the more the whole idea seemed outlandish. If I weren't in the middle of it, I'd think it was all a fever dream of a crazy genius who refused to face reality. Just as he had refused to face the reality of my dying when I was a child, and had instead, foolishly, transferred my thoughts and mind into this body.

Quinten's response to impossible situations was to find an equally impossible solution to it. Sometimes it worked. I was proof of that.

Sometimes it didn't.

I just hoped that he'd found the right impossible answer this time.

18

The Houses have tightened security. Quinten keeps telling me everything is going to be okay, but I don't think I can believe him.
— from the diary of E. N. D.

"This is a cabin?" Abraham asked.

"It used to be," I said.

We'd been hooded and unloaded from the pod into a small room, then put on a bus Neds drove for about a half hour.

Finally far enough from the secret speed-tube drop, Neds had given us the go-ahead to remove the hoods. Not that it would have mattered. It was so dark, none of us would have been able to see anything anyway.

We made it to Pock Cabin by four a.m. The cabin was a block of concrete and metal, with narrow slits for windows. It looked like a cross between a medieval fortress and a postwar bunker.

Neds drove the bus around back of the place and parked it there.

"This is it," he said. "As close to the property as I can get us and still be safe for the night."

I stood and stretched, trying to loosen muscles without making the wounds in my thigh, shoulder, or hip break open and bleed.

"You done good, Harris," I said. I swung the duffel up over my good shoulder. "Let's go, people. It may not be the prettiest accommodation, but it has all the guns, ammo, and rations you could want."

I was out of the bus first, followed by the others. Quinten and I knew about Pock Cabin, of course; our parents had befriended the crazy old guy who had originally built it. And when he'd passed on, it had sort of fallen into our unofficial keeping.

I hadn't been up here since I was ten. I didn't know the last time Quinten had visited.

The damp forest air and smell of pine wrapped the lonely arms of home around me. We were only out a few miles from our property, and it was making me itchy to get back to where I belonged.

I wanted to make sure Grandma was okay.

"Did you bring the key?" I asked Neds.

"It's not *my* hidey-hole," Left Ned said. "Figured your genius brother would know the secret knock."

Quinten pressed his fingertips along the edges of the metal door, then stepped to the left and ran his fingers along the concrete wall.

"It's been a while," Quinten muttered as he pressed and prodded. "Ah, here."

The door rolled open with the grinding of metal gears and a *pop* of rods.

"It's about time you got here," a man's voice said from the other side of the door.

Abraham pulled the gun, but I grabbed his arm.

"Wait." I peered into the shadows. "Welton?"

The door finished opening and Welton Yellow, ex-head of House Yellow, stood the doorway, eating a chocolate bar.

"I've been waiting for hours," he said. "Good to see you're all still breathing."

Behind him, taller even than Abraham, was the mountainous galvanized, Foster First. His thick yellow stitches tracked through the scar tissue across his craggy face, almost glowing against the albino white of his skin and hair.

"Come in," Welton said.

"We trust him?" Gloria asked.

"I think we need to," I said, walking into the structure.

Abraham was right behind me, and clasped Foster's hand in his own. "Foster, my friend."

Foster gave him a crooked smile, and they leaned in and gave each other a fond embrace.

"Do you know what Welton is up to?" Abraham asked.

"Helping," Foster said in his crushed-boulder voice. "Helping."

He stepped aside and waited for everyone else to walk in before he scanned the shadows behind us and closed the door, setting the locks.

"Food and weapons this way," Welton's voice echoed down the hall.

It was cool and dimly lit here in the highly defendable entryway. More light poured from the hallway. "Are you and Welton the only people here?" I asked Foster.

"Yes."

The hall ended at a large, brightly lit room filled with sturdy but homey furniture. Communication devices, tracking gear, screens, and feeds that almost rivaled what we had at our house spread across the walls.

"I don't recall all this being here last time I stopped in," Quinten said.

"I brought a few toys along with me," Welton said. "I've always wanted to test a few of our newer designs in the field."

"Are you sure you're not being tracked?" Left Ned said. "Or that any of your equipment isn't being tracked?"

"Of course I'm not being tracked," he said with mock offense. "I made sure of that before I left the House rulership in Libra's hands."

"Your cousin?" Abraham asked. "She's . . . a little chaotic to be standing as ruler, don't you think?"

"No," Welton said. "I think she is a *lot* chaotic. Which means she is making all sorts of crazy choices and decisions right now. Trust me when I say technology will not be easy for any of the Houses to access or use for a while. It's . . . delightful." The smile spread into a grin, and I couldn't help but shake my head.

"You are a troublemaker. You know that, Welton?" I set my duffel down next to one of the couches and sat.

"Please. I made this world a better place when I took over that House. Any trouble that comes out of Libra is long overdue, if you ask me. Now, food, drinks, kitchen — that way. Bedrooms there." He pointed the opposite direction. "There is a fully stocked basement and some interesting storage in the attic, if you're the curious type.

"Abraham," he said as he dropped down into a stuffed

chair, propping his heels up onto a matching hassock. "I have a question for you, my friend."

Abraham was standing with Foster near the hall. He walked a little farther into the room. "Ask."

"Did you shoot and kill Slater Orange?"

Quinten hadn't taken a seat yet. Gloria was halfway to the kitchen. They both paused and looked over at Abraham. Neds and I were looking at him too.

His eyes narrowed and the muscle at his jaw worked. Then he very calmly said, "No."

Welton's expression was unreadable as he studied Abraham. "He has video that shows otherwise."

"I assumed he would," Abraham said evenly. "Do you think I'm lying?"

Welton shook his head. "I do not. You take the moral ground so high, you could step over heaven. I'm not surprised he framed you for the crime, though. He has never liked you."

"He hates all galvanized," Abraham said.

"He hates all living creatures," Welton said.

"And what about you?" Quinten asked. "I am not as convinced that we should trust you, Welton Yellow."

"Just Welton," he said, pushing his fingertips together in front of his mouth and peering over the top of them at Quinten. "Listen, Quinten. If I wanted to betray you, I wouldn't have hauled my ass all the way out here in the middle of nowhere. I would have taken you down while you were on that seaplane or in San Diego or down that underground train line. Oh yes," he said at Quinten's sudden stillness. "I knew where you were every step of the way."

"But we removed the bugs," Gloria said.

Welton nodded. "Very practical of you. But I have eyes everywhere. Well, I did."

"Matilda," he said, switching his gaze to me. "I knew you lived on a farm off grid, but did it have to be out in the middle of the scrub? I'm practically blind out here."

"Farms are funny like that," I said. "So far away from cities and such. You're saying we can trust you?"

"Don't you already?" he asked with a slow smile.

"I'm not the one you need to convince." Yes, I trusted him. But Quinten had known him longer—hell, he'd worked for the man. He must know a lot more about Welton than I did. It didn't hurt to be a little cautious.

"All right. Proof," he said. "It's probably best we get this out of the way quickly. You are running out of time. You have—what—eight hours left?"

Quinten nodded, and my throat was suddenly too dry to swallow. No one had said the exact time. Eight hours. Not even a day left.

And we still didn't have Grandma's journal.

"You will want to see this news feed from the past two days since the gathering," Welton said. "I'll give you a moment to take it in."

He tapped his finger against his palm, and the upper part of the wall across the room filled with dozens of images. Dozens of voices; dozens of text scrolls in dozens of languages. It was pretty easy to understand exactly what all those images and voices added up to.

"We are so screwed," I said.

The screens scrolled through the gathering where galvanized Helen Eleventh shot Oscar Gray, the head of House Gray, in front of all the world's watching eyes.

An act that broke the treaty between the galvanized and the Houses they served.

A flurry of images showed each of the Houses taking their galvanized in chains to a high-security compound. Once inside the heavily armored solitary-confinement cells, the galvanized were pumped full of drugs that sent them into medical comas.

Helen was confined even more harshly: bound, blind-folded, and intubated, she was locked in a close-fitting body cage that was welded onto a medical table in a fea-tureless metal cell.

Foster made a soft sound in the back of his throat: sorrow.

"It's all right," Welton said comfortingly. "You're not going there. Ever. I won't allow it."

I knew Welton genuinely cared for Foster's welfare.

Being the oldest of the galvanized meant Foster had been experimented on the most and carried the most flaws and scars. He rarely spoke, but I'd seen him stand by Welton out of more than a sense of duty—out of fond-ness.

On the screens, the heads of each House gave speeches and promises. Most of them said they would go to all ends to find Abraham and me and put us down like the inhuman criminals we were.

Some were even more blunt and bloody about what should be done with us when we were found. Cutting off our heads seemed to be the most popular option.

But most interesting to me was Slater Orange, in the body of Robert Twelfth. He gave a short, convincingly humble speech insisting he would serve House Orange with the careful oversight of Reeves Silver, his actions and decisions fully transparent to the other Houses and public at large.

It was chilling to see Robert not acting like Robert, not even speaking like Robert. I didn't know how other people couldn't tell that it was the mind of Slater Orange in that galvanized body and not Robert Twelfth.

Seeing the proof of my brother's handiwork made my stomach sick. Robert was truly dead.

The image of Oscar's face repeated on the screen many times, along with the face of Slater Orange and, of course, my face and Abraham's.

Following Oscar's face was that of his brother, Hollis. The man didn't look a bit like Oscar's affable, absent-minded scholarly image. Hollis was clean and slick as a snake, his dark eyes dead, his smile a practiced thing. If he was grieving his brother's murder, he didn't show it. He looked like he was pleased with things going his way, now that the control of the human resources of the world had fallen into his well-manicured hands.

Abraham had gone a deathly kind of still watching Robert, a galvanized, one of his dearest friends, demanding his death for murdering Slater, head of House Orange.

"Robert certainly takes after Slater," Welton said, watching Abraham's reaction.

"That's not Robert," I said.

"Oh?"

"I am at fault," Quinten said. "I put myself and my . . . skills with galvanized right into Slater's hands. He forced me to implant his mind, personality, and thoughts into Robert's body."

Welton straightened in the chair, suddenly very focused on my brother. "How?"

Quinten pressed his lips together and said nothing.

"Fine," Welton said. "But if you won't tell me how, you must tell me why. Or I will find myself unable to trust *you*, Quinten Case. Why did you do such a thing?"

Quinten's gaze didn't leave Welton, but something in him tightened, as if he were trying to speak around a great pain. "He said he'd kill her," he whispered.

"Who?"

"Matilda."

A wash of shock spread over my skin. "Me?"

"How?" Welton asked.

"Assassins. He had snipers covering her twenty-four hours a day. He . . . showed me."

Oh, God. I couldn't imagine that fear, that pain. I couldn't believe I'd been used against him.

It was my fault that Robert had died. My fault my brother had been used to do this horrible thing. I pressed my palm over my face, wishing I could be anywhere but here.

"I'm so, so sorry," I said.

"Did you know?" Welton asked.

I pulled my hand away, sniffing back tears. "No. But it's my fault that Robert is dead," I said. "If there's blame, I will bear it."

"Oh, for heaven's sake," Welton said, "you've been hanging around Abraham too much. This isn't about blame. It's about truth and information. Who has it and what they'll do with it.

"We know that Slater is in that body. And he knows you, Quinten, guard his secret. If I were him, I'd want you dead."

"Galvanized don't have the power a head of House

has," I said. "We aren't even considered human. Why would he want to be galvanized?"

"Nothing better than an immortal body," Welton said. "A chance to live forever. Given enough time, House power can be bought, bribed, won. He was the one who released that recorded message from your mother, by the way. To flush you out, Matilda. Or, rather, to cause Oscar Gray to send Abraham out looking for you, to see if you were real—a modern mind in a galvanized body. You were his proof that he could gain immortality. He was . . . no, he *is* a very clever man."

"I walked right into his plans," Quinten said. "I put this madman in a position to take head of the House and to order us hunted down, blamed, and destroyed."

"This madman," Abraham said evenly, "has always been the head of a House. The only thing that is different now is that he is in a galvanized body."

"Immortal," Welton said. "Well, until noon today, if my calculations are correct. Are they correct, Mr. Case?"

Quinten nodded, pulling the screen out of his pocket. "This is . . . beautiful," he admitted. "I tried for years to nail down the exact timing. How did you do it so quickly?"

"I cheated." Welton shrugged. "I watched you while you researched. Paid moderate attention to the texts you were going through."

"I took no notes," Quinten said. "I never take notes for just this reason."

"I might have also analyzed your eye movements, body temperatures, pulse rates." Welton pulled his fingers back through his hair, and it slipped back into place like a silk curtain. "Recorded the pages you read, acquired said pages, went through them myself, paying attention to the pages you reacted to. I didn't say it was easy, but, then ... I do like a good puzzle."

"From that you extrapolated I was looking for the mending point in time?" Quinten asked.

"No. From that I extrapolated you were trying to isolate *a* point in time. So, this does have something to do with the Wings of Mercury experiment?"

"You've been watching me for years, haven't you?" Quinten asked.

"I do admit you're a very interesting person, Mr. Case," Welton said. "Your meteoric rise to the head of House Brown—"

"I'm not the head. House Brown has no official leader."

"But if they had one person they all looked to in times of trouble, it was you, and your remarkable sister, wouldn't you say?"

Quinten just nodded.

"I wasn't the only head of House who was interested in your family. Certainly Reeves Silver had his thumb on you and people in place to watch your moves." He gave Neds a look.

"They know," Right Ned said. "But I'm not working for him anymore."

"I know. He is very unhappy about that."

"Don't it just break my heart?" Left Ned drawled.

"How much do you know about the Wings of Mercury?" Quinten asked. "Any detail may help."

"Rumors, stories, theories? Plenty." Welton sighed. "Hard data? There is very little of that to be found. But

I assume you have your grandmother's journal stashed away somewhere?"

Quinten shook his head. "It was taken with our father's research." He said it in such a way that anyone else might not notice how he clipped off the rest of the facts behind that event. That our parents had been killed, their research stolen. That it had been done by the heads of House Black, Defense, and House White, Medical.

"You know which Houses were behind that, don't you?" Welton asked.

Quinten just spread his hand in a motion for Welton to tell him.

"The vehicles and people were wearing black and white," Welton said. "Since your father worked for House White for many years, I never questioned that House Medical would bring House Defense with them to gather research they must have considered theirs to own.

"But Medical doesn't usually resort to killing people to shut them up. Kiana White prefers a much subtler approach and liked to keep sharp scientists in House, or at least owing to her House. It didn't make sense that she would have your father and mother killed.

"I was curious," Welton said, "so I looked into it."

"You're always curious, Welly," Abraham said, finally sitting in a chair next to me, his gaze fixed on the news feed rolling across the wall.

"What did you find?" I asked.

"Several levels of boring backstabbings and substandard bribes," Welton said. "But the interesting bit is, the order to take out your father and mother came from

House Silver and was challenged by House Orange. Reeves Silver wanted your parents dead, possibly for no other reason than Slater Orange wanted them alive."

"The vans were black," I said.

"Colors are easy to wear, even if you don't belong to that House," Welton said, not unkindly.

I always knew that could be a possibility. I'd worn green or blue, or really any color I wanted, when out on the farm, where I knew no one would see me.

All these years I had thought it was House Black and House White that had killed my parents. And if Welton was right, it was actually House Silver.

Or, more specifically, Reeves Silver. The man who had made a deal with me to return my brother, but had also gotten my agreement to stand aside while he went through with his plans at the gathering. Plans I had not known would kill Oscar Gray.

"Are they still working together?" Right Ned asked.

"Who?" Welton asked.

"Reeves Silver and Slater-in-Robert Orange there." Right Ned nodded toward the screen. "Did they both want Slater in a galvanized body? Did they both want Helen Eleventh to kill Oscar Gray? Were they both behind blaming Abraham for Slater's murder?"

"Last part doesn't make sense," I said. "Unless Reeves Silver double-crossed Slater Orange by telling Helen Eleventh to shoot Oscar. Since Slater is now in a galvanized body, it was possible he would be thrown in prison with the rest of the galvanized."

"Would he do that?" Gloria asked. "Is Reeves Silver the sort of man who would double-cross his partner in crime?"

"Yes," both Welton and Abraham said.

"Swell," I said.

"So, now that we are caught up on the current state of your imminent death or capture by the rest of the world," Welton said. "What can you tell me about the Wings of Mercury event?"

"Well, for one thing," Quinten said, "if we can't get back to our farm in less than eight hours, Abraham, Matilda, and Foster will die. So will all the other galvanized."

Welton went very still and silent. Gone was the cat-like smugness, the lazy nonchalance, the humor.

"All the galvanized will die?" Welton asked softly. "No. That is an unacceptable outcome. We are not going to let that happen."

"No," Quinten said. "We are not. Although changing this fate won't be easy."

"Anything I have is yours," Welton said.

"Good," Quinten said. "Bring up a map of our farm. We need to find the fastest way to my equipment in the basement."

19

Things have been quiet. Maybe there will be peace.

—from the diary of E. N. D.

"That doesn't look good." I studied the frighteningly detailed view of the property I'd always thought was far enough off grid there weren't images of it to be found outside of the original surveyor's map.

It wasn't the images of the farm that worried me. It was our property boundary, which was patrolled by at least fifty men—we were pretty sure they were Reeves Silver's men—and the thirty or more guards who surrounded the house itself. Even more forces were on the ground, moving between the pastures and fields that held our stitched beasts.

I was surprised to see that the pony and Lizard appeared unharmed, though Lizard was shifting about in its enclosure like it hadn't been fed in a while. A restless lizard the size of a barn was a dangerous lizard.

The other beasts were too small to see on the spy device Welton had pulled out of a briefcase. But I assumed the cockatrice were holed up in the barn, and the tiny, land-jumping octopus leapers were either in the trees or content in their apple-filled pond.

We couldn't get a good look inside the house because of those great scramblers we'd installed. I didn't know if Grandma was alive or not. I didn't know if she was tied up, shot, hurt. I didn't know if Boston Sue was still in the House with her.

All of which just made me mad.

"Anyone up for grabbing all the guns we can carry and blasting our way in?" I asked.

Neds lifted their hands as if to volunteer, but Quinten just rolled his eyes at me.

We'd all taken the time to shower, and the place was well enough stocked, there was a change of serviceable clothing for everyone.

"Useful suggestions only, please, Matilda," he said, scanning—for the hundredth time—through a list of supplies and tech we had at hand.

We'd been here for an hour. That meant we had seven left before our time ran out.

"We don't have the manpower to take them out," I said. "We don't have the technology to take them out. We don't have the resources to call them off or pull them away. I think driving straight at the problem and shooting at it until it's done *is* a useful suggestion. Abraham, Foster, and I can take a few bullets."

"No," Welton and Quinten said at the same time. "You are more valuable to this mission conscious," Quinten added. "Don't so quickly put your life on the line."

"I thought *quickly* was sort of at the heart of this matter."

"It is," Quinten said. "Just give us a few minutes more."

That was Brother Code for "I'm going to work on this as long as I want, and you're only getting in the way."

Fine. I needed to walk off some restless energy anyway.

I left Quinten and Welton and Neds in the living room. Gloria had said she was going to check the storeroom for better medical supplies, and I thought maybe Abraham had gone with her.

But I found Abraham and Foster in the kitchen, sitting quietly at the old-fashioned blue linoleum table, playing a game of cards.

It was an odd moment to come in on. Then again, this was far from the first battle either of them had fought. They'd originally been designed to be the ultimate fighters in wars, and had served that purpose many times. Taking over a small piece of land under impossible circumstances probably wasn't the most dangerous mission they'd been sent on.

It occurred to me we were leaving the planning of the attack to the wrong people.

"Have they made a decision?" Abraham asked.

"No." I walked around the small kitchen, dragging my fingertips across the counter, then leaned against one wall, my arms crossed. My wounds were feeling better, and I knew I was healing at an accelerated pace. But I wasn't sure how much range I'd get out of my bad arm by morning.

"They will have to decide. Hopefully by sunrise," Abraham said. "Knowing the two of them, they'll work until the last minute. Maybe you should get some sleep."

"I'm restless, not tired."

He nodded, picked up a card, discarded. The two of

them were the vision of calm and patience, while I felt like ants were eating me from the inside out.

I'd checked on the data we'd dug out of Robert's records so far, and Grandma's journal hadn't turned up yet. I didn't want to admit I'd failed, but it had been a long shot anyway.

Just in case something did sort out of all that information, Welton had given me a wrist screen to wear. It was rigged to set off an alarm if by some miracle the data was uncovered.

"I suggested a direct approach to them," I said.

"I heard. Quinten didn't approve?"

"He hasn't had a chance to cross every T and dot every I in the universe. I just want to . . . end this. Get my grandmother out of that house and out of danger, and get Quinten to the basement equipment he needs to try to fix the time thing so none of us die. But standing here, while minutes tick away . . . I'm not built for this kind of waiting."

"Gin," Foster said, laying down his cards.

Abraham smiled. "Are you sure Welton didn't do something to your settings? Maybe a card-counting application or X-ray vision?"

Foster gave him the crooked smile. "You are bad at cards, Abraham. You always have been."

Abraham just shuffled and dealt again.

"Don't you think approaching right now, while it's still dark, might be a better tactic?" I asked.

"Darkness won't hide us," Abraham said, spreading out the cards in his hand, then sorting them. "The men left behind to guard the property and your grandmother will have the equipment to look for us."

Which brought my restless mind around to other thoughts. "No slight intended, Foster," I said, "but you think Welton would turn us in? Maybe if it meant he could save you?"

"He is my friend," Foster said. "A good young man."

"Lots of good young men do the wrong thing when all hell's coming down."

Foster picked up a card from the deck and discarded.

Abraham picked that card up, slid it in with his cards, and discarded.

"Welton thinks of Foster as family," Abraham said. "He was given into Foster's care at a very early age." Abraham glanced away from his cards to me. "At a very early age, Welton developed a problem with his lungs. He was sick for many years. Foster was his constant companion, refusing to serve the head of House Yellow in any other way than looking after Welton."

Oh. They weren't only friends; they were much closer than that. Foster and Welton were family without the blood bond.

"If we don't stop the time event," Abraham said, "Foster dies. So I'd say Welton is completely on our side."

Finally, Foster spoke. "I told him it is my time. A long life. So many have died before me. The child will not listen."

"Love clouds our eyes and fills our ears," Abraham said. "There is no cure for it."

"Yes," Foster breathed. "Yes."

It sounded like something quoted from a poem, or something they had said to each other over their long years together.

"Foster," I asked. "Do you remember anything about

that day when the Wings of Mercury experiment happened?"

The two men continued with their game in silence. I thought maybe Foster was done talking. Conversation was hard for him, and, frankly, I was surprised he had been talking so much.

"It was raining," Foster said haltingly. "Cold. Dark. I was at their graves."

He paused for a long time, and cards were lifted, placed, discarded with plastic-edged *snick*s.

I took a cue from Abraham and waited patiently.

"My wife. My children. Buried," Foster said. "Blisters on my hands. Shovelfuls of earth."

Snick, snick, snick.

"A girl was crying. Afraid of the tower. The angel. The voice. Afraid of the bell. She ran. She ran. And then the world ended."

"You heard the bell too?" I asked.

Foster nodded. "You were there, child."

That was the thing. I hadn't been there. But this body, this girl my brother had pulled out of cold storage with no memories left in her, no thoughts or personality left in her, had been there.

"I don't remember," I said.

"Gin." Foster placed his cards down in a careful row.

Abraham sighed. "Good. My strategy to lure you into a false sense of security is working. Up for another hand?"

Foster nodded, and Abraham shuffled and dealt.

"We have a few hours yet, Matilda," Abraham said, sorting through his hand. "Rest. Make your peace with your life, with your death. You'll want a clear head."

"Please don't tell me that was your pep talk," I said. "Because if it was, you should stay out of coaching."

He smiled. "How about: 'Worrying won't change anything'?"

"So, your plan is to just sit here and play cards?"

"My plan is to let those two geniuses out there work out a plan. If they haven't come up with anything by daylight, we'll chose the best route using the equipment and resources we have, and get your brother into that house's basement one way or another."

Right. That was the plan. Get Quinten in so he could activate the countermeasures to try to travel back in time. Then he would try to talk our ever-great-grandfather into adjusting the hammer on his time-smashing machine so none of this happened.

That was, of course, if Quinten had guessed right about the calculations. Without Grandma's journal and the original code, everything—all of this—was a guess.

"There are too many unknowns," I said. "We don't even know if he'll survive the trip through time. And if he does and he fixes the experiment so it doesn't break time, what happens to us? To you? Do we survive the adjusted experiment? Or will we just be mortals who live out a short life? What if Quinten's adjustments make things worse?"

"Well, if he's wrong, we'll certainly die," Abraham said. "If he's right, we'll probably die." He put down his cards, pausing the game. "I thought you had worked that through by now. No matter how tomorrow ends, we won't be here to see it."

He said it so casually. He wasn't smiling, wasn't joking. This was his end, our end. Something he must have prepared for hundreds of years ago. Something I'd had only a couple days to get my head around.

And I supposed a clean death, a clear end, was much kinder than perpetual awareness and a bodiless life in a cage.

"You're glad, aren't you?"

He frowned.

"Maybe you aren't excited about death," I said, "but you want it. You want out of this life and this struggle. If I'd been through everything you have, maybe I'd want out too. But I haven't lived three hundred years. If there is any action I can take, any sacrifice I can make, we are not going to die tomorrow. None of us. Just . . . no."

Abraham stood and turned toward me. "You assume too much."

Okay, now he was annoyed. Well, good. I'd rather have an angry Abraham going into a fight than a man who had already picked out the font on his headstone. It didn't matter if he was angry at life, fate, Slater, or me.

"Oh?" I asked. "So you haven't given up? Because this"—I waved at the cards—"looks like you're saying good-bye. Permanently."

"You can't be more wrong."

"It's your last day on earth and you spend it playing cards with one of your oldest friends? Tell me another story, Vail. You're cashing in your life chips."

Foster watched us for a bit, then gathered up the cards and laid them out in a game of solitaire.

"I am not cashing anything in." Abraham advanced, stopped just inches in front of me.

I was still leaning, one foot planted on the wall behind me, my arms crossed over my chest.

I tended to forget just how big a man he was. Until he was standing right up against me and I had to crane my neck just to get in a good glare.

"You're telling me this isn't last-day, fond-farewell behavior?" I said.

He clamped his jaw, nostrils flaring. Those hazel eyes of his still had some red in them, which meant he was still hurting. Also I'd just put a different kind of fire in them. He leaned in even closer, his palm flat on the kitchen wall next to my head, his arm blocking my peripheral vision so all I could see was him.

He smelled good. A mix of the eucalyptus soap from the shower and a deeper, warmer note that was all his own.

"No," he said, low. "If I thought this was my last day on earth, I would be doing something *quite* different."

"Sure. Like what?"

His exhalation came out in a soft growl, a sound of utmost frustration.

Oddly, I heard Foster chuckle.

Then Abraham caught the side of my face with his free hand, his thumb pressing on the edge of my mouth. I opened my lips on a gasp, suddenly realizing just what it was he would do on his last day.

Me.

He lowered his head, his mouth hungry, devouring mine. His lips tugged, his tongue stroked and teased, sending electrical zings through my already pounding blood. I slipped my arms up around his neck and pulled him closer.

This. Yes. This is what I wanted too.

We left the kitchen and found a bedroom with a door

that locked. I'd like to say I was calm and smooth and patient. But as soon as the door was locked behind us, I pulled him closer to me, not caring if he was hurting, not caring if I was hurting either.

He responded with another low sound in his chest, wanting that, wanting me. I stretched my body to press against his, so far up on my tiptoes, if he moved away, I'd collapse. His arm shifted to my back. He bent, his hand scooping under my butt, and lifted me up, bending me into him.

I wrapped my thighs around his hips, and he pressed me down into the soft bed, coming down with me. Everything in me came undone. I was liquid; I was warmth. Heat sparked and crackled in my bones and pulsed through me, stealing my breath.

I dragged his shirt up and over his head so I could stroke my palms across the muscles, ridges, and stitches of his back. Then I ran my fingers across his stomach and the hard line of his hip bones that plunged downward. The world swayed as if I'd drunk a bottle of booze.

He tugged on my pants and I waited, licking the taste of him off my swollen lips, staring at the wooden ceiling. I groaned in frustration.

"What is taking you so long?" I panted. "Haven't you ever undone a girl's britches? That top thing is a button and you just push it through the hole, and then there's a zipper. Undoes easy if you tug it."

He huffed out a breath on a chuckle, but still wasn't doing anything to further my undress.

"Here, let me show you . . ." I started.

His hands clamped over mine, catching my fingers before I could get ahold of my waistband. He crawled up over me and leaned forward, eyes glittering with heat, a wicked smile curving his lips and making me want to lick him.

He stretched my arms up over my head, held them there with one hand loosely around my wrists. "You are disturbing my romancing moves, woman. Stay put and let me untie your boots."

I opened my mouth to ask him if that was an euphemism, in which case I'd be happy to stay put, but he headed me off with a kiss that made my back arch and toes curl, which was, I'll admit, less fun in combat boots.

He pulled away, and I spent a minute or two trying to catch my breath and not squirm. Then he spent a minute or two untying my boots and pulling them off.

"Now," he said, his wide hands massaging up the inside of my calves, knees, thighs, urging the heat inside of me to build. "Let's see to those britches."

20

They say the plague is in the cities. We don't know how long it will be before it reaches House Brown.

— from the diary of E. N. D.

A knock woke me from of a deep, glorious sleep. I opened my eyes onto a darkness broken only by the wedge of yellow light coming in from under the door.

"Matilda," Quinten said from the other side of that door. "We need to be moving out in a half hour."

"Mmm?" I was still picking the dreams—very nice dreams, I might add—out of my waking thoughts. Abraham had been in my dreams, and he'd done such things. . . .

"Tell Abraham too, please," Quinten said after a slight hesitation.

"I heard," Abraham said from behind me. No, not so much behind me as wrapped up tightly around me, his hand on my bare stomach, his leg tossed over one of mine, his body bent around mine, as I used his arm for a pillow.

Okay. So those weren't dreams. I smiled.

And while I was very much awake now, I was not sure what to say to my brother. Silence seemed the safest way to go. I bit my lip and after just a short pause, I heard the retreat of his boots on the wooden floor.

"Morning," Abraham said into my hair. "Sleep well?"

I smiled, then rolled over toward him, untangling from his embrace and then tucking myself back into him, snug, as he shifted onto his back.

"My arm's asleep," he said. "That's annoying."

I tipped my face up from where I'd rested my head against his chest. "Sorry?"

"Don't be. I haven't had this problem in a couple hundred years. It's worse than I remember." He shook his hand and hissed, then chuckled.

"About last night," I said.

"Mmm?" He reached across to tug my hair off my face, absently twisting his fingers in the curls.

"I don't want you to get the wrong idea about this. About us," I said.

He was silent for a couple seconds. "All right. So what is the right idea?"

I propped up beside him so I could look down at him through the dark. There was just enough light coming in through the door that I could make out his face, relaxed, his smile softened by more than sleep, and the ridges of scars and stitches marking his face, neck, chest. Those scars were the mark of a warrior's life, battle scars of being galvanized, of strength.

And, yes, I got a little fluttery just looking at them and the man who wore them.

"Matilda?" he asked softly.

"The right idea," I said, "is that this, what we just had, what we just did . . ."

"Twice?"

"Shh, I'm talking." I pressed my fingers over his lips, and he gently bit my fingertips and raised an eyebrow. "What I'm trying to say," I said, pulling my finger away before I just forgot all words, all needs, all hungers except for him.

"Yes?"

"You said you'd do this only if you thought it was your last night alive," I said simply.

"Mmm?"

"I don't want this to be your last night alive. I don't want that to be the only reason for this. For us."

He paused, his fingers halfway to the curls that refused to stay in place behind my ears.

The rest of what I was thinking and feeling came out of me in a rush. "I don't want you to think we can't win this fight. I don't want you to think this is all we'll ever have, you and I. We are going to get to Grandma, make sure she's safe, then trigger that machine Quinten built in the basement and thread that loophole in time. We are going to save the world. Our world."

"All right," he said slowly. "And then what, Matilda? Don't you think that if someone, if your brother, goes back in time, that just his presence there will change things? Let's say he does adjust the Wings of Mercury experiment so that it doesn't break time. We don't die. No one dies. We live our lives. Mortal lives. No break in time means there will be no galvanized, no immortality.

"The chance that he's worked through all the possibilities that will allow this"—he tucked my hair behind my ear and cupped his palm over my cheek—"to play out in the same manner, is so finite as to not be logical to contemplate. Your brother's going to change time. That will change the world. He'll change our lives. He'll change our deaths. And this . . ."

He drew his hand down my neck and shoulder, his gaze following. "This will never have happened, because I will never have met you."

It was logical. I'd been worried about the same things. Quinten was amazing, but no man knew what would happen if time were altered. I knew Quinten wanted a way to save me, and he'd even said he wanted another chance at saving Mom and Dad. I didn't know how he intended to work that out while also restoring time.

If, as Abraham had just said, we mended time or adjusted the Wings of Mercury experiment so that it no longer broke time, then all this . . . this world, the Houses, my almost death, my life, and the man lying beneath me would be gone.

Dust.

"We can find a way . . . if I was a girl back then . . ."

"No," he said softly. "The body was a different girl. You were born in the modern world, Matilda. If I live my life, one life, a mortal life, I will be two hundred years in the grave before you take your first breath."

"I hate that," I said, tucking against him again and wishing I could stay here forever in this quiet room, under these soft blankets with him.

"There is always the chance I'm wrong," he said. "I

am not educated in the sciences of time or in what your brother intends to do with it. He might have investigated an angle I'm unaware of."

"Maybe," I said, wholly unconvinced. "But just in case you're right . . . kiss me one more time."

And so he kissed me one more time. And I kissed him back, as if there were no more time, no more tomorrows for us.

I expected a bit of teasing when Abraham and I finally emerged from that bedroom and joined everyone else in the living room. But other than a quick smile from Gloria and an approving thumbs-up and wink from Welton, everyone was more than happy to get on with the real business at hand.

"We've scanned the property for hours." Quinten stood in front of the wall of images, a cup of coffee in one hand. "The guards are from House Silver, we're fairly certain. They don't appear to be too concerned about being attacked. Which probably means they have their own surveillance team off-site looking out for them, looking out for us. That's going to work in our favor."

"How?" Right Ned was busy strapping on guns, knives, and grenades. He hadn't made eye contact with me yet, and I was a little worried my late-night decisions had put a dent in our friendship.

I'd told him before we were running for our lives that I was in love with Abraham. So it couldn't be a surprise to him. But I didn't always know what was going on in their heads.

"That's where I come in," Welton said. He'd changed

into very practical boots, jeans, and a heavy jacket, and had a duffel next to him, packed and ready to go.

"I'll throw false signals here, then, as we get closer, I'll throw a few other tricks into the mix. The goal here is misdirection and subterfuge. Also, we're going to set that dragon of yours loose."

"Lizard?" I said. "Don't hurt it."

"Can anything hurt it?" Welton asked.

"There will be no lasting damage to Lizard," Quinten assured me. "We're going to cut the fence and prod it a little. You know how that will go."

"How?" Abraham asked.

"Lizard doesn't like being bothered," I said, spotting a couple extra cups of coffee. I handed Abraham one. He gave me a short smile, and I had to look away so I wouldn't be tempted to do anything about that.

"The last time it was irritated," I continued, "it tore down half the barn and cut a swath through the forest. We turned the cleared land into a nice pear orchard."

"Those guards are armed, aren't they?" Gloria asked.

"Yes." Quinten said, "But they'd have to have a lot more firepower than they currently have on hand to slow Lizard down, much less stop it."

"We get in while they're looking somewhere else," Left Ned said, "then set off the reptilian killing machine in the middle of the property. Fine. How do we get in the house and to the grandmother without her getting killed?"

"That's a little less tasteful," Welton said. "We're going to walk into the house and surrender. We can take out the guards patrolling the perimeter of the house, but inside . . . we can't get a good lock on that. Your property, and the house specifically, Miss Case," he said to me, "is a little too well blocked."

"Thank genius over there," I said, pointing to Quinten.

"No," Quinten said. "These weren't blocks I put up. You must have put them in while I was away."

"That was me," Right Ned said. "Thought the place needed an upgrade, so we jimmied in a few nonstandard systems."

"Mr. Harris," Welton said, "you are officially hired once we get out of this mess. Well, if I go back to being head of House Yellow."

"You can do that?" I asked.

"Oh, it's never been done before," he said. "So yes. I might just do it."

Foster First sighed and shook his head slowly.

"Now, don't give me that sour-lemon look," Welton said. "It might be fun to pick up the mess Libra is leaving behind. She might even want me to."

"What, exactly," Abraham asked, "do we have for fire-power?"

"The second basement of this place is an armory," Gloria said.

"There's another basement?" Quinten said, stealing the words out of my mouth.

She nodded. "I was looking for medicine. Found a trapdoor down. Bunker chock-full of things that go boom. From heavy land-to-air munition all the way down to can openers."

"Well, hell," Left Ned said. "Let's go get us some can openers."

*   *   *

I thought the whole plan of diversion, distraction, dragon, then walking in the front door to surrender seemed a little too vague to go on. No one else appeared concerned about it.

When I brought it up, Neds just told me to keep my hands on a gun, my finger on the trigger, and my eyes on the targets.

We were loading our supplies into the bus behind the cabin. Quinten spent a little time trying to convince Gloria to stay behind. She refused to do so and finally just gave him a gentle kiss, then got on the bus, a gun on her hip and a case of medical supplies in each hand.

"This is crazy," I said to Quinten, who couldn't seem to pull his eyes away from the bus window where Gloria sat.

"Yes, it is," he said. "But that doesn't mean it won't work."

"Will it?" I stepped around so I was in front of him, so he had to look at me. "Even if you manage to get back in time and change the settings on the Wings of Mercury experiment, you can't know what that will do to today, to the future. You can't know that I won't be dead. That Mom and Dad won't be dead. You can't even know if you'll be born."

"Do not doubt me," he said through clenched teeth. His eyes glittered with an anger I'd never seen in him. "You of all people. Do not doubt the years of my life I have lost to searching for this answer. Do not doubt what I have *sacrificed* for this answer, for this single chance to make this right. Right for *you*, Matilda."

Wow. That was a strong reaction.

I pulled back my shoulders and straightened but did not step away from my brother. Why the sudden rage?

"I don't doubt you, Quinten. I love you. Do you want to try that again?" I asked.

"Yes," he said a little cooler. "Yes, it will work. You will survive. All of the galvanized will survive. Yes, our parents will survive and I'll be born. I have considered every angle of this problem. I have broken the code."

"Without the journal."

He stared at me, finally dropped his gaze. "I can do this. I promise you."

He stepped past me and stormed up onto the bus.

I stayed where I was for a minute, the heat of confusion flashing across my face. I didn't know if he was angry at my questions, at my doubt, at Gloria for refusing to stay behind, or, hell, at me for sleeping with Abraham.

What I did know was that the brother who had walked out from those years of being imprisoned by House Orange carried wounds with him. And somewhere deep in that brilliant mind of his, those wounds still twisted and cut.

Just like the death of our mother and father still twisted and cut.

My big brother hadn't been capable of letting me die when I was sick. He had been thirteen years old when he'd transferred my thoughts and memories into the galvanized body. He also didn't find it easy to forgive. It just wasn't in his nature.

He'd never forgiven himself for our parents' deaths and he wouldn't forgive himself if time snapped back and killed me.

The wind picked up a bit and I smelled rain on the air.

I turned my gaze up to the sky, where clouds churned in every shade of gray. A stray drop struck my cheek just below my eye and tracked down to my chin.

A second followed.

If I were the sort of woman who prayed, I'd be on my knees. Instead, I adjusted the semiautomatic over my shoulder, strode to the bus, and got on.

21

I miss my parents every day. I want to tell them I'm sorry, tell them I love them. Tell them that I know this was my fault.
                    —from the diary of E. N. D.

We left the bus half a mile out from the northeast border of our property and made our way on foot down the old washed-out road as quickly and quietly as we could. It was eight in the morning, raining, and we had three hours left before the world ended.

I was worried about being spotted, but Welton assured me that the rain would do a lot of good to keep us off certain tracking devices, and the thing—whatever it was—that he carried in his briefcase would pretty much blind or fool anything else mankind had invented.

I hoped he was right. The Houses wanted us captured or dead. And they had drones, satellites, and droppers that could be on top of us at the push of a button.

Every time we were under the tree cover, tromping through wet underbrush that made a lot of noise, I was sure we'd be caught. Out in the open made me feel even more vulnerable. Too much sky, too much loud gravel, mud, and broken stretches of concrete.

If anyone else had worries, they kept them to themselves, so I did the same.

At least the rain hadn't turned into a downpour. It was just a steady sort of wet September misery falling out of the sky that had me thinking more than once about the warmth of the covers I'd left behind.

And the warmth of Abraham's arms around me.

"How close do you need to be?" I asked Welton quietly as we took the hitch in the road that would set us right down along the creek. If we followed the creek, we'd end up at the pump house.

"I'll throw the monkey in the gears when we have visuals on the perimeter patrol," he said.

"Cutting it a little close, aren't you?" I asked.

He shook his head and water trickled down from his bangs into his eyes. He'd put on a wool beanie and insisted Foster do the same, even though the big guy couldn't feel the wet or the cold. "They're not stupid. They'll quickly discover our ploy, and we'll want to be moving in fast right about then."

"And what's going to stop them from lobbing a bomb at us?" I asked.

"That dragon of yours."

"Lizard."

"Whatever you want to call it, it is a delightful beast. I do not know what your father was thinking of using it for, but as a thing that can cause sheer chaos, it should be unparalleled.

"So," he continued, "distraction, dash to the pump house where we can cut the electric to the fence around the dragon, poke the beast—I understand it is sensitive to certain high frequencies—and let the fun and frolic begin."

"You have a twisted sense of fun, Welton."

"Yes. Yes, I do. Your brother, on the other hand." He shook his head and we both stared after Quinten, who was walking ahead of us, just behind Abraham. Foster brought up the rear with Neds, leaving Gloria, me, and Welton in the middle.

"What about him?" I asked.

Welton just shrugged. "Smart man, I can say that. I would like to have met him in better times."

"Then you would have never have known him," I said. "We haven't really had better times."

"Hm." We walked for a bit, and then Welton said, "I've met men like him before. Running House Technology brings a person in contact with staggering minds—brilliant, savagely genius people. I've seen men like your brother lock on to a problem they are determined to solve."

We walked for a while more. The next bend would drop us at the actual edge of our property. We were close now. Almost there.

"And?" I asked.

"They all have the same blind spot," Welton said.

"What's that?"

"They do not see how much of themselves they give away to the problem. They do not see how much that focus makes them perceive only one thing: the problem. Your brother has cracked the code on the Wings of Mercury—or thinks he has. Impressive," he said with a single nod. "But he has put too much of himself into that solution. Men are not pure enough to endure such heat."

"A little less poetry and a little more clarity would be nice," I said.

"I think . . . no, I know that if he manages to catch the moment and travel back in time, he will cease to exist."

At my silence, he said, "That means I think he'll die."

I wanted to roll my eyes at him but was too busy dealing with the idea that my brilliant brother's brilliant idea was going to kill him.

"He knows, doesn't he?" I breathed. Now that little outburst by the bus made sense. He wasn't angry about all the things he'd sacrificed for me in the past; he was angry that he was going to sacrifice his life for me now.

He was going to die so I could live.

No wonder why he didn't want to talk to Gloria and tell her he cared for her. He knew what the endgame would be. His death.

"Yes," Welton said. "I'm sure he does. I just thought you would want to know. I never had siblings, but . . . well, there are those of whom I am fond. I'd want to know if my time with them was about to be cut tragically short."

"Thank you," I said. "But I'm not going to let that happen."

"Oh?"

"He's my brother. He's done his job looking after me, protecting me. For all our lives. Now it's my turn to protect him."

"Spoken like a true galvanized," he said.

"Spoken like family," I replied.

"That too."

Abraham stopped, held his hand up. We all paused. We'd been walking for just over a half hour. We had two and a half hours left.

Abraham pushed forward through the thicker brush. I could hear the creek rushing by. It was such a familiar sound, so much a part of the pulse and breath of my home, that a surge of homesickness poured through me.

I wanted to grab my brother's hand and run home. Forget this fight, forget these guns, forget our time slipping down to zero. I just wanted to be home with him and Grandma, my arms wrapped around them, together as the world wound down.

But that was a child's dream, a child's longing.

It was much too late for that.

It might be much too late for everything.

Abraham scanned the creek long enough that I was getting a little itchy from the rain and sweat.

Then he strolled back to us, and we all pulled in close, bending our heads together in a huddle so he could speak quietly.

"The creek is just down the other side of this hill." He pulled a palm screen out and it displayed the property. Our location was a small red dot more than a quarter of a mile from the house itself. The guards were indicated by yellow dots that surrounded the house, moving along the road that ringed our pasture, and in clumps of three spaced about a mile apart that were walking the outer edge of our property.

"The next patrol out this far should be passing by in about five minutes." He pointed at a clump of approaching yellow dots. "Does everyone remember where they are going and what they need to do?"

Everyone nodded.

"All right," he said. "No heroic crap. I expect each of you to stick to the plan. Your death will not change time. It will not improve this mission. You will each make decisions that will keep you alive. Do not fear for Matilda, Foster, or me. They want us more or less in one piece, and it is very difficult to take us down. We are the mostly likely targets. Do not be surprised if more than a few bullets hit their mark. Stay safe. Even if that means standing down. Are we all gold on that?"

I had to smile at his use of that old saying. "I'm gold," I said.

"Gold," the others echoed.

"Good," Abraham said. "Welton, you're up."

Welton pulled back his sleeve to reveal a watch. "Quinten?"

Quinten dug around in his pocket and pulled out his pocket watch. He and Welton must have done some upgrades. The shapes inside the liquid face were shifting in precise rhythm to the watch on Welton's wrist.

They held both time devices close, waited; then each touched something on the watch faces.

"Good luck to you, Quinten," Welton said. "And thank you for letting me come along for the fun."

Quinten nodded. "Just stay on track. Any deviation could be catastrophic to our objective."

"Understood." He patted Quinten politely on the shoulder. Then Welton shifted the case in his hand, placing four fingers into indents at the edge of it. "And ready," he said. "On three. One, two, three."

He pressed down.

I thought I heard a buzzing just outside my range, but then it was gone.

The yellow dots on Abraham's screen paused, turned,

and headed in the opposite direction. "Let's go," Abraham said.

Whatever Welton had done was supposed to draw all their attention to the far side of the property and send most of the patrol there.

What we needed now was speed, not quiet.

We scrambled through the underbrush, wet limbs and brush slapping at us, the leaves under our feet slippery on the downhill slope.

The rumble of an engine fading into the distance was a welcome sound. That would be the nearest patrol moving away to close the circle, thinking we were approaching from the south.

But we still had about a quarter of a mile before we hit the pump house.

We ran along one side of the creek, using it as our guide to the pump house. Rain came down harder. Each footstep sent wet up to my knees. My wounds were healed enough that they weren't bleeding. While running in the rain wasn't exactly my idea of easy, I was in good shape and could handle it.

Welton seemed to have some trouble keeping up, his breathing going too hard too fast, and I remembered that Abraham said he had had lung problems when he was a child.

Foster, who was still bringing up the rear, finally knelt and refused to go a step farther until Welton got on his back.

I thought Welton would argue, but he just cussed, then got on Foster's back.

As for Foster, he was a tireless machine, a mountain

of muscle and scars and stitches and wires. Grim as a gravestone; determined as death.

Gloria ran beside me, and Neds clipped along at our heels. None of us wasted time on talk.

Finally, finally, the pump house came into view. There was only one narrow door into the little structure. As far as I could tell, no one had thought it was anything more than a pump house.

Which was true. It really did pump the water up to the property and out to the fields. Beneath it, however, was Dad's lab.

I wasn't sure that we needed Dad's lab, but the feed to the electric fences could be controlled from there.

We slowed our approach. Just because most of the patrol was dealing with the diversion south didn't mean they wouldn't have eyes out here.

Abraham checked the screen again.

No sign that we'd been spotted. I strode up to the door and opened it, and Foster and Welton rushed inside into the dark with me, the others waiting outside, hidden in the trees that surrounded the pump house.

"Are you ready?" I asked, my hand on the breaker for the electric fences.

"Just. A second." Welton opened the briefcase, looked up as if getting his compass bearings, then nodded. "Do it."

I pulled the toggle, breaking the feed.

"And now: chaos." Welton turned a dial and flipped a switch.

Nothing. I couldn't hear anything.

"Is it working?" I asked. "Welton, tell me that thing of yours is working."

He held up one finger, his head bent, as if listening for a faint call of a whistle.

That's when I heard it. The not-at-all-faint scream of a man, followed by gunfire and the warbling hiss of a very angry Lizard that sent chills through my bones.

"Music," Welton said. "Why haven't I made a dragon? I really should do so. Such a fun beastie."

"Lizard," I said absently. "Are we clear yet?"

Abraham and the others were outside, waiting for our signal.

"Hold on." Welton scrolled through what appeared to be a couple dozen camera feeds on my property, focused around the house.

The guards who had been stationed on the porch by the kitchen door and around the perimeter of the house had all left to take care of the three-story reptile tearing its way through the outbuildings.

Bullets bounced off the beast's thick hide. Lizard was lightning fast when it got going, and it was going now: a streak of muscle and scales that moved too far, too fast between each eye blink, stopping only long enough to smash guards, vehicles, and weapons into an oily mash.

"Can't see inside the house, but that's as clear a path as I think we'll get," he said.

"Good enough." I racked a round in my rifle and walked out of the pump house. I signaled the others in the brush to follow.

Sneaking up on the place wasn't going to do us much good. Welton insisted he had control of all eyes on the place and had blocked or false-fed the other drones and satellites and spy devices that any other House might have put in place.

Abraham, Quinten, Neds, and Gloria strode out of the trees, guns ready.

We broke into a jog and made quick work of the old path up to the yard, where Abraham made us pause to scope out the house.

"Still no guards," I said.

"Ain't right," Left Ned said.

"Nothing's right," I said. "Ready?"

Abraham nodded.

We exited the scant cover and crossed the yard to the kitchen door. In the distance, Lizard threw a vehicle that came crashing down to the west, taking out a good section of our pear orchard. An explosion rocked the air.

I was a step ahead of Abraham. Quinten was behind him, then Gloria and Neds.

I opened the kitchen door and strode in, rifle tucked against my shoulder.

The kitchen was pretty much as I'd left it: mostly clean, smelling of freshly brewed tea, and no new blood on the floor.

I heard voices in the other room; one of them sounded like Boston Sue. The other was my grandmother. My heart rattled in my chest. She was alive. Alive enough to be talking. That was a good start.

"Come in, Matilda, Quinten," Reeves Silver's voice called out from the other room. "You too, Abraham and Mr. Harris. We've just brewed the tea."

22

*Quinten won't stop making stupid, rash deci-
sions. I'm worried he has a death wish.*
                        —from the journal of E. N. D.

Reeves Silver was in my house, with my grandmother.
I glanced at Abraham. His lips were pressed together, and he frowned. Probably thinking something
along the line of what I was thinking.

If we stormed into the room, shooting, Grandma was
bound to be hurt.

We had planned to surrender, after all. I lowered my
rifle and walked through the short adjoining hallway to
the living room.

"Matilda Case," Reeves said. "You are looking well."

The head of House Silver wore a casual sweater and
slacks, his white hair brushed up and back from his
tanned face, giving his blue eyes a glacial glint.

He stood at the far side of the room, leaning on the
old stone fireplace.

Grandma was in her comfortable chair, which had
been placed in the middle of the room. She was knitting,

the three pocket-sized sheep in her lap. To one side of her was the generously proportioned Boston Sue, who had a cup of tea in one hand and a gun pointed at my grandmother in the other.

Three guards, heavily armored and heavily weaponed, stood near Reeves, their guns trained on us.

"Why don't you put your weapons down?" Reeves suggested. "We'll have some tea, and we'll see if we can't all get through this little business conversation unbloodied."

The clack of guns behind us made me glance over my shoulder. Three more guards stepped into the room, guns aimed at our heads.

Neds flicked me a look, and I shook my head slightly. I refused to get into a shoot-out that would kill my grandmother before the smoke cleared.

"Call off your men," I said, "and we'll talk."

Reeves pursed his lips. "You're saying I should stand here, without any weapon in my hands"—he lifted his palms just to prove that point—"while each of you has a gun? That is called an inhospitable negotiation climate. Not my favorite way to do business. So no. However," he continued like he was just warming up to the beginning of a meeting, "if you put *your* guns on the floor, I will have my men leave the room so that we can get on with our talk."

"There's nothing to talk about," I said. "This is my land, this is my home, and this is my grandmother. You are trespassing. And you are going to leave. Now."

Reeves smiled, but there was no warmth in it. "You know what I like about these kinds of stalemates, Matilda?" he asked. "They can last for hours. Or days. I have all the time in the world. What about you?"

My heart tripped into a fast beat. He knew. He knew we had no time—well, very little time. He knew that I'd do anything to keep my grandmother safe, just as I'd done anything to keep my brother safe.

What I needed was a quick solution. Bloodless and bulletless, if possible.

"Fine." I placed my rifle on the coffee table to my left. "My gun's down. Tell your guards to get the hell out of my living room."

"Done." Reeves wrapped his hands together. "Please," he said to the guards, "wait outside."

I signaled for Abraham and the others to put their weapons down, which they did, Neds the most grudgingly.

The guards walked out the front door, and I heard their boots cross the porch and crunch in the gravel. I also head the Lizard warbling and the thunderous crack of a tree being uprooted.

If we got out of this, I'd have months of repair to do on the place.

"Now," I said, "you are going to give me one good reason not to shoot you."

"Other than Boston Sue has a gun on your grandmother? I suppose if you'd like to risk her point-blank aim, then by all means . . . take your shot. But the moment you do, all the forces I called off when I got here— not just my guards, but all the other House forces who had surrounded your house, including drop units that were carrying a squadron of soldiers armed with incendiary rounds—will be crawling over you. In seconds."

It might be a lie. It might not.

"What do you want, Reeves?" Quinten asked.

"Mr. Case. I hope you're feeling better now that you've gotten a bit of fresh air. Your release from Slater Orange's prison seems to suit you."

"You wouldn't be here, in person, trying to hold all the cards in your hand, if you weren't desperate for something we have," Quinten went on as if Reeves hadn't even spoken. "What do you want?"

"I want a deal."

"For what?" Quinten asked.

We were still standing on one side of the living room, and Reeves still leaned on the fireplace.

Bo hadn't said a word since we'd come into the room, other than to give me a smug sort of smile that made me want to slap her.

"I trusted you," I said to her.

"Oh, baby sweet," she said, "that was your mistake. Trust is fine, but money makes much louder promises."

Grandma finally noticed all the commotion going on around her. She stopped knitting, her face a mix of confusion and worry. Then she noticed me.

"Matilda?"

"I'm here, Grandma," I said. "It's okay. You're okay."

"What is wrong?" she asked. "Is something wrong?"

"No," I said, "everything is good. We were just saying that everything is going to be fine. You have some tea there you could drink."

She looked around, spotted the cup on the table next to her, and made a happy sound.

"My proposal," Reeves said, "is a simple merger between our two Houses. House Silver and House Brown. Over the years I've been working with people from House Brown and I have been pleased with their . . .

flexible sense of morality and *infinite* need for money. Wouldn't you agree, Mr. Harris?"

"Fuck bricks, Reeves," Left Ned said. "Cut your deal or call your troops before I get it into both my minds to blow your head off out of boredom."

"You want me to cut to the chase?" Reeves asked. "Fine. Here's the chase: I want House Brown. All of it. Off record, of course. I want full access to every pocket and farm and compound and bunker stashed away in the world. Names, numbers, resources, capabilities."

"We don't own House Brown," I said. "It can't be bought. It's a collection of people who make up their own minds on how they live and what they do. Those people's lives are not up for sale."

"What I want," he repeated, "are your records, your contacts, names, and the history you have on every member of House Brown. All of them. I want all the information you own. You are the communication hub for House Brown, are you not? That is what all that equipment in the basement is for. Well, that's what all the equipment *was* for, wasn't it?"

A chill washed through me and an unshakable fear clutched my gut. That equipment in the basement was what Quinten was going to use to trigger his time travel. If Reeves had damaged it, destroyed it, taken it, our plan would be worthless and I'd be dead in a few minutes.

"You can't own something we have no influence over," Quinten said, refusing to react to the idea that Reeves had destroyed the equipment.

"But you *do* have influence over each and every person in House Brown. You will explain to them that you've made a deal with House Silver that is in their best interests. Of course, they can stay off grid and under radar—that is one of the things I most like about House Brown. But they will do business for me whenever I call upon them to do so. I will pay monthly stipends. A little more credit in their pockets for nothing more than their silence and occasional help."

"Help?" Quinten asked. "Help for what? Smuggling illegal compounds and products below House notice? Transporting or killing people and the other unfortunates who cross you or get in the way of your power plays and House politics?"

"You want House Brown to be your pet criminals?" I asked.

"Not at all," he said. "I want House Brown to fall under my care. I want to nurture it and give the people in the House the niceties they currently lack. In return, I will help House Brown become fully recognized among the world powers. It will have a voice among the Houses. Isn't that what you wanted, Matilda? Wasn't that the price you expected House Gray to pay for owning you?"

"House Brown won't have their voice," I said. "They'll have *your* voice. This isn't about charity, Reeves. This is about you claiming people and using them however it suits you."

"Well. These things do tend to happen that way. I am offering to lift House Brown out of the squalor, dirt, and shame of its past. The past of a failed rebellion and a war that they lost—decades ago. I am offering them victory. I will stand beside them and help House Brown become strong. A force in the world."

All the pretty spin he put on those lies didn't change the fact that he wanted House Brown for reasons that would only benefit him. He already was in position to take over House Orange, and if he owned House Brown, he would become a very powerful man indeed.

He once told me all the world was a game board, and he was the only one who knew how to make the pieces dance. And they were dancing right into his control.

The last thing House Brown wanted was to be under another House's rule. Reeves Silver was right: people who were now a part of House Brown were the sons and daughters of those who had fled from being owned by the other Houses.

Freedom was more than an empty word for them.

It was not a coin that could be traded.

"No one owns House Brown," I repeated. "Not us, and certainly not you."

"I don't think that you own it, Miss Case. But you are respected within it. You and your brother. All I need is your approval on a few key matters. When I call on you to endorse my desires, you will do so. Quickly and without falsity. In exchange, I will ask your fellow House Brown neighbor, Boston Sue there, not to murder your grandmother."

I didn't look at Bo or Grandma; I just kept my eyes on the devil.

"We contact House Brown," I said. "Tell them we approve of the new management, and you walk out of here, leaving us all to live happily ever after?"

"Oh no," he said. "Not at all. There is a price on your head. Yours and Abraham's. You will both come with me—your lovely grandmother too. We'll leave your brother to send out the message to House Brown."

"No," Abraham said, speaking up for the first time since we'd stepped into the room.

"This is the *only* offer you are going to get, servant," Reeves snapped. "You shouldn't even be breathing right now. You're mine to do with as I please, Abraham Seventh."

"I am no man's property," Abraham said in a low rumble. "My allegiance is to House Gray, not Silver."

"Such delusions of your station in life," Reeves said. "Oscar was soft. You liked him that way. You made him that way. You used him and that soft head of his so you could get what you wanted. Oh yes. I know how you made him think you were his friend while you made decisions behind the scenes. But Oscar is dead now. And that death is on *your* hands."

"*You* killed him," Abraham said in a way that was a promise, a threat.

"No," Reeves Silver said, "my bitch of a galvanized, Helen, killed him. Do you really think I would order her to shoot another head of a House in plain sight at the most publically viewed event of the year? Do you know what that did to my plans?"

"I know *exactly* what you would order her to do," Abraham said. "You know we talk, don't you? The stitched? Helen was more than happy to tell me what you had done to her. And what you'd told her to do. If Slater hadn't shot me, I would have been there to stop her."

That surprised me. I didn't know if Abraham and Helen had talked in the short amount of private time the galvanized had spent together before the gathering. I did know Helen didn't seem to like me much. But maybe she was just angry and trying to get out of doing something she didn't want to do. Something that could lock her away for life.

Although I'd seen her eyes when she shot Oscar. There had been no regret in them.

Truth or bluff, Abraham's comment was enough to make Reeves pause.

"Willing or unwilling," Reeves said. "You are mine. All of you. Mr. Case here has convinced you both that he can do something to stop you from dying today. That is not true. There is no break in time from that ancient experiment. There is just this sorry, desperate child-man who can't get over Mommy and Daddy dying in the front yard. He has convinced himself he can travel through time."

He was angry, yelling. And he was wasting our time.

"He's deluded!" he said. "The only reality here is my generous offer, the gun in Boston Sue's hand, and the snipers who have you in their sights. You will deal with me, or, so help me, I will just *kill* you all and remove you from my list of problems."

"We'll do it," I said. "We'll give you House Brown."

Abraham didn't look my way, but every muscle in his body tensed, his fists curling into a white-knuckle grip.

"Tilly," Right Neds warned.

I wasn't listening to him. And I didn't believe Reeves about the time event not being true.

I wanted Grandma out from under that gun, and I wanted access to the machine in the basement. I didn't care how greedy or crazy Reeves Silver was. Let him think we would do what he wanted. He could have his game.

There were only minutes left before time was going to end me.

Anything I agreed to would either change after I died

and Quinten fought for what he really wanted out of the deal with Reeves, or I went back in time and changed this so that none of us had to talk our way out of a life of servitude.

"I'll say whatever you want me to say to House Brown," I said. "Just take the gun off Grandma and keep her out of the negotiations. I'm agreeing to be yours, Reeves. You own me. I will stand and do as you ask as long as you leave my grandmother out of it. Out of all of this."

Reeves's gaze flicked between me, my brother, and Abraham. I didn't look at either of them, but I didn't have to to know how angry they were.

Well, I hoped we'd have time to argue about how stupid I had been to play into Reeves' hands and agree to his deal.

But first we'd need time if we were going to save our asses.

"And do you also agree to bend knee to me and my rule, Abraham Seventh?" he asked.

Abraham was a stubborn, prideful man, for all the humblest of things he had done for the people in this world. He had sacrificed his own life and freedom for the lives and freedom of others. But I didn't think he was going to do Reeves any favors.

"I will not stand in the way of House Brown following Matilda and Quinten Case's orders," Abraham said.

It was much more than I'd expected him to concede. It was not a yes. It was nowhere near a yes, but it was not exactly a no either. I just hoped it was enough to satisfy Reeves.

"That is a very hesitant acceptance," Reeves noted.

"I follow my sister's word," Quinten said, with a timely interruption. "As does House Brown. You will have us, Reeves Silver, if anyone in this world can."

"In return," I said, "you will release our grandmother, and you, Boston Sue, and all your damned snipers and guards will get off our property. This land is ours. We keep it. We own it. We will bow to you, and we will give you our service and do what we can to convince House Brown to listen to you, but this land remains ours. Is that enough of an agreement?"

He considered it for what felt like an hour. How long had we been talking, negotiating? How much time did we really have left?

"Yes," he said. "It will do." He stepped away from the fireplace. "There's just one more thing."

Guards rushed back into the room, guns trained on each of us.

I twitched toward my weapon.

Reeves raised his voice. "Uh-uh. You are outnumbered, and they are in full body armor and shock shields. Your bullets will do them no damage. They, however, are armed with hollow-point and Shelley dust rounds."

He strolled up behind Grandma and patted her shoulder. "The lovely elder Case will be coming with me."

"What's that?" Grandma said, craning her neck to look at him. "Do I know you?"

"We're going for a ride," Reeves said, "And so are you, Abraham Seventh."

"No," I said, the wind knocked out of me. "That wasn't the deal. Grandma stays here. Abraham stays here."

"I'll go," Abraham said.

"You will not," I said.

He turned to me. "I will. I'm sure it won't be long before I see you again."

Time travel. If we could still trigger our way into the past, maybe this would all be different. Maybe we'd have time to save Mom and Dad, save Oscar, save Grandma and Abraham, and stay out of this mess completely.

If it worked.

We didn't have the journal. We didn't have any kind of guarantee.

This might actually be the last time I saw him.

"Don't," I said. "Please."

"This isn't good-bye," Abraham said.

"And if it is?"

His eyes clouded. "I'll find you again. No matter how long it takes me. I promise you that."

"You will return our grandmother to us," Quinten said to Reeves. "Unharmed, as soon as we make our announcements to House Brown."

"Of course, of course," Reeves Silver said, looking between Abraham and me and seeing far more than I wanted him to see.

"You have a week," he continued. "Get the message out. Tell House Brown they will be following you in following me."

He snapped his fingers, and two guards moved forward and put their hands on Grandma's arms to help her out of the chair.

"Matilda?" she asked as the sheep tumbled to the floor and ran around in circles, bleating pitifully. "Why are there men here? So many men?"

"It's okay, Grandma. Abraham and you are going for a ride. He'll look after you." It was a lie. I knew Reeves wouldn't let Abraham anywhere near her. I knew Abraham, in volunteering to go with Reeves, had just signed himself up for torture, imprisonment, or worse.

"Here now, Mrs. Case," Abraham said kindly. "Let me walk with you."

He gave the guards a look, telling them to stand aside. To my surprise, they glanced at Reeves, who nodded.

Accusing galvanized of being criminals did not wipe out the decades the galvanized had been seen as stars, warriors, and an authority second only to the heads of Houses. So I supposed it was no wonder that the guards stepped aside respectfully and let Abraham help Grandma out of the house.

"One week," Reeves said as he walked to the door. "I expect results. Don't disappoint me."

Boston Sue followed him out the door, and then the guards all walked out too.

"Son of a bitch," I said. I strode to the door and watched as Abraham, Grandma, Reeves, and several guards climbed into a heli that was ready for takeoff. The rest of the guards climbed into vehicles.

Lizard was thrashing its way through the barn, throwing hay and beams and cockatrice into the sky. It was raining harder now, lightning stitching across the clouds.

"We have to stop them," I said. "Quinten, we have to do something."

"Nothing we do will matter if we don't get downstairs. Now." He jogged down the hall.

"Neds, keep an eye on Lizard, okay?" I said before following Quinten. "It should wear itself out soon since there aren't any more people to smash, but if it looks like it's headed our way, yell."

"Got it," he said.

I jogged the hall. Quinten had left the door open. I took the wooden steps down into what used to be our secret communications hub for House Brown.

"Oh no," I said softly.

Reeves and his men had torn the place apart. They had smashed everything: screens, satellite links, radios, video feed, telephones, telegraphs—everything. What had once been an amazing blend of high and old tech—brass, wood, rubber, wire, slick plastics, crystal, and glass carefully gathered together, maintained, and restored—now looked like a shattered junk pile.

"We can still make this work," Quinten said, righting a table that had been thrown on its side. "We can do this."

I didn't think we could, but I didn't tell him that. We had—what—an hour left?

"What do you need from me?" I asked.

"Welton." He hurried to the tool cabinet in the back of the room and scrounged through it. "Get Welton. Quickly!"

I rushed up the stairs, checked the living room. "All clear?"

"We're good," Gloria said. "Quinten?"

"He could probably use a hand. Down the open door at the end of the hall."

Gloria started that way. I jogged to the kitchen.

"Where you going?" Left Ned called out.

"Welton." I jogged out the door and ran down the familiar path to the pump house. Lizard must have calmed down some. It was raining hard and the wind had picked up quite a bit. I didn't hear any demolition or screams of people being smashed. The blades of the heli were already out of my range of hearing and so were the engines of the vehicles full of soldiers.

Just moments ago, we'd been surrounded. We were still surrounded. I knew Reeves must have left snipers on the ground and drones in the air to watch us. But right now the only thing I could do to make any of this better was to get Welton to help my brother fix the device that would give us a loophole to travel in time.

If that worked, I would be the one going back in time instead of Quinten. I would try to convince Alveré Case to change his experiment. To make it right so I didn't die.

This is crazy.

Grandma was in Reeves' hands. Abraham would be tried as a murderer.

My brain was so tied up in the tangle of worries that I didn't even see the man who stood at the turn in the path until I was almost upon him.

Robert Twelfth — or, rather, Slater Orange — raised a gun at my head. "Take me to your brother — now."

23

Quinten was gone for a while again. He doesn't think I know what he's doing, what he's looking for, or how dangerous it is.

—*from the diary of E. N. D.*

It occurred to me that an awful lot of people who had been or were currently heads of Houses were now on my property, waving around guns and telling me what to do.

I had had enough of it.

"Put the damn gun down," I said, wiping the rain out of my eyes. "Shooting me won't get you anything. If you want to see my brother, if you want to live, then get out of my way, Slater."

His face twisted up into a snarl I'd never seen on the kinder Robert, who had once been behind those eyes.

"You will not give me orders, filth," he said.

"Filth?" I repeated. "Fine. Let's do this. Do you know what my brother was looking for before you locked him up? Do you know why he risked hiring himself out to all the Houses—yours included—so he could have access to their histories?"

"He was looking for your grandmother's journal," Slater said. "I am not a fool."

"Good. Then I'll only have to say this once. In her journal was the calculations for the Wings of Mercury experiment. An experiment that killed everyone in a fifty-mile radius, except for the thirteen people who went on to become galvanized.

"You are wearing one of those bodies, and you think it's immortal. Well, it isn't. Today, in less than an hour, we are going to have to deal with the repercussion of time being broken. When time snicks back into place and all the galvanized die, our three-hundred-year extension on life will be over. The bill is up. Done. And you'll be dead."

"I don't believe you."

"I don't care. Dead is dead. Get out of my way while I'm still asking you nice."

The snap of a broken branch made Slater spin.

Just in time to see Foster First rush out of the brush, straight at him.

Slater fired half a dozen shots into the big man. But Foster kept coming. He swung a huge fist and clocked Slater so hard, the slighter man was lifted off his feet before he slammed into the wet ground. That blow would have snapped a man's neck. If Slater weren't in a galvanized body, he'd be dead.

I scrambled for the gun that flew out of his hand, dug it out of the brush, then turned it on Slater before he regained his feet.

"Just stay down," I ordered.

Foster stood above him, rain soaking the hat Welton had made him wear and sending rivulets down along his stitches, his scars. His fists were locked at his sides. Hatred burned in his eyes.

"Thanks, Foster," I said. "Is Welton around?"

Right about then I heard footsteps. Welton walked up the path at an even pace, his breathing more labored than it should be, a slap of red spreading from his cheeks out across his wet pale face.

"Was coming to get you," I said. "Quinten needs you at the house, quick."

He nodded, then stopped just behind and to the side of Foster, looking down at Slater.

"So, you found a way, didn't you?" he asked, searching Robert's face for signs of the transplanted Slater Orange. "A way out of that death-trap body of yours you filled with chemicals to keep alive. But this solution is cruel. You murdered a man when you implanted Robert Twelfth into your dying body."

"Galvanized aren't men," Slater said.

"I've never agreed with that," Welton said. "But you know the laws. Galvanized can't rule. You will never be the head of a House. Reeves Silver is just using you. He will kill you and take over House Orange the moment it suits him."

"*I* will be the first galvanized to rise to power," Slater said. "I am immortal. I have all the time I need to make the world mine." He stabbed at his chest. "I will continue long after you mewling mortals are dust and forgotten."

Welton's eyes flicked up to me. "Did you tell him about the time break?"

"Yep."

"Did you tell him he's about to be dead?"

"He had too much megalomania in his ears to hear me."

Welton flashed me a bright grin. "He's always been a little tight-screwed."

"Well, right now he's in my way."

"Oh?" Welton waved a couple fingers toward Foster. "We need him to be quiet."

Slater pushed back, trying to get his feet under him, real terror on his face as Foster grabbed hold of his shirt in one hand and pounded him in the face with the other until he was unconscious.

"Will that do?" Welton asked.

"Perfectly. I have rope at the house. Let's talk and walk."

Welton patted Foster's shoulder. "I've wanted you to hit Slater in the face for years," he said. "I'm just sorry it's your friend's body he's wearing. Are you okay, buddy?"

Foster looked like he still wanted to pound something, but he gave Welton a grunt and a rusty nod.

"Good," Welton said. "How about you pick him up and bring him along?"

Foster bent and picked up Slater as if he didn't weigh any more than a wet kitten.

We headed back to the house as quickly as Welton could walk. Which wasn't nearly fast enough for my spinning thoughts.

Less than an hour left.

"I was coming your way for a reason," I said. "Quinten wanted you."

"Do you know why?"

"Reeves destroyed our equipment."

"Reeves? As in, Head of House Silver Reeves?"

"He was here. You were right: those guards were his. He held our grandmother hostage."

"Where is he now?"

"Gone. With Grandma and Abraham."

"Reeves Silver has Abraham?" Welton stopped talking for a short distance so he could get his breathing under control. "Why did he leave you here?"

"He wants us to sign House Brown over to him."

I didn't know if Welton was taking a little time to think that over or if he just didn't have any extra breath. We were nearly to the house when he spoke again.

"I always thought he had his thumb on House Brown," he said. "All the smuggling rings and so on."

"Nothing official that I've heard about," I said. "All the Houses use members of House Brown to get what they want. Mostly none of us care, since House Brown is just folk trying to get by on their own. If a House hires them for legal or illegal work ... Well, I can understand doing something because you need to keep food on the table."

"Still ... odd," Welton said.

"To negotiate with us and tell us to step down from running House Brown?" I said. "Not that odd. A lot of people trust Quinten and me to give them good information. With the Houses currently in such chaos, a lot of House Brown is going to hole up, pull stakes, and hide away until things sort out. Those who remain in contact with the outside world will be looking for clean information from us. Reeves wants to be in control of what information we give them."

"There's more," Welton said. "Must be more that he wants."

"Oh, I'm sure of it," I said. "Right now, I don't care."

We'd finally made it to the house, taking a good ten minutes for a walk that shouldn't have taken more than half that. Ten minutes we didn't have to spare.

I glanced at Slater, who was still unconscious in Foster's arms. I didn't think he'd wake up before we handled the time situation, but just in case, I wanted him tied down tight. Slater might not be a man who knew how to physically fight, but that body he was wearing was just as uncommonly strong as mine was.

I pushed open the kitchen door and nearly walked into Ned's shotgun.

"What the hell is he doing here?" Neds asked, the barrel of the gun notching toward Slater.

"Taking over the world, apparently," I said. "Drop him in a chair, Foster. We'll truss him up."

Foster pulled a chair out with his foot and dumped Slater unceremoniously into it.

"Neds, get the rope," I said. "The strong stuff. And remember he's galvanized and can snap that chair if he flexes right. So don't be shy with the knots."

"I know how to keep a man still," Left Ned said, "stitched or otherwise."

"Good." I measured Welton's breathing. It seemed a little less labored. "Think you can handle some stairs?"

"Up?" he asked with a little dread.

"Basement."

"Lead the way."

Foster took a step to follow us, but Welton shook his

head. "Stay here and watch him." He pointed at Slater. "I'll be fine with Matilda."

Foster frowned, and his pink eyes flicked up to meet my gaze.

"I'll make sure he sits and rests," I said. "We need his brains more than anything else right now. I can do whatever repair work needs to be done on the equipment."

Foster reluctantly moved back closer to Slater, positioning himself within punching range. Between Foster's obvious dislike of the man and Neds' shoot-first-and-apologize-never attitude, I wasn't sure what kind of shape Slater was going to be in when we came back upstairs.

If we came back upstairs. Time was falling away, faster and faster. We had—what—thirty minutes?

"And tell Neds to frisk him, okay?" I said to Foster. "If Slater was stupid enough to bring our grandmother's journal out with him, it'd be all kinds of useful."

I led Welton down the hall and through the open door to the basement.

He took a deep breath at the top of the stairs and then walked down them at a steady pace, his hand gripping the rail.

"How's it going?" I asked, following Welton.

"Just fine," Quinten said. "I should have it up and running in a month." He was crouched in front of the crate-sized timetable he'd made. It seemed to be in one piece, though it canted slightly to the right, one wooden foot on one corner broken off. He didn't seem concerned about the casing that surrounded the invention.

Instead he'd pulled out yards of wires, bits of metal and glass, and thin, flexible tubes filled with liquid. I had no idea what any of it did or was supposed to do, and wouldn't begin to guess which parts of it might be broken.

Gloria stood next to him, a cloth packet of tools spread out on a table next to her. She had a calm but sort of grim expression, as if she knew the patient wasn't going to pull through but the doctor hadn't figured that out yet.

"This is, well, this *was* impressive," Welton said, stepping out into the rubble of our dreams. "I knew you had your hands on most of the modern communication and computing technology, but a telegraph?" He walked over to the huge wooden desk that was demolished, where the telegraph key lay on top of the debris. "And is that a ... shortwave radio?" He chuckled and clapped his hands together. "Delightful!" he declared. "What other old tricks did you have up your sleeves? Smoke signals and lanterns in the night?"

"All we have right now," Quinten said, "is a problem. How much research did you really do into the Wings of Mercury experiment?"

Welton walked over to where my brother was systematically soldering wires into a network of plastics and crystals and rare metals he had carefully balanced on a tray across his lap.

I jogged over to the broken bank of screens over the curved desk and picked up a chair. I brought it over for Welton.

"I scoured every record and lead I could find," Welton said. "It was the beginning of Foster's experimentation, and I wanted to know the source of it. Before I gave him any modifications, I wanted make sure I wasn't doing him any harm."

"So, you know how time broke?"

"No, not at all."

I offered him the chair, and Welton nodded his thanks and sat. "You do know it's mostly myth and legend, that experiment? The records, the *real* hard evidence, has been lost, and the scattered mentions and notes that survived in the histories are suppositions and hearsay."

Quinten didn't stop, didn't even pause in what he was doing. "The journal was the records," he said.

"We don't have the journal," Welton said.

"I understand the situation," Quinten said, carefully placing a thin glass tube with wires attached at both ends back into the cabinet. "And I'm as certain as I can be that my calculations will change the event so that we all don't die in a few minutes."

"Wait," I said. "What do you mean, *we all don't die?* You told me when the break in time mends, it will just be the galvanized who die."

"I omitted some details," he said.

"You *lied* to me?"

"No, I just didn't tell you all of the outcomes."

"That's called lying."

"What," Gloria said, "is going to happen, Quin? If you don't fix that? If time mends without us doing anything about it?"

He carried on with what he was doing, steady hands, steady progress, like a man who had only moments to defuse a bomb. And I supposed that was pretty close to what he was doing—only the bomb was time, and his wire cutter was a pile of broken junk on the floor.

"The blast will kill everyone in an hundred-mile radius. Maybe a thousand."

A thousand-mile radius would wipe out most of the big cities on the eastern seashore, and everything between here and the Mississippi.

"Thousands," I breathed.

"Millions," Welton said. "Millions will die."

"How much time do we have left?" I asked.

Gloria looked at my brother's pocket watch. "Eighteen minutes."

24

*I didn't want to tell him. That I remember the
infinity bell. That I remember time breaking.
That I know he gave up everything to change
the world.*

—from the diary of E. N. D.

"Quinten, you have to get out of here," I said.

"No."

"I can make you leave."

"No, you can't. And there is a chance, a small one, that if
we are close enough to the time event, we might survive."

I did not believe him. "How?"

"Think of it as the eye of a storm," Quinten said.
"Time will mend around us, but the repercussions from
that event will radiate outward. Destroying half of the
people on this side of the country."

I didn't know where Reeves had taken Abraham and
Grandma. But it hadn't been enough time for them to be
thousands of miles away.

Which meant Grandma and Abraham were in the
blast zone too.

And so were all the people—families—who were a part of House Brown, and all the other people who worked for the Houses and were trying to make their way through the world as best they could.

Billions of peoples will die.

Unless he went back in time to try to change the experiment.

Except I was the one who was going to go back in time. I couldn't let him die. But we weren't going to have a chance to fight about that if we didn't get the device of his up and running.

"What can I do?" I asked.

"Here," Welton stood stiffly from the chair and walked over to kneel next to Quinten. "This will be faster." He reached into the cabinet and adjusted something while Quinten nodded and continued soldering.

"Is there something I can get you?" I asked. "Either of you?" I hated standing here with my figurative hands in my figurative pockets, while the world not so figuratively came to an end.

"Nothing," Quinten said.

"Now, if you had the journal . . ." Welton said.

"Or our grandmother," Quinten said.

"For what?" Welton asked. "Cookies and milk?"

"No. It's her journal, and since she wrote it, we thought we could get the information from her."

"Your grandmother had the equation all along?" Welton asked. "Why didn't you just stay home and talk to the woman?"

"She's very old," Quinten said. "Her memories are scattered. We'd hoped . . . well, it doesn't matter."

Except that it did. We needed the journal or someone

who had read it. Quinten and I had never read it, but Slater owned it. He must have read it. Somewhere in that head of his might be the information we needed.

"Slater!" I said, running for the stairs.

I rushed into the kitchen, where Foster stood in the exact same position, staring at the unconscious Slater as if waiting for him to wake up so he could punch him out again.

Neds rested one shoulder against the wall where he could see into the living room and out the kitchen window at the same time, shotgun still in his hands.

"Touch him," I said to Neds. "Touch Slater and see if you can get the vision of what he read in the journal."

Right Ned frowned. "I don't think that will work, Tilly. I can't pick and choose what I see."

"Try. Please try. All we need is the calculations, so Quinten can check his against them."

"Which could be pages and pages of formulas," Left Ned said.

"Please."

They held my gaze for a moment, maybe as surprised as I was at the desperation in my voice.

"Get a piece of paper," Left Ned said.

"Thank you." I opened a drawer, the wrong one, then opened two more before I found paper and a pencil. "I know you don't like doing this. I know what I'm asking you. If we get out of this somehow, I want you to know I'll pay you back."

"And if we don't?" Right Ned said, taking the pencil.

"I want you to know that I've always considered you my friend even when I was angry about you spying on us."

He smiled and set the paper on the table, switching the

pencil to his right hand so Left Ned could write, and then reaching out with his left hand to touch Slater, who was trussed up tighter than a ham hock, his eyes still closed.

Neds touched Slater's hand. I knew skin-to-skin contact worked best for him to see the visions in other folks' minds.

Right Ned jerked his head back and grunted, scowling like he'd just caught a whiff of something rotted and foul.

Left Ned swore under his breath and clenched his fingers around the pencil, not looking at Slater, not looking at anything but the visions in Slater's mind.

"Are you okay?" I asked, but he wasn't paying attention to me.

A loud crash from outside the house had me running to the window, Neds' shotgun in my hands. *Lizard?*

Not Lizard. There was an army coming this way, fronted by vehicles that crashed over our fences like they weren't even there.

The vehicles were black. The soldiers wore black.

Dozens of trained fighters moved out to surround the house with more weapons than I'd seen in my life. Reeves Silver hadn't called off the troops. The lying bastard had called them in.

Shit.

"We have company," I said, glancing at the clock on the wall. Five minutes left. "Neds," I said. "Anything?"

"It's . . ." Right Ned said in a strained voice, "impossible to sort a mind in seconds."

"Keep trying." I ran into the living room and gathered up all the guns I could carry. Then I ran back to the kitchen and handed Foster the semiautomatic. "You know how to use this, don't you?"

His expression didn't shift, but he handled that weapon like he'd been born with it. All those wars he'd fought, all the lives the Houses had made him take had left their mark on him. His hands and his eyes were steady as an assassin's.

"I'm going to flip the house locks, if they haven't been cut yet," I said. "That will take care of doors and windows."

I ran back to the pantry on the far side of the kitchen, where one of our main lock stations was set up. There was another control in the basement and one in Dad's lab below the pump house.

Abraham had said he'd never seen scramblers and blockers like those my father, genius brother, and Neds had built, improved, and installed on our house.

I just hoped they'd be enough to buy us five minutes.

I triggered the locks, then the emergency feeds.

A blast my dad called dark static, which had something to do with cosmic physics and good, old-fashioned nuclear electromagnetic pulse, exploded about thirty feet out from the house.

That blast disabled weapons and weapons systems, and would knock a man unconscious for a good five minutes.

I rushed out of the pantry and glanced out the window. A lot of soldiers were on the ground, some of them moaning.

They'd be on their feet soon. Too soon.

"Are you done?" I asked Neds as I grabbed the rifle out of the broom closet. "Did you get the calculations?"

"No," Right Ned said.

"Did you get anything?"

"Tilly," Left Ned turned the paper so I could see it. I took it and the pencil from him. The paper was blank.

"It's a mess in there. What I saw . . . it's not going to do any of us any good."

I nodded, even though everything inside me went a little numb and my ears were ringing. That was it: our last chance to make this right. We had no calculations. My crazy brother was going to try to save the world on a guess. If he could get the machine running in time.

"Thanks for trying," I said. "And, Neds, I'm glad you're my friend."

He nodded. "You too, Matilda," Left Ned said.

"More like family," Right Ned agreed.

I handed him the rifle. "So don't die."

"Back atcha," Right Ned said.

I left the kitchen and started down the stairs. We'd just have to make the best of this.

Something was chiming. A sweet, electric-bell sound. I looked down. The wrist screen Welton had given me was lit up. The chime had been ringing off and on for a half hour; I just hadn't heard it in all the commotion.

I paused, halfway down the stairs, my heart beating hard. That chime meant my crawler had found something. My hack into Robert's records had a hit.

But had it found Grandma's journal?

I coded the unlock sequence.

One item located. I keyed that up. It felt like it took a day, a year, a forever to download the file. I opened it.

Scanned pages in my grandmother's looping handwriting that appeared on the screen. Slater had scanned the journal and copied it to Robert's files!

I let out a whoop and ran down the stairs. "Quinten!"

In the very short time I'd been away, Welton, Quinten, and Gloria had piled a wild array of mismatched instruments and equipment into three stacks, with the timetable cabinet in the center.

Wires of every kind strung out from the cabinet and knotted and looped into and out of the piles of things. It looked like a mechanical spider had gone mad in a junkyard.

"What?" he asked, not looking up.

Quinten and Welton were both sweating hard, hands shaking as they crimped, strung, and shoved things into place, all the while reminding and correcting each other as they rattled out half sentences involving ratios and oscillation rates and words I'd never heard before.

"Is this it?" I jogged to them and shoved the wrist screen in front of him.

"I don't have time," he started angrily. Then his words trickled away.

"Where did you get this?" he demanded. "Where?"

"It's her journal, isn't it?"

"I think so. I think it is. Welton?"

"I'll keep working on this. Look for the calculations."

Quinten flipped through the document so quickly, I was sure he had already missed the information. We didn't have enough minutes for him to read through it a second time.

"Oh," he said softly. "Oh."

He pulled a grease pencil out of his back pocket and grabbed the blank paper I still had clutched in my hand. "This, no." He scratched out a line of letters and numbers and replaced them. "It's this. Easy. Much easier than I thought."

Welton leaned over to look at the paper.

"Yes?" Quinten asked, turning so Welton could better read the paper.

Welton took it out of his hand, his eyes scanning across the page in record time. "Yes. Though it will kill you, Quinten."

"What?" Gloria asked. "We'll be safe in the eye of the storm, right?"

"*We* will," Welton said. "Quinten wants to thread that loop and travel back in time. It will kill him. Any of us humans, actually."

"That's inconclusive," Quinten said. "There's every reason to expect I'll live."

"No," Welton said. "Hardly any reason at all."

"It doesn't matter anyway." I said as I pulled the paper out of Welton's hand. "I'm going instead of you."

"Give me the paper, Matilda," Quinten said.

"I'll live, right?" I asked Welton.

"Don't—" Quinten warned.

"It's more likely that you will, yes," Welton said.

"You son of a bitch," Quinten said. "Don't listen to him, Tilly. I'm going to fix this. I'm going to change this. I'm the one who should risk it. This is my problem to solve."

From that reaction, I knew he'd known all along that my going back was the best chance for survival. He just couldn't stand putting me at risk to do it.

"No," I said, "it's our problem, and I'm going. If I die going back in time, well, I was gonna die here anyway. But you're not going to die now, and I'm not going to let you die in the past. Stay here—stay alive. Love Gloria, if she'll have you. And if everything works out, then we won't even remember this argument, right?"

"She's making sense, Quinten," Welton said. "You know that she is."

"Matilda, please . . ." Quinten searched my face, looking for hope. Everything in my heart was breaking to give it to him, but it was my turn to put my life on the line. To do the right thing for us, the galvanized, and the world. There was no bend in me on that.

"Alveré just needs to see this paper to understand what to change, right?" I asked.

He swallowed and nodded. "Alveré Case should know what to do. It's not a large adjustment. You'll need to find him before he triggers the experiment. Give me the paper," he said. "We need to make sure it can go back with you."

I hesitated. If he took it away, would he give it back?

"I need to put it in this." He pulled his pocket watch out of his pocket and twisted it, revealing a space big enough for the paper if we folded it down tight.

I held out my hand for the watch, and he pressed it into my palm.

"This is the countdown," he said while I folded the paper into a small square and slipped it into the watch.

"It's calibrated with . . . never mind—that isn't important. Press the button when I say *one*, and it will trigger the force to catch the break in time. When you cross back into the past, it will reset and begin a countdown to when the Mercury Wings experiment is triggered. Get to the tower and Dr. Case before time runs out, and show him the paper."

"I will. I promise. And if I don't . . . well, even if I do, I want you to know I love you."

He placed one hand on the side of my face, his fingertips curling at the edge of the stitches tracing the curve of my cheek. "Just look for the tower. It will be huge and somewhere to the west of here. He built his lab beneath it. That's where he'll be."

Then he pulled me into a hard hug, and I hugged him back, wishing I could stay here, wishing my life had never come down to this moment. This might be the last thing I ever did before I died.

"I love you too," he said in a fierce whisper near my ear. "Never forget that."

I nodded and bit the inside of my cheek so I wouldn't cry.

"Time," Welton said. "Now, Matilda. Now."

Quinten stepped to the side, and Welton motioned me toward the center of the contraption.

"Anything else I should know?" I asked, suddenly panicked that I hadn't gotten enough specifics or details about . . . well, anything.

"You know what I know," Quinten said. "But you . . . well, your body was alive back then. You need to avoid her. She was young. Still a child."

"And if her body meets her future body, that's bad, right?"

"Let's not risk it," he said.

A roaring explosion from somewhere above us rattled the ceiling and sent dirt sifting down to the floor.

"They're coming!" Right Ned yelled.

A second explosion blasted so bright, the light spearing the basement was blinding.

"Five!" Quinten yelled, but he might as well have been whispering, for all that I could hear him over the insane rattle of gunfire.

Neds stumbled down the stairs, half of him covered in blood and unresponsive, Left Ned's head lolling to the side.

"No!" I yelled.

"Four!" Quinten said.

Gloria was running past me, trying to reach Neds in all the dust and debris that exploded through the door.

Slater, no longer tied to the chair, was tossed down the stairs. He scrambled to his feet, bloody but still mostly whole.

"Three!" Quinten yelled.

Foster was the last down the ruined stairs, firing round after round of ammo at the surge of soldiers clotting the doorway.

Foster was missing an arm and was drenched in blood. But he held that staircase like a lion taking a last stand. When the bullets ran out, he roared up the stairs and tore the soldiers apart limb from limb.

"Foster!" Welton screamed, "no!" Welton ran toward him, but Slater had found a piece of metal the size of a bat. He swung for Welton's head.

Welton crumpled and fell.

"Two!" Quinten said.

A massive blast pulverized the basement.

It blew Quinten in half before he could say *one*, his mouth half-open in surprise, the top half of him twisting off while the bottom somehow stayed still.

My brother was dead. Gone. Dead.

Everything in me stopped, except my heart that throbbed hard once, twice.

The basement collapsed. Stone, wood, metal, dirt buried Neds, Gloria, Welton, and Slater. They were dead.

Even before I'd had a chance to try to save them, even before the break in time had mended.

Everyone was gone.

We had failed.

Then a great bell rang out, a sound that built up out of the marrow of my bones, filling me, filling the air I breathed, my skin, my muscle, my blood with a single cosmic peal of sound that was more than sound. The universe paused, its voice raised in ecstasy.

I thumbed the button on the watch ...

... and screamed as the infinity bell shattered me to dust.

25

*You gave up everything to change the world
too. I never had the chance to thank you.*
    —from the diary of E. N. D.

Cold rain falling upon me, wet earth below. I was
curled in a ball, shivering. Alone.

I opened my eyes. Darkness. Faint light just beyond
me between slats of stone.

I was not in my basement. I was in the middle of a
field, and it was the middle of the night.

Had I been thrown in the blast? Had I been knocked
unconscious?

The light ahead of me moved, swinging in a long, slow
arc. A single flame burned in the darkness and rain.

A lantern?

I pulled myself up straighter and was surprised when
rain pattered against my bare legs.

I wore a dress and boots and a hat on my head. Even
though I felt all the right proportions to myself, my arms
were short and so were my legs. And in the nearly nonex-
istent light, I could see something else that had changed.

I had no stitches. Not on my hands, my wrists, my ankles. I ran my fingers across my neck, up the side of my cheek. Nothing but smooth skin.

What happened?

I ran away, a tiny voice said.

I jerked and looked around. There wasn't anyone I could see in the tall grasses surrounding me. But the slats of stone were curved at the tops, some shaped like crosses.

A graveyard?

By the church, the little voice said. Only this time I realized the voice was inside my mind. More than a thought or a random impression. This voice belonged to a whole person. I could feel the heavy weight of memories and ideas and fears and needs coiled up in a tangled ball in the middle of my mind.

Are you an angel? the little voice asked. *I prayed for an angel to find me.*

What's your name?

Evelyn Douglas. What's your name?

Matilda.

Okay, this was all kinds of weird. Was I hallucinating? Possessed? Was there a little girl somewhere nearby and my ears were thrown off because of the rain and stones— correction: gravestones—surrounding me? And why was I crouched down in the middle of a graveyard at night in the pouring rain anyway?

I ran away, Evelyn said again. *Can we go to heaven now?*

Why did you run away? I asked. I thought about standing up, and I did. A moment of vertigo swept over me, and I put my hands out to catch myself on the gravestone. Beneath my fingers was carved Douglas 1910.

Whose grave is this? I thought.

Mother and Father. They went to heaven. I want to go too.

Her sadness filled me, and I tried to think comforting thoughts, filling her with warmth and the image of my arms around her, rocking. She calmed almost immediately.

Can we go now?

Not yet. It's not time yet, I thought.

Time. I wondered how much I had left.

The watch! The paper. I checked my dress for pockets. Nothing. Then I crouched down and searched the grass. My fingers finally brushed the cool, smooth curve of the pocket watch, and I clutched it to me like the lifeline it was.

I knew where I must be—or, rather, I knew *when* I must be.

What year is it, Evelyn? I asked.

Nineteen hundred and ten, she said. *Are you a new angel?*

Yes, I thought. *Very new. Is this your dress, Evelyn?* I asked, touching the cloth at my waist.

Yes.

And I'm inside your mind. Talking to you?

Yes, she said a little doubtfully. *A dream. You are a dream and you are going to take me to Mother and Father. Aren't you?*

I will. Of course I will. But I need your help. There's . . . People are going to be hurt if we don't . . . give a message to a man. Do you know a man called Dr. Alveré Case?

No.

Do you know a doctor or scientist who lives nearby?

No.

I got the distinct impression of her turning away from me and pushing shut something like a door between us. She found a pocket of her mind so far away, I couldn't sense her anymore.

Evelyn? Evelyn?

She wasn't answering. Maybe she thought she was still asleep and didn't have to dream me if she didn't want to.

I tucked the watch tightly in my fist—her fist? Our fist, since I was sharing her mind and body—and walked toward the lantern light.

The rain eased a little, but I had to watch the ground so I wouldn't trip on the clumps of heavy wet grass.

That was probably good, because if I had the luxury to focus on anything else, I'd be in a panic. I'd gone back in time like Quinten had supposed I would, but he had been wrong about one thing: it was just my mind, my personality, my thoughts that had survived the travel and were impressed on the brain of this girl—the girl whose body I had been stitched into all those years ago.

Quinten certainly wouldn't have survived this. I'm not sure any mortal human could.

He was right about the pocket watch traveling with me, though I didn't know why it, of all things, would.

That didn't matter. I had to find my great-great-and-then-some-grandfather and convince him I was a grown woman from the future with a highly advanced set of calculations he needed to use to adjust his experimental time machine.

He'd never listen to me in this little girl's body.

I didn't even know where to find him.

Quinten had told me to look for the tower, but it was

so dark out, I couldn't see the top of the steeple on the church ahead of me.

Just take it one step at a time, I told myself. Quinten had said the watch would count down to when the Wings of Mercury experiment was triggered. How much time did I have left?

I tipped the watch in my palm, trying to catch the watery light from the lantern a very tall man was holding just a ways off.

Yellow slipped across the wet pewter, revealing the watch face. Instead of a circle of numbers and two arrow hands, the watch was exactly as I'd seen it last: a liquid screen with a set of geometric shapes floating across it.

And in the center was a very plain digital countdown. Five hours, and steadily decreasing minutes.

That wasn't enough time. Not nearly enough to find the tower, the scientist, and the machine in a world I didn't know, in a time I didn't know.

I hurried over to the man holding the lantern. Since I appeared to be a lost child, I hoped he would be willing to help me.

The lantern—a basic kerosene, lit-wick sort of affair—was low in his hand. The man was tall and wore a long black coat, slick with rain. He had on a brimmed hat and was leaning on a shovel, staring down at a fresh grave.

Seeing him nearly shocked me to silence.

I recognized him.

"Foster?" I said in a voice too young and too quiet. Then, a little louder, "Foster?"

He didn't move for so long, I wondered if he could hear me. If maybe I wasn't even substantial enough in this time to be heard.

Could I be a ghost? Could I be nothing but a stray collection of memories and random neurons firing in this girl's mind?

Was I dreaming?

I tried again, this time reaching out and tugging on the sleeve of his coat. "Foster? Can you hear me?"

Finally, his head moved and he looked down at me.

Even in the uncertain light, I could see that there were no scars, no stitches crossing his face. He didn't look younger, but he was not galvanized. His hair under his brimmed hat was still ghost white and so was his skin. His pink eyes were the same too, and so was the deep, wrenching sorrow in them.

"Go home, child," he said in a rumbling whisper. "There is nothing but death here."

"I'm lost," I said, and I was not lying. "I need to find my family. I need to find Dr. Alveré Case. Please help me. Please."

He stared at me for so long, I wondered if he was in a trance.

"Who did you bury?" I asked.

"My wife," he whispered. "My son."

I place my hand over his, my palm just wide enough to cover his knuckles. "I am so sorry for your loss. I know you need time to grieve. My family . . ."

The image of Quinten ripped apart, dead, filled my mind, and I couldn't breathe past my sorrow.

"My family is dead too," I finally said. "Except for Dr. Case. Please, please help me find him."

"Go," he said. "Run home. The night is dark and cold, and morning will be here soon." He turned away from me and lowered the lantern to the ground. Then he sank the shovel into what remained of the freshly dug ground, spreading muddy soil onto the graves. The lantern caught rain in gold sparks falling like a veil across the graves.

But the light did not touch his face, as if the shadows of his grief were too dense to pierce.

"I know when the world is going to end," I said.

He just kept digging, dirt falling in steady rhythm on top of a grave already buried too deep.

"My world has already ended," he said.

"No," I said. "You are going to live a long life. Much, much longer than any man should, and it's going to be filled with pain. But at the end . . . way at the end, you are going to be among your friends, among the other thirteen people who survive the disaster that's going to hit this town in just a few hours."

He stopped shoveling. "What disaster?"

"Dr. Case is a scientist. He's going to experiment with . . . time. It will kill everyone in a hundred-mile radius."

"What will kill people? Fire? Flood? Landslide?"

"I don't know," I said. "Not exactly."

He shook his head. "Who has been telling you stories?"

"No one. The disaster will happen. I can prove it." I wanted to yell at him. Wanted to tug him with me, make him run, make him help me find the tower before it was too late.

Maybe I couldn't talk him into helping me. Maybe his grief was too deep and my story too fantastic.

"Please," I said, my voice soft but steady. "He built a tower that houses a great machine. He built a machine to break time. He wants to find a way for man to travel in time."

"And how do you know this?"

"Because he did it. Only he did it wrong. His calculations were wrong. I've traveled back in time. To now, to stop it and try to change what he did before people die. Before my family dies."

Another long pause while he considered me. "What is your name?"

"Matilda Case," I said.

He bent, picked up the lantern, and rested the shovel over one shoulder. He started walking, the lantern swinging in his hand. Dawn was just starting to thin the fabric of night. The rain had stopped.

"Come with me, Matilda Case," he said. "You are soaked to the bone."

I hurried to catch up with him, and realized I was shivering. Evelyn hadn't been wearing a coat out here, huddled on her parents' grave. Maybe there was a reason she'd assumed I was an angel who could take her to heaven. Maybe she was hoping to die.

Foster's stride was impossibly long, and I had to jog to catch up. Soon we were out of the tall grass and onto a trail that wound past a church to our left and then opened on a narrow lane.

A horse-drawn wagon waited there, trees lining either side of the lane. Foster pulled back a canvas tarp under which I caught a glimpse of saws and hammers and other tools. He set the shovel in with those tools, covered them, and hooked the lantern to the front of the wagon. He swung up easily into the driver's seat and I stood there, feeling tiny and cold and lost.

"Go around the back to the other side," he said.

I did so, and got a foothold on the passenger's side of

the wagon. I pulled myself up. He reached over and gripped my arm, his hand warm, work hardened, and blistered, and helped pull me onto the plank of wood that served as a seat.

I braced my foot on the front edge of the wagon and held on tight.

Foster snapped the reins and clicked his tongue. The horse started off at a slow walk.

Too slow. At this pace, I'd never find the tower in time. I wrapped my arms around myself, shivering in the wind but keeping my eyes open for any horizon line where I might spot the tower.

"Is that what you're looking for?" he asked.

The wagon broke out from the cover of trees. We were on a slight rise, the lane leading into the town, where little flickers of light—lanterns and candles—shone from the windows of a dozen houses.

Behind those houses, not by more than half a mile, rose an eighteen-story tower that I would have guessed was a lighthouse, except the top of it was a rounded dome—an enormous bowl tipped upside down and balanced on top of the tapered column.

Dawn was smearing muddy yellow light low in the sky, and the sound of living and moving—a rattle of wooden wheels, the clanging of a hammer on metal, the *thunk* of an axe in wood—filled the air.

"That must be it," I said. "Is there a building below it or near it? Do you know where Dr. Case might be? I need to go there now."

"First we'll get you dry," he said.

"No. I don't have enough time. I need to get to that tower."

"I am taking you home," he said, sending the horse down toward town.

"You don't believe me?"

His face was illuminated by the pale sun rising. From his slightly annoyed expression, I knew the answer to my question.

"I can prove everything I said."

"That you are from the future?" He slipped a look my way.

I held out the pocket watch.

He took it out of my hand, stared at it, then rubbed his thumb over the face and frowned. "What is this?"

"A pocket watch that has been in my family for a long time. My brother modified it—changed it—so it would count down how much time I had before Dr. Case's experiment triggers the disaster."

"How is this powered? How is it lit?"

"Batteries and light-emitting diodes. Future stuff," I said.

"This is a countdown?"

"Yes. And when all that time runs out, everyone in this town is going to die. That"—I pointed at the tower—"is going to do something.... Maybe it's an electric pulse; maybe it's sonic. I don't know, but when the experiment is complete, we die."

"You told me I'd live a long life."

I took in a breath and shivered hard before letting it out. One thing Foster was right about: I was soaked to the bone and miserably cold. But cold was the least of my worries.

"The experiment will begin soon. When that happens, everyone dies within a hundred-mile radius," I said, "except for thirteen people. Those thirteen people live. Well, they go unconscious and are brought back to life by scientists in the future.

"The thirteen become known as the galvanized— living creatures who were raised from the dead. You are one of them. The first of the thirteen galvanized who wakes. I'm one of them too. The last."

He shook his head. "Stories. This can't be true."

"It is." He didn't believe me. I wasn't sure there was anything more that would convince him.

"How do these future scientists wake us?" he asked.

"Painfully. They experiment on you, on us all, until they find a way to wake us. When they do, they'll think we're immortal. We'll think we're immortal. Until the time that is broken by Dr. Alveré Case finally mends."

"When does that happen?"

"About three hundred years from now."

"And what happens when time mends?"

"I'll watch my brother die, my friends die. I'll watch you die, trying to keep us safe. You all gave up your lives so I had a chance to come here, three hundred years in the past, to change the experiment. If I can change it, we don't have to die. Millions of people in the hundred-mile radius of this experiment in the future won't die. It's important, Foster. This is important."

"Mr. Sanders," he said. "My proper name."

"This is important, Mr. Sanders. I promise you I am not making this up."

"Millions?" He frowned. "How old are you, child?"

"In the future, I've lived twenty-six years. In the future, you've lived over three hundred."

He took in a deep breath and let it out. "Where are your parents? Tell me the truth. Now."

"They're dead."

"You must live somewhere."

So much for trying to convince him I was telling the truth. Best to get off here and try to find Alveré Case alone.

"There." I pointed at the nearest house. "I live there."

"The jail?"

Crap.

"Behind it. That other house."

"Jacob Laine doesn't have any children."

"Not that house. The other one." I smiled. "You were right, Mr. Sanders. I was just telling you crazy stories. Thanks for the ride back to town. I'd better go now before I get in trouble. Can I have my watch back, please?"

Okay, if being honest with him had been a mistake, I quickly discovered lying and trying to pretend to be an eight-year-old girl wasn't working very well either.

He did not give me the watch back. "Where do you live?"

"Fine," I said, cold, exasperated, and out of patience. "You know what? I'm sorry I asked for your help. I don't care what you believe, and I am very sorry for your loss. Really, I am. But that watch is my property. Give it back to me, and I'll just find my way home on my own."

He stopped the wagon next to a small house and jumped down to the ground. I scrambled out of the seat, my boots hitting the hard dirt of the road, and stumbled. I caught myself and ran around the back of the wagon.

"That is mine," I said, running after him as he strode

toward the house. "Give me back my watch, Foster. Now. You can't steal that from me."

A few people were out on the street, but I didn't care if they heard us. As a matter of fact, maybe a commotion would make Foster give me back the watch.

"Come inside and get dry," he said. "We'll find your family."

"I don't want to find my family. I want my watch."

"Matilda," he warned sternly, as I suppose any adult would when facing down a strong-willed, and probably delusional, eight-year-old. "Come inside. Now."

"Not unless you give me my watch." I crossed my arms over my chest.

"Matilda," he said again, louder. "Inside."

"Matilda?" a voice asked.

I turned.

Standing near the wagon was a boy—well, he was physically older than me. I'd say fifteen or so. He had sharp features and thin brown hair that was wet against his head. His eyes were blue enough I noticed it from a distance. There was something all-around familiar about him.

"Do you know this girl, Robert Chapman?" Foster asked.

"Robert?" I said.

The boy smiled, but there was no kindness in that grin.

And that's when I knew exactly who it was. Robert Twelfth, Abraham's friend. Only it wasn't Robert behind those eyes. It was Slater. Slater Orange.

26

It has been too long since I've written. Quinten is keeping secrets from me. I just hope the Houses haven't discovered what he's been doing.

— from the diary of E. N. D.

I'd been thrown back in time, riding Evelyn's body, my thoughts and personality woven into her mind. There were only two people who had ever had their minds, thoughts, memories transferred into a galvanized's body.

Me and Slater Orange.

Slater had been pulled back in time like me.

"Do you know me?" I asked, hoping a bit of Robert was still in there, just as Evelyn was still in me. "Matilda Case?"

"Yes, of course I know you, little girl."

That wasn't Robert. Not at all. The cruelty in his smile was all Slater.

Hell.

"Do you know where her family is?" Foster asked.

"Indeed I do." Slater sauntered forward. He had a rifle resting over one shoulder, but Foster didn't even blink at it. "I was hunting for you, Matilda," Slater said.

"Why?" Foster asked in a dubious tone.

Slater ignored him. "You and a dozen of our acquaintances. Why don't you be a good little girl and come along with me to find them?"

"No." I backed up until I ran into Foster, then clutched the edge of his long, wet coat. "I don't know you. I don't know him," I repeated for Foster's benefit. "Don't make me go with him. I won't go with him."

"That's too bad," Slater said. "Because I was just going to hunt down a friend of yours: Abraham. Remember him?" He shifted his grip on the hunting rifle. "He and I are going to have a grand time."

He was going to kill him. Slater was going to shoot Abraham before the Wings of Mercury experiment went off. Abraham wouldn't survive the experiment because he'd be dead.

"Where is he?" I whispered.

"You don't know?" He shook his head slowly. "If you come with me, I'll take you to him."

My heart was pounding so hard, it was throbbing in my ears. Four hours left before time would break. If Slater found Abraham—worse, if he already knew where he was—Abraham would be dead.

He must be bluffing. I didn't know where anyone was in this time. He couldn't know either, could he?

Or maybe Robert was in there, in his head, telling him things. I could feel Evelyn still curled in the back of my thoughts. She was little and sad and missing her parents.

Robert would be older. He would know the people in this town. Maybe Slater had mentally overpowered him.

Maybe Slater had locked him away at the back of his mind and was forcing him to give him information.

I was breathing too fast, panic strangling all the air out of my air, my head gone dizzy. A small, fearful, childish noise escaped me.

Foster's wide hand rested against my chest, pulling me closer against him. He was a warm, safe, solid barrier between me and Slater.

"Don't worry yourself about her," Foster said. "I'll get Matilda home. Go on now, Robert. I'm sure your father is looking for you."

The rage that twisted Robert's face was sharp and sudden. He swung the rifle down and pointed it at me. "You aren't going to be there to get in my way this time. House Brown won't be there, because I won't let it. Abraham won't be there to start the Uprising for it. And I will kill every last galvanized I can find."

Foster stepped fully in front of me and took the distance between me and Slater so fast, the younger man had time to get off only one shot.

It went wide, maybe because Slater wasn't familiar with the weapon or the younger body. Maybe because he carried the memory of what had happened the last time the huge man had come at him.

Foster snatched the rifle out of Slater's hands and emptied the bullets into his palm. "What has gotten into your head today, Mr. Chapman? You get on home before I tell your father what you've done. Go on."

He held the rifle at his side, barrel pointing down, bullets in his other hand. "Go."

Slater glared at the gun and then up at Foster.

"I killed him, you know," Slater said. "Your precious

Welton. Bashed him over the head and watched him bleed. And I will kill you too. All of you. Your parents, Matilda? When I find them and your brother, I will kill them too."

Foster took another step toward him, but Slater backed away fast, almost tripping over his feet as he ran away, disappearing around the corner of the nearest building.

I wasn't filled with panic anymore. I was filled with anger. If Slater had found one gun, I was sure it wouldn't be all that difficult to find another. He remembered the future and he was planning for his long life inside a galvanized body. Maybe he was planning a long life where he was the only galvanized who survived.

No. I'd get the calculations to the tower. I'd make Alveré listen to me. Then I would come back here into town and stop Slater before he found Abraham and the others. There was still time. There had to be time to save the people I loved.

"Please," I said to Foster's back. "I just need my watch."

"He knew what you know," Foster said. "Galvanized. The experiment." He turned, the watch held loosely in one hand. "Who is Welton?"

"A dear friend of yours. He was sick as a child. You cared for and helped raise him, then stood beside him as he took over ruling a very powerful . . . um . . . business."

He stared off into the distance for a long moment. Then seemed to make up his mind.

"I know Alveré Case," he said. "I helped build that tower."

"What?" I said, stunned.

He ushered me toward the house, opening the door and stepping in behind me.

"I know Dr. Case's work," he said. "I also know what his experiment is intended to do: time travel. I thought someone had been telling you his secrets—a parent, a family member. But you know it and Robert knows it, though he has revealed his intentions to no one. How?"

"This girl." I pressed my palm against my chest. "Her name is Evelyn Douglas. She fell into a deep sleep—a coma from which she never woke when that experiment went off. But her body was preserved by scientists. I, Matilda Case, was born in the future. When I got sick, my brother transferred my mind into Evelyn's body."

"And Robert?"

"He was tricked. A powerful man named Slater forced my brother to transfer his mind into Robert's body, which killed Robert. Slater hates the galvanized, but wanted the immortality our bodies possess. Or will possess if I can convince Dr. Case to change his experiment."

Foster glanced down at the watch in his hand. "Who is Abraham?"

"Abraham Vail is a galvanized who stood up for liberty and justice when the world was falling beneath cruel dictators. He started an uprising for freedom that eventually became a peace treaty between men like Slater and us common people."

"Robert wants to destroy Abraham because he will take away Robert's power in the future?" he asked.

"Slater, in Robert's body, wants to destroy Abraham because he was the one who brought the galvanized together—will bring them together." I took a deep breath. "This is all a little confusing for me too. But trust me, Abraham will be the one who sacrifices his own freedom for the rights and freedom of humanity."

"Is he a hero? A great man?"

"A lot of people believe all the galvanized are heroes. They have saved so many lives and done so much selfless good. But Abraham thinks of himself as just a man."

"I live to see this? Three hundred years?"

"Yes. But not before enduring a lot of pain. A lot."

Foster walked to the far side of the room and picked up a towel hanging there and handed it to me. I dried my face and rubbed it over my hair, then wrapped it around my shoulders.

"What do we need to tell Alveré?" he asked.

We. He believed me. All the anger and panic washed away in a relief that almost made me feel like I'd forgotten how to breathe.

"I need the watch," I said.

This time, he gave it to me.

I flicked open the back of it and pulled out the folded paper. "We think this is the formula that needs to be corrected. You'll have to convince him to do so before the numbers on the watch reach zero."

"*We* will convince him," Foster said. "You are coming with me, Matilda."

I shook my head. "He won't believe an eight-year-old child. I won't matter to him. What I say won't matter. But he'll believe you, though, because you're a friend, a peer?"

"A friend."

"Then you will be the best person to convince him. Please hurry, Foster. Please make him change the experiment. All the future depends on it."

"I will," he said. "But you must be there with me."

"I can't," I said. "Slater is planning to kill people. Kill the galvanized. He's going to turn this town upside down to find them and kill them. I need to stop him."

"You are eight years old. How are you going to stop Rob— Slater?"

"I don't know," I said honestly. "But I will." I snapped the watch closed again and checked the face. Three and a half hours. That was all the time the world had left.

Again.

"It's Abraham, isn't it?" Foster asked.

"What?"

"In the future," he said, crossing his arms over his chest. "Do you love him? Is that the reason you came back into the past? To save him?"

I shook my head. "I came to stop Alveré from going forward with his experiment without changing the calculations. That's all."

"Then why don't we tell him to stop the experiment altogether?" he said. "If it never happens, the disaster won't hit, we won't become galvanized, and the world will go on—changed, without us, without the galvanized."

He was making sense. Changing time in any manner just seemed like a recipe for disaster. And, yes, I loved Abraham. I didn't want him to die in the future when time ticked down and the explosion took out half the continent. I also didn't want my brother, Quinten, to die, to be blown apart by the soldiers who had come to kill me. I didn't want Welton and my grandmother, Neds, and, hell, Foster to die.

I'd been the cause of enough pain for the people I cared about. But this had all started with Alveré Case. I wanted the chance to make sure that when time mended in the future, those millions of people wouldn't die.

"Millions of people will die in the future if we don't change the experiment," I said.

"Hundreds will die today if we do," he said.

And that was true. No matter what we did, there were going to be a lot of deaths.

"I'm trying to save my world, Foster," I said. "I have to try. Do you really think you can talk Alveré out of ever trying the experiment?" I asked. "Do you really think you can make him dismantle the machine? Can you promise me he will never be curious as to what would happen if he set it in motion?"

"No. I can't guarantee that."

"Someone, someday is going to stumble upon this research. And then they will break time. If this experiment is going to happen, and I fear that it will, then let's make sure it is done correctly and controlled. With those calculations." I handed him back the watch. "Agreed?"

He nodded. "Agreed."

"Then please hurry, before it's too late." I ran past him, but he had a heck of a reach. Foster caught my arm. "I can't let you go, Matilda."

"What? No!"

He lifted me up and carried me out of the house to the wagon. I struggled, but I was an eight-year-old girl and he was a full-grown, very strong man.

"I have to save him," I said. "I have to save Abraham. Slater's going to kill him. I can't let him kill him."

"What will be will be," Foster said grimly. "You aren't going to do this world or yours any good by throwing yourself in front of a bullet meant for another. If Abraham is half the man you say he is, he will handle Slater on his own."

"No," I said. "Please."

But Foster climbed up into the wagon and held me down with one arm while he urged the horse into a gallop, quickly putting the town behind us.

27

The day is coming soon. You were twenty-six when we first met, and I am twenty-six now. Your time was so short. I know mine will be too.

—from the diary of E. N. D.

We rattled down the street at breakneck speed. If I threw myself off the wagon, I'd either knock myself out or snap a bone. And there was no guarantee Foster would continue on to the tower and tell Alveré to change the experiment.

If we had only three hours before the experiment went off, Slater had only three hours.

But he had read my grandmother's journal. There might have been something in there that said where Abraham had been during the experiment.

He could already have found him.

He could already have a gun on him.

Evelyn? I thought, reaching out gently through my mind, hoping the girl could still hear me.

Yes?

Do you know a man named Abraham Vail?

No. Why haven't we gone to heaven yet? I want to see my parents.

You will, I promised. *I'll take you to your parents. But there's something we need to do here first. And if we do it right, we will save a lot of other people from dying today.*

Silence.

It's a really good thing, Evelyn. You can help me help a lot of people. You can help them not be sad.

I can?

Yes.

Who?

My brother, for one. He's very nice and very smart. And my grandmother, who knits all day long with the wool from tiny sheep who fit in her pocket. And a woman doctor who is brave and smart, and so many other very nice people.

I want to help them. She sounded tiny but brave.

Good. I want you to help. In just a few minutes, I'm going to be talking to a man about a machine he's built. If there's anything you know or want to say, tell me.

All right.

It made me feel a little better that she wasn't behind that door, hiding away from me. I was the intruder here in her body, in her life. I didn't want her to be frightened.

The road, if that's what it could be called, changed, becoming nothing but rain-filled ruts that wound up the hillside.

If I continued on with Foster, Robert would surely kill as many of the galvanized as he could find.

If I jumped ... If I tried to save Abraham ... It would

be foolish. *Wouldn't it?* I'd spent all of my life trying to save others, help others.

Saving Abraham was choosing the one over the many, and that was never the right choice.

Or was it? Without him alive to lead the galvanized in their fight against the Houses, no one would have broken out of servitude. House Brown wouldn't exist. There would be no place for freedom in the world.

House Brown wasn't recognized as a power in the world, but it was made of people who were determined to make their own way and do no harm. People who didn't want to be owned. People who believed they could make their own paths, their own destiny.

They were my people, my family, my friends. I couldn't imagine a world in which House Brown didn't exist.

I like brown houses, Evelyn said.

I'd forgotten she was in my mind with me, listening to me.

I do too, I told her.

I didn't have the watch, so I didn't know how long we'd been traveling. Certainly more than fifteen minutes. Now that the horse was moving slower up the hill, it felt like it was taking hours.

"How much longer?" I asked.

"Just up a ways," Foster said.

"But how far?"

"Not too much farther."

I swear I could walk faster than this horse. "We need to hurry," I said.

"We are hurrying," he said. "How do people get around in your time?"

"A lot faster than this. Combustion engines really

catch on. After that, a lot of other power sources will be used to make wheels go around."

"And how did you get here?" he asked. "Into the past?"

"I don't know, exactly. My brother . . . he's brilliant. He knew he could catch the energy of this time event . . . the moment Alveré Case's machine breaks time, and use it to step back in time."

"Do you think you could you do it again? Go back in time?"

I wondered why he would ask that. Then I remembered. He'd just buried his wife and son. Maybe he thought there was a way to go to them. To change their deaths.

"I'm sorry," I said. "I really don't know how to do it. I just know that I did it. My brother was fairly certain most humans wouldn't have survived the trip."

"I understand," he said. Then he fell silent again, sorrow closing around him as sure as a shadow.

He still had one arm braced across the front of me. Maybe to keep me from bouncing out of the wagon on accident, but more likely to keep me from jumping out on purpose.

"Foster?" I said.

"Mr. Sanders," he corrected.

"Mr. Sanders," I said, "Thank you for believing me. About time. About the experiment. About everything."

"You may have convinced me of this truth," he said, "but I am not the one who matters."

"You matter to me," I said. "A lot."

He looked down, sorrow and compassion warring across his features. Then he looked away. "Dr. Case is a very . . . focused man. He is willful. Proud."

I took a deep breath. Let it out. "He'll listen. We'll make him listen."

After what felt like hours, we topped the hill, and Foster pulled the horse to a stop.

A smooth road drew a straight line to the long brick building that had six proud, two-story windows and a columned porch that sat snugly among the trees.

Rising to the west of the building was the tower—a beautiful construction of brick and wood with small windows that rose a strangely dizzying eighteen floors, topped by a half globe covered with what appeared to be glowing copper tiles.

"How much time do we have left?" I asked. A drop of rain struck my bare arm; another. The storm was rising, clouds drinking down the morning light.

Foster pulled out the watch that glowed like a cup of moonlight. "An hour and ten minutes."

"Let's hurry," I said.

By the time we had jumped down out of the wagon, it was raining even harder than before. We ran up onto the covered porch. Foster pounded on the door.

"Is he here?" I said. "Are you sure he's here?"

Foster stepped away from the building, scanning the windows. I didn't see any light behind them. No movements.

"This way." He jogged off toward the tower, his boots splashing through the growing puddles.

I hurried after him. Alveré must be here. If he wasn't, then there would be no time to find him, no time to stop the experiment.

No, I refused to give up. If he wasn't here, I'd find

some way to break into his lab and change the experiment myself.

I was freezing and soaked by the time we made it to the tower. The wooden door seemed modest and inadequate for the grand structure. Foster knocked once, then tried the latch.

The door swung inward.

He reached over and pressed his wide hand on my back, and I stepped into the tower. He shut the door behind us.

"Dr. Case?" he called out as he took off his hat and held it in his hand. "Alveré, it is Foster Sanders. I need to speak to you, please."

The room was built a lot like an old-fashioned lighthouse. The walls were a crisscross of bare wooden braces and beams; the wooden floors polished to a soft glow; and a curved, darker wood staircase arced up along the far edge of the wall.

A man came walking down that staircase.

Lean, light skinned, with dark curly hair that stood up off his forehead. He wore dark trousers, a light gray tailored vest, buttoned, the gold chain of a watch fob hanging in two short loops into his breast pocket. His white buttoned shirt was rolled up to his elbows, and a gray bow tie sat under the starched, round-edged collar. His eyes were bright and brown in a thin face full of curiosity.

He looked so much like Quinten, he could be his sibling.

"Foster," he said in a voice half an octave lower than my brother's. "What brings you out on this terrible morning?"

"This young girl."

Alveré Case, my very-great-grandfather, looked down at me.

"Who is she?" he asked.

"She tells me her name is Matilda. Matilda Case."

He shook his head, one hand paused on the banister, one foot still on the bottom stair. "Matilda," he said. "I know of no relation with that name."

"She says she is from the future. And she has brought this device to prove it." Foster crossed the room, his boots leaving wet, oblong marks behind. He handed Alveré the watch.

"A pocket watch?" Alveré's eyebrows arched. "No. Not quite, is it?" He turned the timepiece in his hands, then glanced at the face of it again. "Why are the numbers counting down?"

"She says it is a countdown to the moment you will execute your experiment," Foster said.

Alveré frowned at Foster.

"I believe her," Foster added solemnly.

Alveré walked past him to me.

I stood by the door, dripping and shivering.

"Who told you about my experiment, little girl?" he asked.

"When you trigger that experiment, it will kill everyone in a fifty-mile radius. Except for a few people who will fall into comas, then be revived by scientists. I'm one of those people. Or I will be. And in my time, three hundred years in the future, the repercussions of time mending will kill millions."

He shook his head, a curious smile on his face. "You've memorized those words very well," he said, "for someone so young. This is a joke." He turned to Foster. "Why are you playing a joke on me?"

"It isn't a joke," I said. "When time breaks, everyone you know will die. And when time mends, everyone I know will die." I walked around in front of him. "This paper is what we believe will alter the experiment. Enough so that when time mends, it won't destroy millions."

I held the scrap of paper out to him. He shook his head again but wasn't smiling this time. He took the paper and read through the formula. Then his head lifted and he glared down at me.

"Who sent you?" he asked, his voice growing louder. "Who knows this? Who has been spying on me and my experiments?"

"No one!" I said. "You have to believe me. This isn't ... I came a very long way to tell you this. So that you can fix the mistake you made. I lost everything trying to get this information to you. So many people's lives depend on you, Dr. Case. The entire world depends on you. Please, please believe me. Please change the calculations."

He crumpled the paper in his fist and threw it across the room. "Go home and tell your parents or whoever sent you here to *mock* me that I will find them and bring them to task for their trespass."

"Alveré," Foster said calmly.

"No." Alveré spun on Foster. "I will not tolerate being mocked. I understand you have been grieving, so I will forgive you this gruesome lapse in judgment. But I will not allow a child to make a fool of me."

I jogged across the room and picked up the paper where it fell.

"This isn't a prank," I said. "This is the lives of millions you are throwing away, because of what—your pride? You are just the first domino tipped over in the cascade of disasters that befall this world. Wars, uprisings, social and political failure. Millions die. *Millions.*

"And you have a chance to make things better—you have a guarantee that this"—I shook the paper—"would make things better, *save lives*, but you refused to glance at it. Are you so afraid of being wrong? Of having made a mistake, that you would rather continue making it than to correct it? I'm ashamed to call you my family, Alveré Remi Case. And I wish the Wings of Mercury experiment was never built."

At that last, he went very pale. "How do you know the name of the machine?" he asked.

I was so angry, I wasn't following his question. "What?"

"The name of my experiment. How do you know it?"

"Wings of Mercury? It is written in my grandmother's journal. And it's a legend, a myth. The machine built by Alveré Case that broke time," I said.

"I've told no one. No one." He breathed.

"That watch isn't anything I've ever seen before," Foster said. "Nothing I believe you've seen before. I don't think the child is lying, Alveré."

I threw Foster a look of gratitude.

"This," I said, carrying the paper to Alveré, "is a minor, *minor* correction to your calculations. Brilliant men have studied your experiment. Brilliant men who want to save lives. They believed enough in their work—in your work—to send me back in time to bring this to you. Please."

I held out the paper again. "In all your studies, in all

your research, you must have seen the possibility that someone from the future would come back in time." I shrugged. "That someone is me."

He nodded, and this time when he took the paper out of my hand, he smoothed it and studied the numbers more carefully. "I believe I understand." He walked across the floor, his eyes on the paper, and then started up the stairs, still looking at it. "I will see what I can do."

I watched him for a second, undecided if I should follow.

"Let's see that he does it right," Foster said as he walked to the stairs. "It will be warmer up there. I'm sure his assistant, Lara, could find a blanket we can wrap you in."

Foster believed me. Foster was going to make sure Alveré changed his calculations.

I made my decision.

"No," I said.

Foster paused. "No?"

"Don't worry about me," I said as I ran to the door. "Just make sure he changes it!"

I had to stop Slater, and I had only an hour to do so. I opened the door and ran out into the rain.

"Matilda!" Foster called after me, but I was running with all my heart.

Yes, I was an eight-year-old girl. But that didn't mean I wasn't strong enough to save Abraham. Save the others too.

Alveré Case believed me. Foster would make sure he went through with the adjustments.

The rain fell, piercing and cold, but I didn't feel it anymore. Didn't care. My boots hit the road, splashing through puddles. I needed to find him, find Abraham. I needed to find Robert. Stop him from killing the man I loved. Stop him from killing my friends, my kind.

I ran, counting seconds with my stride, minutes slipping away to the rhythm of my fearful, pounding heart.

Down the winding road, down the hillside, down into town.

By the time I reached the first houses, I had lost my hat and was exhausted, my feet too slow for my racing mind. I sucked down gasping, wet lungfuls of air, pushing this small, strong body to keep going. I looked into the faces of everyone I passed, hoping for the familiar features of a friend, a galvanized, Abraham.

Hoping for a miracle.

How long had I run? A half hour? An hour? How many minutes were left before time broke and the ringing of the infinity bell ended my chance of saving Abraham, my hope of saving the galvanized?

That's him, Evelyn said, startling me. *On the corner.*

I followed her direction. And then I saw him: Slater. He walked into a building at the end of the street, a revolver in his hand.

No, no, no, I thought.

I ran for him, fast, faster down the wooden sidewalk. The sky flashed with blue-white lightning, and thunder pounded across the heavens.

Over that great noise I heard another sound: gunshot.

I skidded to a stop in the open doorway of the building. This wasn't a house; it was a jail.

To my left was a holding cell, the old-fashioned kind that was just metal bars creating a box on one side of the room.

To my right was a desk, coat rack, chair, and chest of drawers.

In the center of the room were two men. The taller man must be the sheriff. He was slumped down in a pool of his own blood.

The man who stood above him, revolver still gripped in his hand, was Slater.

"Go!" a familiar voice yelled.

That's when I noticed the other man in the room. Behind the bars stood Abraham. I wanted to cry out with joy. He was alive, whole, strong, not a stitch on him.

Then Slater lifted the revolver, a grin hardening his face. "Filth," he yelled. "This time you will die forever, Abraham Seventh."

"No!" I yelled. "Slater, stop!"

I threw myself at his knees. I was only eight, but he wasn't fully grown either.

We fell, tripping over the dead sheriff. The gun fired. The shot went wide as we hit the floor. I knocked my head and yelled at the pain.

Lightning flashed; thunder rolled.

How many minutes did I have left? I scrambled to get to my feet, searching for the gun. Slater already had it. He was marching over to the cell.

Abraham stood with his hands out to his sides. "You don't want to do this, son," Abraham said evenly. "Put down the gun. Everything's going to be all right. Let's talk this out."

I knew Slater would never listen to him. He could never be talked out of killing Abraham. Hell, he'd already tried to kill him in the future.

But maybe Slater wasn't the only person in that body, in that mind.

"Robert," I said. "Don't let Slater do this to you. You can stop him. You don't want to kill a man. Don't listen to the voice in your head, Robert. Fight him!"

Slater's hand shook, and confusion shadowed his face. "I don't understand," Slater, or maybe Robert, whispered.

Abraham took the moment's hesitation and reached from between the bars, grabbing the gun out of his hand.

The boy stumbled away, pressing both palms to the side of his head.

I didn't know why there weren't other people here already. Was the sound of gunfire so common in this town?

Lightning flashed. There was no pause before thunder growled, shaking the windows.

A bell began ringing.

And there was no more time. For anything.

I ran to Abraham. "Listen to me, Abraham Vail. My name is Matilda Case. I'm from the future. You must find me on my farm in Pennsylvania in the year 2210, or the world will end."

"What?" he yelled over the building, growing, roaring sound of the great bell. "When?"

"Twenty-two ten. Matilda Case. I am a galvanized. So are you."

He shook his head.

"You will live a long life, but you must find me. Foster will know. Foster Sanders. He will understand. He will be a galvanized too."

"Watch out!" Abraham yelled.

I turned. Just in time to see Robert—no, Slater—stepping up behind me, a nightstick in his grip.

There was no time to duck as he snarled and slammed it into my head.

I screamed.

A bullet exploded through the air.

And then there was nothing but falling and falling, the world rushing away forever, as the infinity bell rang and rang and swallowed me whole.

28

In case you see this, in case you read this be-
fore I can tell you, I had a good life — your life.
Thank you for letting me live it. Now it's your
turn. Good luck, Matilda. Save the world.
                    — *Evelyn Natalie Douglas*

My hands were in the sink. Warm, soapy water lapped up to my wrists. I gasped, and the air felt new in my lungs, as if I'd been holding my breath for too long.

"You okay there?" Right Ned asked.

I turned.

I was in my kitchen. Neds, both of him, were sitting at the table, sharpening that machete of theirs they called a pocketknife. And in the corner, Grandma was knitting, the little pocket sheep nibbling at the laces of her shoes.

Was I okay? Neds had been bloody and half-dead when I last saw him.

Images flashed behind my eyes. A jail cell, a gun, blood, lightning, Abraham.

And through it all, a bell rang.

"What?" I whispered, feeling a little faint. I had been there in that jail, but at the same time a life's worth of memories poured through me.

I had woken stitched, afraid. I had been accepted into a family who had lost their little girl named Matilda.

But I was Matilda.

"Evelyn?" Left Ned said, "you gone deaf?"

Evelyn, that was my name too. I sorted through those memories, but with every thump of my heart, they faded and faded, as if they didn't belong to me. As if the life I had lived and loved wasn't mine, had never been mine.

There was a moment, fleeting, where I almost thought I could hear her voice, a moment where I felt Evelyn's joy at having a childhood, at having the love of parents, of living until she was a woman, with a family who loved her—my family, who had taken her in as their own.

And then the sense of other that was Evelyn lifted, and with a last, gentle warmth, was gone.

Leaving me just me: Matilda.

"Matilda," I said.

"Better not bring her up," Right Ned said. "You know how your brother gets."

"How does her brother get?" Quinten strode into the room.

"Quinten!" I rushed over to him and wrapped him in a tight hug. He was wearing a cotton shirt with a heavy flannel overshirt, and I could feel the gun holster he wore under that.

"Ev, are you all right?" he asked.

"Matilda."

Every inch of him stiffened. He pushed out of the embrace and took two steps back. "What about her?"

"Me," I said. "I'm Matilda. I'm your sister." I checked my hand. My familiar stitches were there, damp from the dishwater. I held them up as if it would prove who I was.

"Don't, Evelyn. That's not funny. It's cruel." He walked the rest of the way into the room and pulled a beer out of the fridge.

That was my brother; that was Quinten. He looked stronger, a little unshaven and tanned, as if he'd spent more years on the farm than in the city reading books, but otherwise, everything about him was my brother.

I was so confused.

"The lizards are fed," he said, "but we lost power to the pump house." He popped the beer, took a drink. "Fences will be down. Neds, you want to handle the pump house? Ev and I can run fences and send a back-link signal on the down line so the Browns don't panic."

"Can do," Left Ned said.

"Matilda," I repeated.

Quinten shook his head in warning. "That won't ever be funny. Drop it."

"You implanted my thoughts into Evelyn's body when I was sick, right? And . . . and this is crazy, but I'm guessing something changed when I got thrown back in time to change the settings on the Wings of Mercury experiment. You remember that, right? You tracked down the calculations for time travel, you built a . . . I don't know. Portal, I guess. When time mended from the original break, you were going to go back in time, thread the loop. but I did it instead because this body—Evelyn's body—was alive back then and survived the initial blast when time broke. Tell me you remember that. You have to remember that."

He was holding very still. So was Neds. It seemed the only thing in the world that was moving was Grandma, who softly sang her knitting song, and my pounding heart.

"Wings of Mercury?" he asked softly. "What do you know about that?"

"It was triggered in 1910; killed hundreds; and created the galvanized, thirteen infinitely repairable, immortal people."

Silence, from him and Neds.

"Ten," Quinten finally said. "There are ten galvanized."

My stomach dropped with dread. Slater must have killed three people before I could stop him. "Who?" I asked, "Who did Slater kill?"

Please don't say Abraham. Don't let it be Abraham.

"Who's Slater?" Quinten asked.

"The head of House Orange."

"Uh, no," Left Ned said. "Head of Orange is Barwick. Well, was Barwick."

Quinten nodded. "For the past ten years."

Dread and confusion were mixing up into a rising fear in me. If this was my time, my reality, my world, things had changed. A lot of things. I'd broken it. I'd screwed up reality.

Abraham could be dead. Foster too.

Because of me.

I swallowed hard, trying to calm my shaking. "Okay, that's not how it was. In the world, the time I lived through. I'm Matilda Case. I was born Matilda Case. And all my memories are of a life I lived—Matilda lived."

"You think you're Matilda?" Quinten asked, his voice softened by the futility of hope.

"I *am* Matilda. Evelyn . . ." I shook my head. "She was here with me for a moment, but then she just faded away. Just now."

"Oh," he said, letting out a breath. "Oh."

"I'm sorry," I said. "I know you loved her . . . I could feel how much she was loved, how happy she was. She loved you too."

He pressed his fingertips against his lips, processing information in that genius brain of his faster than I could imagine.

"Matilda?" he finally said.

"Yes."

A knock at the door broke the moment.

Neds were on their feet, picking up the rifle leaning against the wall. Quinten pushed past me, drawing his gun and holding it at his hip, and aimed at the door.

I didn't think a knock on the door was a reason for full alert, but, hey, this wasn't exactly my world anymore. Anything could be on the other side of that door, and if my brother and Neds thought it was dangerous, then I was inclined to follow their lead.

My revolver was holstered on my thigh. I pulled it free.

"Matilda Case?" a voice said from the other side of the door.

Quinten and Neds looked over at me.

I was frozen in place. I knew that voice. I knew who was on the other side of that door.

"Put the guns down," I said, already moving to the door. "Put them down."

"Evelyn, don't—" Quinten started.

Too late. I threw open the door.

Abraham stood there, rougher, more scarred, wearing

layers of well-worn, travel-hearty clothes and carrying a rifle and something that looked like a sword hilt over his shoulder.

Behind and to the side stood the galvanized Foster First, and a woman—no, not just a woman, but Sallyo.

She's running with the galvanized?

"Are you Matilda Case?" he asked, flicking a gaze at my brother and Neds, as if he were noting and dismissing the color beige.

"What are you here for, galvanized?" Quinten said, his gun trained on Abraham's head.

"Matilda," he said, searching my face.

I wondered who he was looking for there: the little girl who had begged him to find her on the farm three hundred years ago, or the woman who'd fallen in love with him.

"I'm Matilda," I said.

Abraham took a step.

Neds racked a round, and then all of us inside and outside the kitchen held perfectly still. "Not a single step closer," Left Ned said, his voice always a little colder and meaner than Right Ned's. "You have not been invited into this home."

"Do you remember the jail cell?" I asked Abraham. "And Robert?"

"Yes," Abraham said. "You told me to find you. It hasn't been easy." He glanced at Quinten and Neds with sharper eyes this time, noting every detail.

"We're all on the same side here, right?" I asked. "House Brown?"

Abraham's eyes flicked back to my face. There was no recognition of our time together; there was no hint that he cared for me. This Abraham, in this now, was hard as stone and steel. "We might be," he said.

"You want us to trust a galvanized?" Right Ned said. "I don't think so."

"*I'm* a galvanized," I said. "Okay, here's how this is going down: Quinten, Neds, lower your weapons. Abraham, Foster, Sallyo, keep your hands off your guns and knives, and come in the house so we can talk this out. Someone needs to tell me why House Brown—" I paused and looked over at Quinten. "We do still stand with House Brown, don't we?"

He had the most incredulous look on his face, as if he were having a hard time understanding the language I was speaking. "Yes," he said.

"Good. So someone's going to tell me why House Brown and the galvanized are at odds, and we're going to do it indoors, at the kitchen table, like civilized people."

"I already miss the other, less-bossy you," Left Ned muttered.

"Just sit yourself down, Harris," I said.

He threw me an odd look, then glanced over at Quinten, waiting for him to make the call.

"Quinten, this is important," I said. "Please. Let them come in."

Quinten lowered the gun but didn't welcome them into the room. "Why are you here?"

"There's a price on her head." Abraham nodded toward me. "And on yours. Death."

"So what's new?" I said.

Everyone in and out of the room looked at me.

"Okay," I amended, "maybe this is new for you, but not from where I came from. What else brought you out here? I can't imagine you coming all this way to make sure we're still breathing."

"There's that price on your heads," Sallyo said.

Neds swung the barrel of the gun her way.

"Stop," I said to him. Then to her: "You're here to collect it?"

From the looks on the faces around me, I could guess the answer to that. "Okay," I said. "Let me get this straight: House Brown exists on its own without the benefit of befriending the galvanized, and the galvanized are all ... standing on their own, or with mutants, against the Houses, including House Brown and us?"

"All the galvanized stand alone," Quinten said rather patiently, considering the situation from his perspective, which was that his sister Evelyn had just gone crazy ... or been replaced by his sister Matilda, who, for all he knew, might also be crazy.

"They hire themselves out to the highest bidder, no matter which House or individual is paying."

"Which makes the galvanized—"

"Murdering bastards," Right Ned said.

Abraham tipped his head down and gave Ned a dark, heated look that, yes, I could imagine belonged to a murderer.

Holy shit, things were not the way they used to be. Not at all.

Neds smiled and lifted the rifle again.

"No. No guns," I said. "Fine. Galvanized and House Brown don't get along. And House Brown and all the other Houses don't get along. And, hell, galvanized and galvanized don't get along. But we have resources. We have options. We have clever minds. We can find a way to resolve this price-on-our heads mess and keep all of us breathing by the end of it."

"You think they came here to discuss this at our kitchen table?" Quinten asked.

"I don't see why not. We're all here talking, aren't we? No one's gotten shot yet."

"We'll talk," Abraham said.

Quinten shook his head and walked away from the door. I motioned for Abraham and the others to enter.

"I'll make tea. Have a seat." I moved over to the stovetop, picked up the kettle, and filled it with water from the tap. At least we still had indoor plumbing. That was going in the plus column.

"What are you doing?" Quinten whispered.

"Making tea," I whispered back.

Yes, things hadn't gone exactly as planned with fixing the world. But I was home, my brother was alive. My grandmother was knitting in the corner, and my two-headed friend was glowering at our guests.

Foster was alive, and so was Abraham. My pulse settled just a bit knowing that I had them. All of them. That I wasn't alone.

Abraham might not remember me, but that didn't matter. Not right now. There would be time to fix that. To know each other again. Maybe to love each other again.

"You've just invited the galvanized into our home," Quinten said. "Our *home*, Evelyn."

"It's Matilda," I said. "And I think we all need a cup of tea before we get down to planning how we're going to fix this misunderstanding and save the world."

"Galvanized don't want to save the world," he said, "they want to take it over."

"All right. Then we need a cup of tea before we take over the world. What are you so worried about?"

"You—whoever you are, whatever you are—don't know what you're playing with," he said. "You have no idea of the dangers you're dragging us into. The Houses are on the brink of war, and paid mercenaries just walked through our kitchen door."

"What I know is there is a price on our heads. We should do something about that. The paid mercenaries have information we need. We should do something about that. And if there's a way to stop the war, we should be a part of it. A part of making sure House Brown and innocent people are safe, no matter what the Houses do. We are Cases. We've got a world to save. Again. We happen to have a pretty good record on that so far. So we'll figure it out. Get the cups, will you?"

Quinten studied me for a long second, then turned to the cupboards to retrieve the mugs.

I wasn't at all certain I was doing the right thing. I wasn't even certain I was in the right time. But what I did know was that this was my world now. My family, my friends, my home, and maybe my mercenary lover walking into the room, carrying that murderous look and an arsenal of weapons.

If anyone could fix the world, if anyone could make this mess we'd made right again, it was going to be us. It was going to be me.

"So." I took a deep breath and turned with the cups in my hands. "Who wants some tea?"

Read on for an exciting excerpt from the next
House Immortal novel,

CRUCIBLE ZERO

by Devon Monk.
Coming in September 2015 from Roc.

"This is a bad idea, Evelyn. A bad idea." My brother, Quinten Case, paced the dirt patch just outside our farmhouse door, one hand stuck stiff-fingered in his curly dark hair. His other hand kept drifting toward his gun holstered on his thigh, while his gaze flicked constantly toward the kitchen window. The flannel shirt and work boots he wore didn't disguise who I knew he really was: a restless genius and a brilliant stitcher of living things.

I should know. After all, I was one of the living things he'd stitched together.

"Matilda," I corrected him gently. I was sitting on top of a rain barrel, thunking my bootheels absently against the hollow side of it, and wondering what else about my farm and my world had changed since the Wings of Mercury experiment had broken and then mended time. "I'm not Evelyn anymore, Quinten."

He pulled his fingers out of his hair and waved impatiently at me. I guess he was still trying to get used to the changes in his world too.

I understood why he was calling me Evelyn.

I'd been born his sister, and named Matilda Case. But when I was a little girl, I'd become deathly ill. Quinten and his genius mind had found a way to transfer my thoughts, my personality, my mind into the comatose body of a girl named Evelyn. A girl who had been asleep for over three hundred years.

He had stitched everything that made me *me* . . . into her. It had been a desperate, risky thing to try. But he had succeeded. In my world, my time, I'd woken up in her body as Matilda and had lived until I was twenty-six.

That was when we'd done something even more desperate: Quinten had sent me back in time to change the Wings of Mercury experiment. We hadn't had much choice, really. If I hadn't gone back in time, billions of people would have died.

That was how I remembered it. That was what had happened in my time.

But in this world, in this time line, Evelyn had been the one who woke up when my brother had tried to transfer my mind into her body.

She'd lived until today, just a few minutes ago, when I'd found myself standing in the kitchen. I'd felt Evelyn in my mind with me. Then she had lifted, all her memories and thoughts fading like smoke in the wind.

My going back in time was supposed to save the world. And it had.

But it had also changed it in massive, chaotic ways.

So far, I'd been told there was a war going on between the Houses who ruled the resources in the world. House Brown, or House Earth, as Quinten had told me it was referred to now, was the House made of a loosely connected network of people who had escaped servitude to the other Houses to live free, was now apparently several walled strongholds scattered across the world.

Another huge change I was still trying to wrap my mind around was that the galvanized, people like me who had survived the original Wings of Mercury experiment and whose brains and bodies were over three hundred years old and stitched, were some kind of wanted criminals.

Back in my time, the galvanized had done a lot of good for the world, and for people and human rights.

"You have a price on your head," Quinten said, back to pulling at his hair again. "They—those killers in our kitchen—shouldn't even be here."

"I know." In my time I'd had a price on my head too. That, unfortunately, hadn't changed. One of these days I'd figure out how to avoid such trouble in my life.

"How can that even be possible?" he demanded. "No one except Neds and Grandma knows you exist."

"Someone knows," I stated, waiting for him to turn and start pacing back the other way.

"No. You can't be a wanted criminal if no one knows you're alive."

"I take it you registered my death when I was young?" It was a weird thing to ask, but then, I'd led a weird life.

He nodded, his palm resting on the top of his head so his elbow jutted out. "We never registered Evelyn as alive, since she wasn't technically or medically supposed to be alive. She was just a forgotten medical experiment Dad got his hands on before things really went to hell. There is no Matilda Case on record."

"Still, you couldn't have kept Evelyn in the basement all her life," I said, hoping to lighten things up a bit. "We must have had neighbors or friends who'd seen her and maybe thought she was me?"

"Yes, we have friends. But they think Matilda died. And we told them Evelyn was a child our parents took in after the One-three plague killed her parents."

"One-three plague?"

He stopped, lowering his hand finally. Stared at me, his eyes flicking across my face as if looking for a lie there. "It's . . . eerie," he said. "Knowing you're not you."

"I am me," I said softly. "I'm just not her."

He nodded and sorrow darkened his eyes. "For the last fifty years, we've had a plague hit each decade. One-three spread widely enough. It wiped out millions."

"Oh," I said. "Oh." There had been no widespread plague in my time. I was still reeling with the changes of this world, and I knew Quinten had his own things to get his brain around.

But in my time, Quinten had died from a terrible explosion. We had been hunted by the Houses who had chased us to our farmhouse. The House soldiers had killed Quinten, our farmhand, Neds Harris, and the galvanized Abraham and Foster. They'd killed the others who had helped us too, Welton, head of House Yellow, and House Brown's doctor, Gloria.

Even though this news of plague wasn't exactly welcome, so far I preferred this time and this world, in which my brother and the people I loved were alive.

Whatever else was wrong here we'd make right. This was the only world left to us. That time-travel trick had been a one-shot deal.

"Could it be the stitching?" I asked. "If someone had seen my stitching, they'd know I was galvanized, right? And galvanized are . . . criminals?"

He pulled up the sleeve of his flannel, his eyes locked on mine.

I glanced down at his tanned forearm. Muscular, a few lines of scars that had healed too white against his tanned skin. A row of neat, small stitches ran at an angle below his elbow.

Everything in me chilled.

"Everyone is stitched, Ev—Matilda," he said. "At most times, anyway."

I couldn't take my eyes off that tidy row of thin gray thread piercing my brother's arm. "Why?"

"The One-one plague made healing slower and more difficult. Things go necrotic more often than not. Especially open wounds. If you want a cut to heal, you need to stitch and keep it as clean as possible."

"So those stitches aren't permanent?"

He shook his head and rolled his sleeve back down. "I'll take them out at the end of the month if everything looks okay."

"Are mine permanent?" I asked, a small hope catching in my heart.

"Yes. You are galvanized. But since nearly everyone goes around with stitches, spotting a galvanized isn't easy. And no one I know thinks you are a galvanized."

"So people just assume I'm recovering from injuries," I said.

He nodded. "You—I mean, Evelyn keeps her stitches covered when anyone from House Earth stops by."

"I thought you said no one knew I was alive."

"No one except the people in House Earth, whom I trust explicitly. Well, and the Grubens."

I shook my head. "The what?"

"Family down a-ways. Closest we Cases have to relatives. They're an . . . energetic bunch, but loyal to the grave."

"So stitches aren't rare, and my being galvanized isn't why someone wants me dead. That's different."

"Are the galvanized the only stitched where—I mean, *when*—you came from?" he asked.

"Yes. Twelve of them plus me. They were owned by the Houses. They were celebrities, in a way. World changers. Heroes. They did a lot of good, Quinten. We did a lot of good. I knew Abraham. I knew Foster." I pointed toward our house, where both Abraham and Foster were drinking tea, probably at gunpoint. "We trusted them then with our lives and they died trying to protect us."

"What's your point, Ev?" he asked.

"Matilda," I said. "We should trust them."

"That would be suicide."

"Because they're galvanized?"

"Because they are here to collect on that price on your head," he said.

"Abraham said he came to warn us that there was a price on our heads."

The crease between his lowered eyebrows deepened. "They're mercenaries, Matilda. All galvanized are mercenaries. Guns for hire. No loyalties to anything other than money. No loyalties to Houses, people, or one another. It's what they do."

Oh. "Well, that's not going to happen. We should at least get as much information out of them as we can, don't you think?"

"There's nothing they know that I want or will pay for," he said flatly. "I do not do business with galvanized."

"Well, I do." I hopped down off the water barrel, my boots landing with a crunchy thud in the dirt and gravel. I dusted off my hands. "They came to our farm looking for me and for *you*," I said. "I'm not the only one some-one wants dead. We don't know why someone wants me dead since no one should know I'm alive. But from the way you're acting, all nervous and hair-pully, I think you know exactly why your head is worth hunting."

"It's a mistake," he scoffed.

"No, I don't think it is. What did you do that has made someone want to kill you, Quinten?"

He pulled his shoulders back and tipped his head up as if I'd just punched him in the chest. It took him a mo-ment or two before he answered.

"You are not at all like Evelyn," he said slowly. "Do you know that? She was kind. Trusting. She was the sweetest girl I'd ever known. And she would never have accused me of doing something worth being killed over."

His words stung. Quinten and I had been close. Hell, I practically worshiped the ground his boots trod upon. It hurt to hear him tell me I wasn't as good as the sister he had loved more than me. A girl I could never live up to. A girl I could never be.

But I knew him. He had a habit of striking out when people got too close to the things he didn't want to talk about. I refused to back down on this.

I lifted my chin and stared him in the eyes. "I'm sorry I'm not her. Really, I am. I'm sorry you've lost her. I'm sorry she's gone. But that's not an answer to the question I asked," I said calmly. "Tell me what you did, Quinten.

If I don't know why someone wants to kill you, I can't help you stay alive."

"No."

It was my turn to study him to look for clues. His body language said he wasn't going to budge on his silence. His eyes had gone all sharp and judgy. Closed off.

Fine. He wasn't the only person with information I could talk to.

I had three mercenaries at my kitchen table. They must know who had put the hit out on us. Someone had to be paying them. Maybe they'd have a clue as to why we were suddenly such hot property.

"I may not be as sweet as Evelyn," I said, unable to be angry at him. "But you, brother, haven't changed a bit. You are just as stubborn, smart, and insufferably righteous as you've always been. And I wouldn't want you any other way." I took a few steps and dropped a quick kiss on his cheek. "I missed you." I patted his arm. "But you're being an idiot."

I strode off toward the corner of the house and the kitchen door beyond.

The twisting sensation of an elevator suddenly plunging down flights of a building hit me, and I stumbled but caught myself before I fell. The sharp scent of roses filled my nose and mouth as I gasped, and my ears filled with the distant echo of a bell.

My vision blurred and I blinked hard to clear it. The house in front of me dissolved and was suddenly nothing but a pile of rubble, as if an explosion had reduced it to smoldering dirt and timbers. Men in black uniforms milled around outside it.

My heart raced. Something was wrong. Something was very wrong. I looked behind me, and Quinten was no longer there. But it wasn't just Quinten that was missing. The world had changed.

No. The world had shifted. This world, this property with the broken, burning house was the world and property from my time.

But I didn't want to be in my time. In my time, my brother was dead.

I must have made a sound.

One of the men saw me. "Hey. What are you doing here? This location is under House Black lockdown. There's been an explosion. It isn't safe to be here."

I heard him—honestly I did. But all I could see was my farm—the very familiar land I had grown up on, which was exactly as I remembered it—and not the slightly different world I'd recently woken up in.

And if this was the time I remembered and had grown up in, that meant my brother was currently dead, buried under that pile of rubble that used to be our home.

"Matilda?"

I turned to that familiar voice. John Black, head of House Black, wore a black uniform like the other men but carried himself with a manner of authority and bulldog strength. He had come around the corner of the rubble field and looked just as startled as I felt.

"Were you in the explosion?" he asked, striding my way. "Were there any other survivors? Welton Yellow or your brother, Quinten? Have you seen Abraham?"

I shook my head, my words stuck somewhere in the clot of panicked silence filling my brain.

He stopped in front of me. "You're shaking," he said,

not unkindly for a man who had been sent to bring me in as a fugitive accused of murder. "Matilda, tell me what happened here."

And then the world twisted again, filling with that dizzying rose scent. John Black reached out for me. I reached back. I felt the warm pressure of his fingers on my wrist, and then he was gone—whisked away as if he were a curtain that had been pushed aside to show the open window behind it.

I was holding my breath, my hand cupped over my mouth.

The house was standing, whole, the day quiet and still. In the distance, I heard a bird warble and a sleepy lizard answer with a rumble.

"Ev—Matilda?" Quinten called out behind me.

Relief washed over me, and I finally exhaled. He was alive. Quinten was alive, and I was back in the time where I belonged.

I turned and dropped my hand away from my mouth. The faint ringing in my ears was gone; the flower scent faded.

A very alive Quinten, wearing flannel, jeans, boots, and an irritated scowl on his face, strode up to me. "Where do you think you're going?"

"Did you feel that?" I asked. "Just now, did you get dizzy or smell roses or see . . . anything?"

He paused and gave me a look. "No. Why? Did you?"

I shot a look behind him. This was still the property I'd always known, but the familiar pear orchard wasn't in sight, and a flock of six pocket-sized sheep of various pastel shades shambled along a fence line, stopping to nibble on weeds there.

We had only three pocket-sized sheep in the time I was from.

So I had to be back to the time where Evelyn had grown up.

"I felt something. I . . . saw someone," I said. "Do you know John Black?"

He shook his head. "Matilda . . ."

"He must have been an echo," I said. "No, it was more than that. I saw what this place used to be. What I knew it as. And he was real. He felt real."

"You're telling me you saw something from your own time?"

"Or I somehow stepped into my time. Is that possible? Did I just disappear and reappear?"

He camped back on one foot and stuck his hands in his pockets. "No. You were walking toward the house and I was walking after you."

"Maybe it was just a second for you, but longer for me. Why would that happen? What would make that happen?"

"Don't look at me," he said. "Until today, I would have told you time travel—of any kind—was impossible, and now you're telling me you've experienced it twice. Maybe you're just tired, and your mind can't sort through what's happened. Maybe it's old memories surfacing. Something glitching in the switch between what Evelyn knew and remembered to what you know and remember."

It wasn't a hallucination. That had been John Black. That had been his touch. And that had been our demolished house. I was sure of that. But I had no way to prove that to Quinten.

"Okay." I swallowed and nodded. "Okay. Maybe it's just a onetime thing. I can deal with that." I set my shoulders and turned toward the house. Sometimes experiments had unintended consequences. Maybe seeing into my old time stream was that consequence.

Or maybe it was a fluke of the Wings of Mercury mending time. A wrinkle that hadn't been ironed out yet.

Whatever it was, I would handle it. Right now, here in this time—the real time—I needed to save our lives.

"Where are you going?" he asked.

"To get the information I need to save both our heads," I said over my shoulder.

I heard the sound of his boots as he did a short jog to catch up with me. "Does 'no' mean something else in your time?" he asked.

"No."

That, finally, got a chuckle out of him. "Just. Please. Listen to me on this. Trust me on this. I know the way the world works, with or without time travel."

"I am listening. I am also going to get us some information."

"We do not do business with mercenaries."

"Is that the family motto?"

"It is now."

"Well, I'm still going off the other family motto: do whatever is necessary to keep the people you love alive."

Quinten swore softly.

We'd rounded the house. The big barn, a worn wooden structure two stories high with odd creatures slipping or winging in and out of the windows, doors, and other cracks of it, was behind us now. I hadn't had time to get acquainted with the stitched beasties my brother was keeping, but from the glimpses I'd caught, Quinten had a full-blown menagerie here.

However, I had not missed the half dozen winged lizards of various impressive sizes that skulked a little farther out by the trees, or filled up the dirt road, bellies flat as they soaked up the sun.

"Sure are a lot of dragons around the place," I noted.

"Lizards," he automatically corrected me, just like I had corrected everyone else who had met our single stitched, winged monstrosity back in my time.

"Do you use them for scale jelly?"

"Of course. Other than stitching, it's the jelly that keeps this place running," he said. "But mostly they patrol the property and make sure the things, and people, we don't want here never make it to the house."

"How many do you have?"

"Thirty-six."

I shot him a grin. "We only had one. Big as a barn."

"Still do," he said. "And, well, a lot of others, the size of other buildings."

"As soon as I get the three killers in our kitchen sorted away, I want to see all the critters. We had a unicorn. Well, sort of a unicorn."

Quinten picked up the pace enough so he reached the door at the same time I did. He straight-armed it, his palm smacking flat in the middle of the wood. "Listen to me, Matilda."

I stopped, folded my arms over my chest.

His face was a little sweaty from the jog, but also pale. "We are not on their side. They are not on ours. They want us dead, and they plan to make a profit on our deaths. Anything they say, any information they give us, is suspect."

"I don't see that we have a choice," I said. "Good idea,

bad idea doesn't matter. We need to know who wants us dead, and why, and they can tell us."

The door opened, swinging inward.

Quinten moved back and took hold of one of the guns under his overshirt so quick, you'd think he was on fire.

I stood my ground but didn't draw the gun strapped to my thigh.

In that doorway, filling the most of it with all six foot four of his height and his muscles, was the galvanized Abraham Seventh. The man I'd loved.

In a different world.

In a time that I didn't think existed.

The man who was now a stranger to me.